Gold Fever

The Continuing Tale
of
Discovery, Intrigue
&
Passion

An Original Novel by

Donna Sherry Boggins

&

Robert S. Catan

Dedication

To my Perfect Stranger,
for keeping the adventure alive.
DSBoggins

To my Perfect Stranger
For keeping my brain functioning.
RSCatan

The Letter

If you're readin' this, I'm dead. I was born back in Kansas City, Missouri in the year of our Lord. 1821, September 28. My 3 brothers and 2 sisters I'm hopin' are still alive back there. My older brother, Charlie, Charlie just passed away here, with me. May he rest in peace. I'd be obligin' if you'd let my kin know that he's gone peaceful like with a fever and some dysentery.

Charlie and me, we left Kansas to follow the gold strike in the hills of California. We got signed on to do some surveying along the way and that paid us a dollar a day. We did our fair share of digging but never made a good strike. In fact, most of our surveying pay was lost tryin' to hit a vein of pure gold.

We got signed on to a surveying crew that was headin' out to a new strike in a far off place, New Zealand, so we packed it up and shipped out on a steamer. It took a long time crossin' the ocean and stops along the way to pick up fruit and supplies. We heard scurvy can hit a whole ship full along with sea sickens from the choppy water. Well. Charlie and me, we made it with no real serious sickness.

The sea captain, Marcus Dempsey, anchored off the south tip of New Zealand, a real pretty place. It was all trees and lakes and glacier ice up on the mountains but not much people. It seemed to be just miners and us surveyors buyin' supplies and grub, packin' up a mule train and heading out. We all chipped in a silver piece, some a few gold flakes to get a local guide, named Boris to show us the road to the gold fields.

It was wintertime but hotter'n Hades. Said it was opposite from Missouri, winter was summer and the other way around. Looked a lot like California gold country, to be sure .Maybe one of my brothers or somebody who's got the itch can follow my directions. Charlie and me, we ended up along a narrow little river that was told to be rich with gold as big as your thumb.

The miners started building a town along the river, namin' it Arrowtown and for all my travillin' it looked much like Julian,

California, a minin' town that was just tappin' out. This Arrowtown was full of merchantiles, a stable with a smithy, and gamin' houses with plenty of hard whiskey and those pretty ladies teasin' and smilin' and hopin' to empty full pockets while shamelessly they're droppin' their bloomers.

Charlie and me, well, we did OK. The surveyin' was good and paid regular and we picked up a few gold nuggets, smaller than that here thumb of mine but we lost most of it to the gamblin' halls. Charlie and me, we both have no women back home to speak of so we enjoyed the company of the ladies and we both came down with the clap. So it burned and itched something terrible so we got some salve from the local Doc and that helped some.

After our surveying was finished up, we thought it best to go on our own for a while and see if followin' the river would lead to a good vein. Downriver a ways, we ran into a strange lookin' native, called a Maori poutamu hunter, meaning, jade hunter. For you who reads this and don't know, this Maori was all marked and scarred up on his face and body. Real strange like. Wore nothin' like our dungarees, but coverings from plants and grass. In the beginnin', he stayed clear of us, real shy lookin'. Then we gained his trust by sharin' our evening vittles. Soon, he's sittin' with us around the fire, makin' music with a strange lookin' wood flute. I traded my harmonica for his flute and he seemed pleased with the trade. I taught him a tune and he learned faster than most.

He couldn't understand a lick of what we said but he was good company. He showed us the green jade he collected and I swear, it looked just like that I saw in San Francisco that had come down from the Orient. Real pretty. We made our way down the river until it came to a split and he headed his own way but before he took off, he gave me a little present, I guess for puttin' up with him. It looked to be some sort of fancy bone or horn, all polished up nice and all and some kinda writin' over it. Looked real ceremonial like.

Not communicatin' real well, I figured he made it but he shook his head and pointed back toward Arrowtown. Best I can figure, he got it *from a miner or maybe a ship captain for doin' some trackin'. Don't know for sure but in his way, said it was worth us holdin' onto.*

A few months passed and Charlie and me, we find nothing except more lakes and a few small flakes of gold and our supplies are runnin' low, so we head back to Arrowtown. That's when I overhear some miners talkin' in the saloon about a map carved on some bone that got took and they're out to get it back and kill the dang thief. Well, Charlie and me, we don't want no trouble, least of it to get killed over a bone, so we took it and buried it good, hopin' to dig it up when it's safe, then see what happens.

Before we stuck it in the ground, I used my surveying tools and graphite to draw the markings on some paper. Before you start askin', yes, I had the carved up bone but no, I never could fetch it up. Charlie and me, we had just enough scratch left to book passage on a old sloop headin' north, makin' our way back to Missouri.

The ship, leakin' somethin' terrible stopped in every port headin' up the coast. Finally, we'z both got sea sickness and puking real bad so we get off that blasted ship in South America. Charlie and me, we get good and drunk and sleep it off in a bawdy house and first thing, the dang ship is gone, strandin' us. So right there and there, Charlie and me, we decide to stay a while and get our sea legs. Finally, when we sobered up, we found out we were in Peru ! Never even heard of Peru !

We got jobs doin' some surveying and settled in. Didn't pay much but the girls were pretty like, dark and friendly. That was 5 years ago when we last got stranded.

Now, Charlie's dead. I think he croaked from the clap or something worse. Charlie liked the ladies and they liked him. He got some bad rash all over him and the itching and sweatin' then he started talkin' crazy like. Ramblin' in his sleep. One morning, I find him all sweated up and dead as a door nail. I bury him real nice like outside a little church run by these missionaries. I made sure I carved a cross and wrote his name and birth date real clear.

She came from the church one day and comes every day. She's a blessing. I got a bad case of consumption and everyday it gets more worse. Damn painful, too. I think I'm dyin' though I guess it's my time so I can't complain.

You askin', 'Why all this story telling?' Well, I'll tell you. Charlie and me, we were surveyin' like they wanted and I was restin' on a big granite rock, when I saw a mud brick stuck between the rocks. So, being curious, I broke the clay rock and stuck my hand inside and real careful like, pulled out the damdest thing. It looked like a small, round pumpkin, hard as a stone, deep brown and carved up. Strangest thing, it had those same markings as my bone carvin' down in Arrowtown! I showed it about and someone said I better put it back 'cause there's some curse on it. Then someone broke into our room above the saloon and tore things up bad. But didn't find the gourd. So next week, we go back and hid it under the same rocks. We made a few mud bricks and hid it real good. Seemed like I had some curse followin' us. Then Charlie got real sick and my feet went bad and I've been limpin' around since.

That's part of the curse, Charlie and me thought. Guess we're not much treasure hunters, not even good miners but now, getting' to the end of my sorry life, I'm regrettin' not havin' the chance to write down the writin' and see where it all leads. I drew a map on the back so you can find the gourd and see for yourself. I'm hopin' it's just where I hid it.

Maybe now, whoever gets this letter can finish up where I left off. Find out about what's so special about the bone and the gourd. Pretty strange goings on and kept me awake many nights just thinkin', not doin'.

Dang, I almost forgot to tell you where I hid the bone. No good without it. There's a river right out back a town. You walk around the Arrowtown Bank, down to the river's edge then cross over, then take about 300 big steps, say 900 yards measurement, towards all those giant trees. There was an old pipe used to flush the bank. I found a piece, maybe 3 feet long. I wrapped the bone in a rabbit hide and some old flannel and oil-cloth from a weather coat and stuffed it inside the pipe. I buried the pipe and covered it with a pile of loose rocks. It's plenty safe there and no one will go snooping around it.

Whoever's readin' this last will and testament, I'm wishin' you luck cuz mine just ran out.
Your Friend or Relative, Thomas P. Bratworth, Deceased

So It Begins Again

The 150-year-old letter mesmerized Kate. She was carefully copying Bratworth's symbols by hand, and the small, rough map. When finished Kate photo copied the sketches, and recorded them on her computer disk. This letter was too important to lose.

As soon as they'd have a good visit with old friends and colleagues, they'd plan the next leg of their journey. The die had been cast.

Bill could barely put his arms around all that had happened. Sometime soon, he'd have to level with Kate about the fate of their close friends. And he'd be forced to deal with the Professor who was breathing down their throats. He glanced over at Kate, soundly sleeping, unaware of the turbulence. He wished things could stay that way, especially for her. So much had taken place, and he didn't like events to be out of his control.

William Shepherd, former CIA operative, wanted things to be neat and tidy and they weren't. At least he was able to stop the bleeding. The next twenty-four hours would be telling. He'd do his best to deal with the past and tidy things up for the future.

Flight 641 cut smoothly through the early morning sky. The cabin lights, dimmed during most of the flight, were illuminated, the first announcements made and a light breakfast was served. The coffee smelled good. First Class used premium beans. Their destination was twenty minutes away. Once the dishes were collected, the flight attendants prepared the cabin for a swift arrival. Down below, the lovely South Island began to take form. Kate planted a warm kiss on Bill's lips, smiled dreamily, then focused on the ancient ice fields outside her window. Magically, the glittering ice altered and changed colors, from foreboding grey blue to steel grey. Then, as the sun broke over the jagged ridges, the glacier slipped into lovely shades of pink. The view was heavenly! Early morning in the southern hemisphere sparkled, the air as clean and devoid of polluting smog as the thick haze was prevalent along the densely inhabited shores of the American Pacific.

New Zealand, best known for its millions of sheep and substantially fewer people, lay a mile below in stark contrast to the blue sky above. The descending 737 skimmed the Southern Alps then miraculously broke free, showcasing glacier fed fiords, a light green, elegant carpet of spring grasses and a primary pallet of abundant wildflowers.

Shaggy coated sheep grazed on the fresh clover creeping along the fenced boundaries of the runway, a newly paved landing zone that stretched ahead, ending beside a small, neat terminal. Their flight was the first of the morning to land and the concourses were quiet and nearly abandoned, except for a lone motorized luggage cart alerted to prepare for their approach. Workers, the size of large insects, scampered to their posts and were prepared to guide the big bird to its designated gate.

"Well, my dear, soon we'll be out there taking in a fresh breath of southern air." Bill reached over and returned a warm peck on Kate's cheek. "If we don't suck those sheep into the jets, we'll be home free."

"Fifteen hours is a hell of a long time to sit. I can't wait to take a walk." Bill stretched his arms over his head and rotated his stiff neck and shoulders. He caught movement behind him and latched eyes with Professor Raymond Morrissey, Kate's former mentor/professor, a talented archeologist, who still had an obsessive longing to snatch up Bill's new wife and carry her away.

By now, the professor should realize he'd lost the battle. Kate was bound to Bill, and Raymond would have to stand by and accept the role as academic colleague, nothing more. He should be grateful that Kate didn't put her foot down and send him packing.

New Zealand had lured both Dr. Kate Jenkins Shepherd and Professor Raymond Morrissey to the South Island on separate missions. Kate, to follow the intriguing clues found in a miner's letter, given to her at her previous research site in Lima, Peru and Morrissey, pursuing the unusual discovery of ancient bones from an extinct Peruvian penguin, with close ancestry ties to what is now New Zealand.

If at any time, information surfaced that dismissed the penguin findings, and consequently, the professor's ulterior motives for accompanying them on the plane to the South Island, well, he'd deal with him.

He imagined having him killed, a purely fictional solution, but Raymond would wish Bill had ended things quickly and with little pain. William Shepherd had the power to make his life miserable by drying up the pipeline to his generous grant funds. There were worse things than death to a greedy scholar like Professor Morrissey

"Good morning folks!" Raymond, sitting behind and across the aisle made a point of keeping the banter alive. "Not such a bad trip, was it?" He'd spent most of the flight fantasizing, imagining their roles reversed and Bill seated where he sat and he, unabashedly cuddling and stroking the lovely Kate.

Bill politely acknowledged his salutation, and then turned back to Kate. "Well, here we go. Why do I feel like we're under the Professor's microscope?"

Kate burrowed her head into he husband's shoulder, "I'm afraid we are. He does have a way of getting under your skin. Tell me, how much does he know about our trip south?"

"He knows what I allow him to know."

"Meaning?"

"Before we left Lima, I conveniently let it slip that we were closing the door on Peru, at least for now. It's too dangerous for you right now. And, I hinted that you, as a side bar, had received an interesting, old letter and decided to trace its source. That, along with both of us wanting to take some well earned R & R."

"He isn't aware of the connection?"

"What connection? As far as he's concerned, we're sightseers on holiday. I figured I'd be better off bringing up the letter because you know he'd find out one way or another. That would create suspicion on his part. The sneaky bastard."

Kate sighed and felt relieved knowing Bill was close by. "I feel so much better with you watching my back."

"Just don't worry about him. We'll keep close tabs on Raymond and before long, he'll get bored with us and get wrapped up in his penguin project." Her CIA agent gave her a reassuring hug and a light kiss on the forehead. "In the meantime, I'm looking forward to getting you off this plane and being alone in our private hotel room."

"I can't wait." Kate planted a suggestive kiss on the soft spot under his chin. "A promise is a promise and a warm bed and a warm man sound very good."

Raymond strained to hear their private dialogue but the annoying landing instructions blocked all but a few incoherent phrases, nothing to latch onto. "Hey, lovebirds" Raymond intentionally shook them out of their intimate moment. "I've got transportation arranged. If you hadn't guessed, I knew you'd be on this flight, so…. I made arrangements with an old Kiwi colleague of mine, Dr. Jeremy Marshall. Perhaps you know him."

Kate recognized the name and lit up. "Dr. Marshall? I haven't seen him since I attended one of his lectures back in grad school. What a wonderful character." Surprised that Raymond had never mentioned his name before. "He's your contact here?"

Raymond was instantly put on alert because of Kate's eager response. Perhaps they were too familiar. Managing to rein in his doubts. "Yes, the very same. We've kept in contact since we fulfilled a grant and research project outside of Auckland, let's see, that's going on eight years now."

Searching his memory for a connection. "Haven't I mentioned him before? Hmm, I'm sure I had. Whatever. The latest penguin find got his juices flowing. Not quite his field but he likes to keep in the loop. Curiosity nearly killed the cat!"

Raymond stood up in the aisle to better see Kate, "Jeremy raced down to the South Island with his support team, a couple of talented interns from Auckland and, of course, Dr. Maggie Brown".

Raymond took a breath. He realized his sentences were running together, unlike his trademark, smooth delivery. "Do you happen to know her?"

Kate had strained to converse with the professor over the back of her seat. Now he was directly over her. "No, that name doesn't ring a bell. Is she from the states or is she a New Zealander?"

"Actually, neither. She's a British subject, born in London to working class parents and later, raised in Perth, Australia, a very unusual childhood. Last month, she completed a grant up north. You know, she's one of a handful of authorities on Maori culture and symbolism. Not one to miss an opportunity, she flew down the moment she heard Marshall was invited to join our little party."

Raymond moved closer, directly behind her seat, "Dr. Brown's quite complex and difficult to get to know. When you have the opportunity, look at her hands. Not one callous or broken nail. Unheard of for an earth scientist! You know, hands can tell a lot about a person. And she's more seasoned than she looks. I put her at under forty. She's been in the field for at least twenty years. Then, the time she worked with Jeremy? Doesn't make sense." Raymond continued to ramble on. "Unless, of course, she's a child genius and obtained her degrees years ahead of schedule. But don't ask her age unless you want to make an enemy. She's a private, guarded woman. You know others like her, well, not exactly like her. No one's exactly like her." She's not one for small talk." The Professor was still rambling, trying to stay close to Kate's faint woman scent.

Kate could feel his warm breath as did Bill. He turned in his seat and made solid eye contact with the Professor. "Raymond, would you mind backing off a bit? The air's getting pretty stuffy in here." Bill Shepherd utilized his diplomatic tenor and Raymond, on cue, took a step back.

"Sorry Bill, I didn't mean to crowd you. Just pretty tight in here and I hate to shout. Now, where was I? Oh, Yes. I know Dr. Brown is a well-read, talented earth scientist, and degrees in a number of disciplines, archeology, paleontology and vast studies in Maori culture. She's certainly an interesting colleague of Jeremy. He and Brown have been working together, on and off, for at least fifteen years or did I already tell you that?" The plane came to a stop at the gate. Raymond paused to haul his bag out of the overhead bin.

"Before you ask, no, they are not a couple, Jeremy and Maggie. They never were. Fact is, Jeremy's one of the few men who hasn't been devoured by her. She's strong willed. And Jeremy, well, he's Jeremy. A bit flighty, if you get my drift. Has a separate life off campus nobody talks about it. You know, he's so respected in his chosen field.

Raymond kept up his rambling dialogue. "Maggie had been married to a brilliant scholar who headed up the philosophy department at the same university. I heard he made the mistake of questioning her on some subject dear to her heart and she objected as only Maggie could."

Kate couldn't avoid becoming entangled in long-winded story. This was a woman who could cause them grief down the road.

Raymond continued on. "At the same time, her husband, I believe his name was Randolph, became involved with the English Parliament, some distinguished position and planned his move back to London. But I'm afraid no one crosses Maggie. He lost his post along with his marriage. No coincidence, I'm afraid. She put his feet to the fire and emptied out the closet filled with his skeletons and nearly destroyed the man. He went back to London, alone, a broken man, with his tail between his legs."

Bill rolled his eyes. He knew what Kate was thinking. Life was too short to deal with such difficult people.

Raymond cleared his throat. "I hear she's off men, except, of course, for her worker bees. You're a woman, so you can probably sympathize. She's the queen bee and somehow she finds a steady supply of drones and worker bees to jump at her commands."

'Why so much energy explaining away this manipulative woman?' Kate thought of Raymond's persistent attempts to bed her. "So, Raymond, you tried, and she turned you down?"

Out of the blue, his male defenses surfaced, "Damn, Kate, I don't chase every female I meet. You have no idea, especially in Maggie Brown's case. I just wanted you to get an idea of who she was in case you had to deal with her. That's all." He sounded wounded, offended by her jab.

Bill Shepherd maintained a low profile. This was Kate's skirmish to win.

"No, Raymond. You only chase the ones with breasts!" She had to laugh. "Sorry, Raymond, I couldn't let that one go. It's just that well the way you go on about her. I imagine she must be a rather pretty but difficult challenge."

Bill had to chuckle at her quick comeback. Kate had learned her lessons the hard way and could handle this aggressive womanizer as well as anyone.

The professor noticed curious eyebrows lifting in the rows around the Shepherds and he bristled at the passengers' reactions. He could hear the chuckles and whispers rising around him. He leaned close to Kate's ear. "Please Kate, could you keep it down. Actually, just let it rest, OK." He had chosen the topic but suddenly found he was flustered and uncomfortable with so many strangers eavesdropping on this private discourse.

"Let's move on, shall we?" Kate backed off, flashed him a coy smile then grinning satisfactorily. She turned away from his scarlet face. "OK Professor. No more discussions about your lady friend. The doors will be opening shortly."

Over the past several minutes, Raymond could feel his temperature rise with the familiar tightening in his loins. Kate released a sexual charge that was hard to ignore. His fingertips tingled. He imagined her warm skin under his touch. He changed the subject to something more neutral, like the advancing hands on his watch, "Good, we're nearly on time. Jeremy will be meeting us with a small caravan of vehicles." His voice was suddenly cheerful. Raymond had raised the symbolic white flag. Much to his dismay, the vision of Kate's warm body would never fade from his memory.

The subject changed, Bill felt safe replying. "Old man, we were planning on renting a car but it's kind of your friend to consider us."

"Nonsense. The best way to get where we're going is with Camper Vans. They're very accommodating. You can eat, sleep and maintain a research facility, all in one practical vehicle. We've rented a total of four so you'll have privacy and you can venture off at will."

G'day

"G'day ! G'day! Over here, will you! Yes, Miss Jenkins, Raymond!"

A jovial, round faced fellow with a resonating voice called out and a hundred heads turned towards the exuberant greeting. Raymond spotted the rotund gentleman standing beside a woman of average height, short brown hair, dark eyes and a very pretty face. Rubbery legged, the weary travelers edged their way through the throng of eager greeters to be warmly welcomed by their host.

Jeremy took two giant steps forward, "My goodness, Kate, you haven't changed a day! Every bit as lovely as I remember." He planted a brotherly kiss on her cheek. "And this must be your fortunate husband, William Shepherd." Jeremy's faced danced as she made eye contact with his lively, blue eyes. "Welcome, my friend! I've heard great, heroic stories about you. May I address you as William or do you prefer Bill?" His tone was ingratiating.

"Either William or Bill, whatever is comfortable for you, only if I can call you Jeremy?" Bill Shepherd immediately liked the jolly, affable man.

"Of course, Bill, I feel we will become fast mates. So, yes, Jeremy it is!" His North Island accent was rhythmic and charming.

At the same time, Kate and Bill were swept into his soft, pudgy arms. Jeremy Marshall was surely a very likeable and cuddly sort of creature. How could they have doubted his sincerity? Bill took a firm hold of his hand and Jeremy shook it like he was grappling with a large fish.

"Wonderful, wonderful. I adore these reunions." He placed his broad, soft-lips next to Kate's delicate earlobe,

"You found a handsome bloke, Kate. Good on ya, Kate. I was hoping you'd wait for me!" He winked and gave her a friendly pat on the rump.

An effortless laugh broke free and spilled onto everyone within earshot. Perfect strangers paused and began to mimic his contagious chortling. His manner was so disarming; no one with a warm spot in his or her soul could take offense.

Once released from his generous grasp, the small group followed his dramatic hand motion. Kate and Bill Shepherd and Raymond Morrissey locked eyes with the woman who was idly standing out of the traffic pattern. "And mates, this is my dear friend, Dr. Maggie Brown, the most brilliant scientist I've ever come to know. Her list of accomplishments goes on and on. And a true beauty as well."

Maggie Brown was a beauty. A fine cap of dark short hair framed her nearly perfect features. Her almond shaped deep brown eyes were penetrating as they flitted from face to face. Kate couldn't help but notice that they lingered a moment longer on the men. She was small in stature yet her figure was ample and sensuous. Raymond would pursue her if given the opportunity.

Kate and Bill reached out to continue Jeremy's warm welcoming gestures. Dr. Maggie Brown masked a smile as if well rehearsed. Quite discomforting. She pursed her lips, forming a sealed orifice, like a mother unhappy with her disobedient children. Strangely and inappropriately, Dr. Maggie Brown looked displeased. It took only a moment to pour cool water over Jeremy's warm, bubbling brew. The lips spread in a tight smile. "I'm pleased to meet you."

Her voice was strained and the words sounded rehearsed and awkward. She was the most diminutive member of the group yet she seemed to look down on everyone. "So, you are friends of Raymond as well? Then without warning her voice went through a series of subtle changes, her accent, from classic Queen's English, to Eastern American and finally to Aussie English, as if she was uncertain who she wanted to be. The change was subtle but to a CIA agent's trained ear, it spelled trouble. Bill caught Kate's gaze and rolled his eyes skyward as if to say, 'Oh God, what have we got here?'

Bill was skillfully trained to observe facial expressions as well as body language. He was unconsciously on the lookout for high-risk terrorists or other rogues, of various religious, political or ethnic persuasions, anyone who possibly could pose a national or international threat. Maggie Brown was a case study. He'd make a call to Langley before they ventured out of Queenstown. Not that she was a terrorist but he was curious. Jeremy jumped in with all the enthusiasm a round, monk-like fellow could manage. Apparently he was blind to her strange behaviors. "Now, now, mates, we'll have plenty of time to chit chat later. I'm eager to ask you questions. But right now, I believe we better hoist your belongings and head towards our caravan. I've secured the finest coaches. Vans. Camper vans! All white and comfy! Anyone need the loo?"

Shepherd tailed Jeremy's and Raymond's camper van while the others followed closely behind, first, turning left on Frankton Road, then touring at a comfortable thirty miles per hour. The two lane highway ran along the banks of frigid Lake Wakatipi, a crystal clear deep blue body of water that intimately bordered Queenstown proper then subtly widened as it wound through the impressive, brilliantly green, rolling countryside, meandering through the awe inspiring fiords located a fair distance away.

The ride was short and the view, pristine and quite rural, considering populated Queenstown lay less than five miles down the road.

One by one, the camper vans turned left off Frankton Road and stopped directly behind a series of tall, non descript two story buildings. A pleasant, young Kiwi nicknamed Pepper, greeted the group, and one by one, logged their names and made arrangements to carry their bags to their rooms. A friendly sort, Pepper efficiently led the small party of scientists through the compact entry, where he produced five numbered room keys. Kate and Bill accepted their key and after a brief discussion, walked up a short flight of stairs that led directly to Suite 3A.

Once inside, they were dazzled by a beautiful, panoramic view. Crystal clear water lazily slapped against the grassy banks one hundred feet below. And another two thousand feet across the narrow waterway, lay lush green hills, the same hills captured so beautifully in Lord of the Rings. The view was as spectacular and pristine as late spring in New Zealand promised to be.

The suite was more condo, than hotel room, featuring a comfortably furnished great room a broad deck and an efficient kitchen, completely equipped to prepare meals and easily entertain. The wide glass sliders opened to the spacious wood deck, with two inviting outdoor chaises, a casual teak wood dining table and a view stretching to the quaint heavily wooded center of Queenstown. Lastly, an open staircase led up to two master bedrooms that were nicely decorated, roomy and inviting.

Within minutes, a young bellman tapped on their door then quickly deposited their luggage. After he was properly tipped, they took barely a minute to occupy one of the luxurious king sized beds.

"You know, I really love you." William Shepherd, CIA agent, had that serious, *"I'm tired but I love you still"* look. "Can we sleep first, *then* make love?" His body hit the wall and no amount of urging could change that.

Kate pursed her lips, "I was hoping you'd say that. I'm exhausted. An hour from now, we'll jump in the shower and then see where it goes." She curled in his arms and was asleep before her handsome husband could say another word.

"Sweet dreams, my love." Queenstown, Jeremy, Raymond, the odd Dr. Brown, the miner's letter along with their anticipated love making would have to wait.

Kate awoke to the gentle sound of running water and a familiar hand carefully unbuttoning her Egyptian cotton blouse. Without opening her eyes, she imagined his touch and where his hands would lead. He tenderly kneaded her bare breast, sending chills down her spine, to the warm, moist place nestled between her thighs. She let him take charge. Her man's fondling was pure pleasure. He took his time and feasted on her, a banquet that would last until there was nothing left!

"Oh my!" Kate managed a moan, and then felt her lover's warm, firm body make careful contact, then slide deeply into her warm center. Slowly, they moved to their own rhythm, their heat gradually building. Kate held on as long as she could but the smooth motion got to her and suddenly, without further prompting, little shudders resonated and her dam broke free. At that very instant, Kate's lover followed her lead, consciously controlling his release, then deftly, letting go, their fluids blending into a perfect lovers' cocktail.

Locked in an idyllic pose, the couple drifted back and forth, between fantasy and the reality of their sublime moment. Soon, the two realities merged and they drifted back to sleep.

Bill woke first and utilizing all of the hours spent working out at the gym, he lifted Kate, still a single, connected unit and carried her to the steam filled shower. The warm water traced over her bare shoulders and soon revived her spirit. The perfect conclusion! They reveled in the fresh, restorative mist. "Oh Mr. Shepherd, am I dreaming? Is this? Are you real?" She held him firmly and thanked God for bringing them together. His heart beat powerfully against her breast.

Filling his hand with scented body wash, he let his hands run over the full length of her body, pausing at the spot that brought him greatest joy. "Yes, Kate, you're dreaming!" He found her pleasure and massaged her until she leaned back quivering with another orgasmic release. "I'm dreaming."

"Oh, my God, darling. Oh, my God." She could put no more words together. "I love you."

Queenstown

The Shepherds were the last to arrive at the casual outdoor café in the heart of Queenstown. "G'day everyone! I hope we didn't keep you waiting too long. We fell asleep and well , no excuses. We're here now." They sat around the sprawling picnic table. A young man, yet to be formally introduced, passed two cool Aussie bottles of beer their way.

"G'day, Raymond. I hope you caught up on your sleep!" Bill Shepherd was relaxed and confident. He was happy and glowing with satisfaction. He tried to cover his internal feelings but he was sure they spilled out of him.

Jeremy could no longer contain himself. "Excellent, excellent! You don't know how I'm enjoying this reunion. I hardly see my old colleagues these days." Jeremy downed his beer and waved to the server to bring another round. "I want to hear from all of you. I want to know what you're searching for and how I can help. I know the countryside and the small towns and cities. I'll gladly open doors if it has to be done, mates!"

Kate scoured the table, making friendly eye contact, returning pleasantries and conducting quiet, non-invasive interviews. When she had nearly traversed the rustic table she focused lightly on Dr. Maggie Brown, then she tried to break through the woman's self-imposed barrier. Although Bill had prepared her, Kate couldn't resist pushing the envelope. " G'day Maggie. May I call you Maggie?"

"Actually, I'd prefer Doctor or Dr. Brown. I worked hard for that title and I like to use it. I'm sure you understand the importance of a well earned title."

'Hmm, interesting response'. She didn't like Kate. Yes, it was obvious she preferred interacting with men. "Fine, then Doctor Brown, I hear you just completed a very provocative grant. Would you mind describing the subject? I'd love to hear about it!" Kate tried to balance the Doctor's negativity with her own positive mood. After all, she'd just had some of the best sex since they were married! She was bursting with positive energy. "Would you indulge me Dr. Brown?"

"Maybe later. I get such a headache trying to explain what I do." He eyes studied Kate then Dr. Brown intentionally turned away from her. She was dismissed, just like that. The mighty Dr. Brown had solidly rebuffed her.

Had she believed that Kate, also a brilliant PhD, would have difficulty grasping her project? Kate decided to jump into her little game, "Dr. Brown, I understand completely. You know, I have the same problem. Whenever I'm at the grocery store and some woman behind me in line, wiping jam off her child's face, asks me about ancient DNA markers, I get a headache, too." There was deadening silence. Maybe she had gone too far to make her point. She just had great sex. *'To hell with her!'*

The doctor's lips tightened and nearly vanished. Kate thought she heard her teeth grinding against each other. At the same time, the doctor's eyes narrowed into little brown slits and her skin became noticeably blotchy and flushed.

Both Kate and Bill could read her body language. Anyone around their table could. She was thinking, *'How dare anyone question her intellect, especially another woman?'* She tossed her head, took a noticeable breath to regain her composure. She flashed a smile. *'The little bitch was trying to play chess with her. She'll lose.'*

In a silky smooth voice lacking sincerity, Dr. Brown faced Kate, the contrived smile showed strain in her jaw, "I'm so sorry, Dr. Shepherd, but I do have a headache. Believe me. I didn't mean to be so brusque." She thought to herself, *'But I did mean it and I'd say it again.'*

"Apology accepted." Kate dropped the idea of extending the confrontation so she turned her attention to the young interns who were doing their best to ignore the two women's war of wits. They labored under the affable Dr. Jeremy Marshall and had only recently walked on brittle eggshells dealing with Dr. Maggie Brown.

Each had quickly learned to keep their temperamental and critical thoughts to themselves, unless of course, they found reason to stroke her enormous ego. Kate had stood up to her and lived to tell the tale. Jeremy's interns would sing her praises and laugh about it later, when at a safe distance. *'Someone actually called her bluff.'*

"And you must be Harry! You look like a Harry!" The young man was tall and slim, dressed in a deep green flannel shirt and Levis. His hair was long, curly and carrot red. Kate liked his friendly smile. "I know Miss, sorry, Dr. Shepherd, just like Prince Harry! I hear it all the time. I wasn't named after him but I'm not offended by the comparison. He's a good man." His cheeks were flushed like a young, British gentleman beginning to come to terms with his manhood and the newly sprouted auburn whiskers that curled around the tip of his firm chin. Kate smiled warmly as his shy demeanor warmed her then she let her eyes travel to the young man seated across from him.

"Let me guess. I bet you're Peter!" The medium height, dark haired young man was well muscled, tanned a rich bronze and had a wonderful, open smile displaying straight, white teeth. He was head turning handsome yet he seemed unaffected by his easy sexual presence. He would break many hearts.

Kate was enjoying the surprised looks on their handsome, well scrubbed faces. She had done her homework on the way to dinner. "And, let me guess, Peter, you're an artist. Your job is to interpret and catalogue what everyone else on the team uncovers. And Harry, you're a detail man and you take copious notes in the field."

Pleasantly surprised Harry spoke in a fresh and pleasant voice, "My, Dr. Shepherd, you're good!" Studying his hands and holding up his right hand to the light, "What gave me away? Was it the ebony pencil stains on my pinkie?"

"Yes, that and, I cannot tell a lie. I read both of your dossiers, quite impressive for being so young., and working under Jeremy. Dr. Marshall, that alone tells me a great deal. He only chooses the most talented students!" She laughed at her ruse. "I hope I didn't embarrass you."

"No, you didn't, not at all. Embarrass us, I mean, Dr. Shepherd, but Pete and I are both twenty-four. We're not that young. And you probably already know, by checking our credentials that this is our third trip into the field with Professor Marshall. Trust me. I speak for both Peter and myself we're eager to learn and help out any way we can. That's what it's all about." His sincerity was genuine. Kate thought they were both fine, likeable young scholars.

"Dr. Shepherd, if you ever need an intern in America, I would like that opportunity." Harry blushed and turned towards, Dr. Marshall. "Oh, Dr. Marshall. I didn't mean I don't want to continue with you..." he was flustered. "I meant perhaps when you run out of work for me, I'd enjoy the opportunity to study under her, I mean Dr. Shepherd."

Jeremy laughed. He took no offense. "My boy, I've been trying to work under her for years!" His off color joke sent the group into fits of laughter and the two young men beamed at being included in personal parlor talk.

Dr. Maggie Brown sat quietly, her hands folded in her lap. She smiled briefly and rolled her eyes. She didn't like being left out. She was offended that they didn't beg to work under her tutorage. Dr. Brown was accustomed to being fawned over, now and forever. She knew Jeremy's young men were nothing special or they'd be at her door. Jeremy Marshall would be nothing without her encouragement and knowledge sharing. At a whim, she could shake the tree and get rid of the bad apples, the one's that didn't dance to her tune. Including Dr. Kate Shepherd.

Vetting

What Kate hadn't mentioned to the young interns when they questioned her uncanny knowledge of them was her CIA husband's complete vetting of everyone sitting around the table. William Shepherd was cautious to a fault but after the difficulties they'd encountered in Peru, he made a point of checking into everyone's backgrounds, including the jovial Jeremy and the fractious Dr. Brown.

Jeremy Marshall's dossier came back without a single blemish. He said whom he be and didn't lie. He remained discreet about his sexual preference and never let it interfere with his work either in the classroom or in the field. Within his profession, he was listed among the best, and brightest yet in recent years, his ability to be as effective in the field diminished as his waistline expanded. He attracted the brightest interns and these young assistants were destined to excel under his casual yet thorough tutorage. And Jeremy did his own vetting, turning away young scholars lacking the fire and passion he required.

Years before, Kate had been mentioned as a viable candidate and Jeremy wrote a number of flattering letters trying to gain her attention but Raymond had vied for her as well and apparently had successfully blocked the line of communication between Jeremy and his personal favorite. Kate was unaware that Raymond had guided her career to that extent. She would have been furious, but for now, her husband chose to withhold that information from her. Perhaps that time would come.

Jeremy received a gold star. Dr. Maggie Brown did not. Her thick file was rich with awards yet varied and troubling. It began with her earliest childhood. She was an only child, born to Eastern European parents of the working class. She was the second son her father had wanted. The first son unfortunately had died at birth. The older brother would have relieved the pressure.

Enrolled in a Catholic school, Maggie was tested and the results came back indicating a child of extraordinary brilliance. The problem? She was told the truth and from that point on, she ruled her parents, treating them with unreasonable contempt. She was smarter and no one, including her own parents could influence her choices or control her raging temper and her uncanny ability to manipulate and control her illustrious future. When Maggie became a legal adult, she changed her name to cover her shame of her parents' foreign sounding name that ended in *ski.* Brown was her chosen name and it worked for her.

The Mensa member sailed along, becoming the first and youngest at every level of her academic career. People, including her professors, learned to keep a safe distance. She was never wrong or at least, she would not admit to being at fault. . She never apologized because *"if Maggie's always right, then why the need to apologize?"* And she would never forget. Cross her once and you became a lifelong enemy.

She was the center of her universe and everyone and everything revolved around her. She lacked empathy. She could charm the king but loathe the very sight of him. She'd feed a starving child then rush to wash away the filth.

Still, she was brilliant and excelled in spite of her functional disability, recognized as Narcissistic Personality Disorder. She preferred men to women and treated other females with contempt. On a positive note, a woman plagued with this disorder, could reject, manipulate to get her way and divide and conquer nearly anyone that came under her influence but rarely would a woman with NPD kill to support her desire to control the outcome of her important all encompassing world.

A male, on the other hand, could kill after his five-course dinner! Many of the classic serial murderers matched traits and were equally brilliant, lacked empathy and often experienced grandiose feelings of superiority.

Like athletes with quirky, dangerous habits, Maggie took steps up the ladder of success, predicated on her ability to deliver the goods while intimidating and manipulating anyone who dared challenge her. *"The ends justify the means."*

Earlier in the evening, Kate had read Brown's profile then covered her head with a bed pillow, "Damn, what a piece of work! Give me two hard working interns with normal IQ's and send the oddball back to London for a turn of the century lobotomy! How in the world can she work with anyone?"

Bill had to chuckle. "That's easy. She doesn't. That, meaning anyone who comes in contact with her, works *for* her or not at all. She is no team player. And I don't automatically assume she's without physical risk. I've witnessed women, trained in radical, political conditions, who would slit your throat as efficiently as any well trained, fanatical man. Or hire someone to do the deed. It's unusual but not unheard of. Dear Kate, we'll head off on our own as soon as we can."

"But, Darling, how do we do that without hurting Jeremy? And, come to think of it, how in the world does he maintain a relationship with her? I'm baffled. He's such a sweet guy."

"Well, one thing, Jeremy's gay. I didn't mention anything because it doesn't matter. The guy's a saint and I like him."

"Yes, me too but his being out of the closet has never been an issue with him. He's comfortable with his choice in life partners and the school accepted him because of his brilliance, nothing else. So you think that Maggie, sorry, the Doctor, has something else on him? Or maybe, she just doesn't feel threatened by him?"

"Yes, something like that. She likely outed him years ago and she's used threats to keep him in line. Something damning. If it's to her advantage, she'll use it. Jeremy works with her and uses self-deprecating humor to ward her off. All that laughter covers some, but not all, of his distrust."

"But why now? Everyone is coming out of the closet. What has he to worry about?"

Bill Shepherd gave it more thought as they prepared to meet for dinner. Yes, they were running late but this was important. "I imagine there's more. Jeremy has a few skeletons and Maggie would love to haul them out for the entire world to see. I bet that extra weight he's packing comes from worry. He knows how dangerous she can be. Keep your friends close and your enemies closer."

"Well, she's as close as she can get. Damn her. Just, well, I was hoping for an informative, fun trip. Not another punch to my battered psyche." Kate combed her damp hair back and tied it loosely with a blue ribbon.

Bill came to her side and gave her a squeeze, Don't worry. I'll take care of Dr. Maggie Brown. Knowledge is power and we have both, knowledge and power. So leave that up to me. She'll deal with me better than you. She's programmed to compete with you. With me she'll flutter her lashes.

The Plan

So, as they sat and chatted at dinner, each member of the party downed their third cold beer, along with the sliced lamb, sizzling shrimp on the Barbie and hot plates of bangers. The baskets of chips were greasy and served with a side of mayo, instead of the American way, with catsup, an acquired taste.

"Well, mates, down to business, shall we?" Jeremy, wiped the flavorless mayo from his chin, cleared his throat and continued. " I feel we have a few dreary days ahead. I heard some rain's in the forecast so if I may, I suggest we grab our gumboots and enjoy the fjords, just to keep our sensibilities. The rain may not move in but just in case... then we'll get to work on your little projects!"

Jeremy continued, "Nothing like a boat ride down the lake to Walter Peak and you'll certainly enjoy Milford Sound. I have so much to introduce you to. New Zealand, mates, is quite spectacular".

Dr. Marshall was delighted playing tour guide for his foreign visitors. "You know, my friends, it's all so beautiful and peaceful. It will give you some extra time to catch up on those bloody time differences. Be sure to wear your slickers or oilcloths. Whatever you have to fend off the damp."

"Nice in the drizzle, perhaps it won't rain after all, who minds, mates! Cold beer, and a stop at the Colonel's Farmhouse for a BBQ! My treat! This is my *Aotearoa* ! You know what that means blokes?" Laughing as he put forth the question then just as quickly answering,

"Translated, that's Maori for New Zealand, it means '*land of the long, white cloud'*. Pretty much says it all, doesn't it?"

Jeremy fell back in his chair and rubbed his ample belly. "What do you say?"

Kate responded first to his invitation. "Jeremy that would be wonderful. I'm all for it. Work can certainly wait a day or two."

The others joined in, appreciating the generous offer of a cruise, free beer and an authentic Kiwi BBQ!

The only sour note came as expected, from Dr. Maggie Brown. "Well, I imagine it would be pleasant enough. But I have research to do. I don't know if I can spare the time.

Maggie, who cleverly made herself the center of everyone's concerns, finally gave in to Jeremy's insistence. "Well, if you really need me to help you understand the history of the Sound." She rolled her eyes. "Well then, it's settled. I'll come along."

Bill and Kate gently bumped knees. Dr. Brown might very well be brilliant in her field, but her attention getting ploy was childish and too obvious.

"Jeremy was relieved. His little reunion was a success. He counted heads and planned to phone in a reservation for first thing in the morning. The 1912 coal fired vintage steamship, the TSS Ernslaw, would provide an enjoyable cruise for his little party.

There would be a total of nine, Kate, William, Dr. Brown, the interns, Harry and Peter, Raymond, and of course, Jeremy and his borrowed help, Gregory and Anita, yet to make an appearance. He wished that his lifelong partner, Stephen could have come along, but the Auckland restaurant, Dominos, that he owned and the fine kitchen he oversaw, was serving a flurry of discriminating customers since the fine review had appeared in the local newspaper. "

8.2 On The Richter Scale ,The Earth Quake

It was 5:51AM.

"Honey, what was that?" Kate was burrowed into her husband's warm back when she woke with a start. "Something's bumping the bed."

Bill bolted upright. "Earthquake!" He threw on the khaki's that were draped over the small bench, just before the room erupted.

Kate reached over and flicked on the light, illuminating the room and exposing a phenomenon that was hard to explain. "My God, the floor, look at the floor!"

As if the carpeted floor had turned to molasses, it shifted in dizzying waves. Bill grabbed Kate's hand and pulled her from the bed and away from the expanse of glass windows, into the more secure doorway. They held each other and braced themselves.

The walls bent to and fro while the framed pictures on the walls, bumped and slid back and forth on their wire hooks. Kate could hear her cosmetics, set around the bathroom counter, tumble to the floor, rolling like marbles on the bulging tile floor. The floor to ceiling windows bowed and Bill hoped they had enough play in them not to burst under the stress. The wooden deck and railings bent and swayed like the top deck of a fishing trawler caught in a mighty storm. The earth was groaning. Grinding. Strange.

It was surreal. The scent of concrete dust wafted up the stairs from the great room casting ghostly little images. The Italian, hanging lamps, behaved more like wind chimes, swinging in wide circles. Their bedroom was hauntingly alive, the earth breathing and growling, like grating, rusty gears escaping their well-carved grooves.

The earthquake felt like it went on forever but in reality, it lasted only 90 seconds, long enough to shake up their world. The energy created by the earth's violent movement transferred to their bones and muscles and once the rolling ceased, Kate and Bill continued to feel the earth's power surge pass through them.

When the room finally stood still, the couple stepped away from the doorjamb, still holding each other tightly. The lights were glowing gold as a thin curtain of dust drifted across the room.

"The power's still on. I'll turn on the TV! We need to know where the epicenter was. It could be a six here and an eight at the center." He took careful strides to the remote and flicked on the news station.

The screen miraculously lit up with a map of the South Island area and an expert on seismic activity was already in place alongside the glowing red diagrams. *"As you just felt, we've experienced a major earthquake. The exact epicenter is still being evaluated through our extensive system of sensors"* Shuffling papers. *"Here comes a report! Right now, we show a quake of a magnitude 8.2, a major, catastrophic earthquake, centered twenty-five miles south/southwest of Christchurch on the South Island including Irontown, and expanding in waves through the center of Christchurch."*

"Damn, that's off the scale. Loss of life and property could be astronomical." Bill wiped a hand across his eyes, trying to clear his head from the reality of the moment.

The phone rang and Kate picked up the land line, "Kate Shepherd here, hello,"

It was Jeremy, his voice was high pitched and breathless. "Oh, thank God, are you both OK?"

"We made it OK, what about you and the others?" Kate could hear her own voice, raspy, nervous and unsure.

"Shaken but not stirred. Oh, that's earthquake humor!"

At a moment like this, Kate was startled that the round, robust man could find room for humor.

"Thanks for that, Jeremy. You brought me back to earth! Bill and I are watching the TV emergency broadcast. It looks really bad, especially to the north and east. Can we do anything for you or the others?"

"Our building's faired well but there's bound to be damage. I think it's best to gather your belongings and head to the parking area in front of the buildings." Kate could hear Jeremy speaking to others in their party.

"I'm sorry, I have to go. Please move carefully. We may have more aftershocks perhaps even larger than the first jolt. It was a roller with strong earth movement. My my. I am so sorry for the quake. I was looking forward to a day on the water, but I imagine that is on permanent hold. There is more to be concerned with now."

"Nothing to apologize for, Jeremy. We'll hurry along and, Jeremy, you be careful. And the others…" Jeremy hung up. They began to gather their belongings and Kate quickly picked up the spilled toiletries on the bathroom floor. With everything laid out on the bed, another shockwave passed through them and the floor bellowed. The sound of tinkling glass was followed by another strong rolling motion, their feet caught off balance, like walking on a soft air mattress. They fell back on the bed and waited.

"That was nearly as strong as the first." Kate's breathing was quick but she was under control. "Time to get out of here."

"We just experienced, an aftershock of nearly 6.2. The 8.2 was felt from Christchurch and the coast, north all the way south to Milford Sound. Calls are continuing to come in. Damage is extensive and many are assumed to be trapped in their homes and businesses." The seismic needle grew from a single dark line to severe peaks and valleys.

The earthquake expert continued, *"Please, everyone, remain in a safe place, away from windows, and falling debris. Turn off natural gas and be aware of any leaks. As I speak, all communication is reported down in the epicenter site, and a radius of approximately 50 mile. Keep wireless radios on at all times."*

The earthquake authority was professional but her voice was cracking under the strain. *"Cell phone usage is overloading the system so please, please be patient if you are trying to reach loved ones. And keep close to an emergency radio or TV broadcast with the latest information."*

The emergency system was exceptionally efficient and up to the minute. Had the power failed, the small radio next to their bed could be battery operated and would continue reporting instructions on evacuation procedures, rescue and available emergency centers.

Kate and Bill, quickly dressed in jeans and khaki's, carried their bags down the slightly ajar stairs then dropped them outside the lobby's door. Inspecting for damage, they saw gaping cracks and dislodged roof tiles scattered around the driveway but no major damage.

"We were lucky. It was a roller, not a shaker, at least here. Not as violent and damaging. But that doesn't mean the building is stable. At least the upper floors didn't pancake down on our heads." Bill held Kate close by his side.

"At the site of the epicenter, I'm afraid the damage." As William Shepherd was talking, another wave of aftershocks hit, nearly as strong as the last.

Kate looked past the buildings to the lake, its shores overcome by tall, well-formed waves. "Darling, the water! That's incredible! The power of the Earth! " The waves washed over the footpath that they had walked on last evening, and carried debris into the lower parking lot, fifty feet from where they gathered. There wasn't enough distance and depth to create real concern on the lake.

"*A tsunami warning has been issued....*" The main bodies of water surrounding New Zealand's South Island could be another story.

The group, some dressed and others, still in their nightclothes, hugged and chattered about their personal experiences confronting the quake. Some compared the 8.2 trembler, to others they had lived through. The young interns were pale and silent. They were virgins where earthquakes were concerned. Jeremy instructed them to pack the travel vans then wait behind the wheel while everyone completed their final exit preparations.

The complex manager, sweating profusely, joined the group and apologized. Pointing out severe cracks in the foundation and the place where two balconies had pulled loose from their anchors, he explained that he was certain that the official inspectors would tag his complex as unsafe, at least until a more thorough examination had been made.

He looked beaten down, aware that his income had been suddenly impacted. "Mates, we must consider ourselves fortunate. And God help our mates, especially those in Christchurch."

Sirens blared from a distance and traffic on the road was exclusively fire vehicles and emergency rescue squads. Once the vans were loaded, the group of nine gathered around Jeremy. The earth once again shook, not violently but enough to keep the event first and foremost on their minds.

"Listen please, I've taken the liberty to check with our local emergency center and I've volunteered our help and expertise. I hope you don't mind, but we have tools to dig and I'm afraid there are people trapped in collapsed buildings. Queenstown experienced broken windows, foundation damage and cuts and bruises but nothing, nothing like what lies to the north and east."

There was no debate. They knew the role they must accept. Their options were laid out simply and unanimously the group of archeologists agreed to lend a hand. First, they'd head in a caravan to the Queenstown Central Emergency Office and organize a relief effort under the guidance of the local relief officials

Search and Rescue

Bill and Kate prepared their self contained camper van to aide in the rescue attempts. He got hold of Jeremy and advised him that they had personal reasons to help in Arrowtown, the small, historic town fifty miles to the north and would not go with the group.

Radio broadcasts indicated that, while still away from the epicenter, Arrowtown had sustained major damage to their historic sites. As a town of approximately seventeen hundred people, it had little funding; few rescue assets or any type of infrastructure. Raymond immediately volunteered to join their small party but both Jeremy and Bill insisted that he join the main search and rescue group to add his valuable expertise.

Surprisingly, Dr. Maggie Brown, who'd remained mute to this point, took Raymond's arm and reinforced the position that his knowledge and strong back would be most valuable to her as well as the group. Raymond was thrown off his game and succumbed to a woman's charms once more!

It was agreed that they would all communicate with the local authorities as a way of keeping in touch with each other's progress and location. Time was the essence in reaching the devastated areas and rescuing the trapped and injured.

Once organized, the parties went their separate ways.

They were told that Arrowtown's hotels were filled at the height of the tourist season. The Lake District and Chinese Museum were high points of any trip to Arrowtown, plus the panning sites available to tourists along the Arrow River. They'd have their work cut out for them.

As Kate and Bill Shepherd drove the fifty miles north along the split and cracked pavement, Kate distracted herself by rereading the miner's letter, describing the location of the unusual carved bone they were hoping to locate. It seemed inconsequential now, with the earthquake and the damage and loss of life they were about to witness firsthand.

The carved bone appeared, by description, to have many of the same or similar markings as the gourd they discovered in Peru the previous year. They guestimated the gourd predated the carved bone by hundreds of years. The Maori who had befriended the long deceased brothers had no idea the age or heritage of the relic.

A tree lay across their path and Bill swung the van wide, off the road surface, brushing the branches against the hood and bending the antenna in half, breaking it free of its mount.

"Damn, there goes our radio. Grab the backpack and fire up our Emergency radio band, would you."

Kate pulled the small radio from the pack and plugged the power source into the lighter outlet. The radio, though loaded with static, came to life.

"The tsunami warning for New Zealand has been lifted. The coast below Christchurch was spared. Apparently, the wave energy dispersed into open waters to the northeast, including the Alaskan coast. The warning was still posted. Again, the tsunami alert is lifted for New Zealand, North and South Islands."

The geologic main system was working smoothly and the reports were coming in, as outlying towns were able to relay them.

Kate tried to pick up where she left off, "You know, the letter makes it sound like the carvings have some sort of a tie to gold, so there may be local significance, at least to Arrowtown, what's left of it."

Her husband, looked worried and preoccupied, as he slowed the van, "Kate, my dear, that's all well and good but I think right now, the only thing we can think about is helping mount a rescue." As he slowed further, the outskirts of Arrowtown appeared through a film of dust. " Good God, look at that."

They slowly pulled into the devastated town and were shocked and dismayed at the destruction of the historic buildings. New Zealand was not a stranger to earthquakes but the size and magnitude of this one, 8.2 on the Richter scale, was enormous.

Driving slowly through chaos, the pair searched for emergency relief headquarters. They found an Army field tent and a few official vehicles parked around the side. The mayor and police chief were looking over maps, trying to get a handle on the situation and mount a workable plan.

Around the back of the tent, survivors, covered with dust and in some cases, blood from minor wounds, sat around on benches, looking dazed and disoriented.

Finding a level spot to park the van, they jumped down and pushed the tent flaps back, startling the pair of officials. Agent Shepherd spoke first. "Gentlemen, we're Americans, here on other business but we're qualified to help in the rescue."

The mayor and police chief left the map and firmly gripped the hands of the surprise volunteers. "G'day! As you can see for yourselves, we have quite a mess here. We need all the assistance we can muster." Wiping the nervous sweat from his brow. "Oh, sorry, I'm Arrowtown's current mayor, Albert Dion and this is our Chief Constable, Martin James.

William and Kate warmly accepted their greeting, "And this is Dr. Kate Shepherd, an American archeologist and I am William Shepherd", pausing to construct a believable title, "a former American military man, trained in survival methods The important thing is, we have strong backs and a willingness to help any way we can."

"Excellent, Kate, May I call you Kate? And William?"

"Of course, Kate and Bill. You know I have a special place in my heart for your countryman. I remember fighting alongside you Kiwis during the Gulf War. Good fighters and brave as Hell."

"Good Lord, I was there fighting' with you bloomin' Yanks!" The Constable tightened his grip and gave Bill's back a solid slap.

"Mates, now, we're fighting the wrath of God. He threw us a hard punch, I'm afraid. First, we're concerned about fire. The propane tanks have been partly secured and the gas valves shut off. We need to proceed with the rescue of anyone still trapped in their homes. This quake rattled us early in the AM so most were home tucked in their beds".

Mayor Dion added, " And right now, we think a dozen or so are still unaccounted for. People in Arrowtown are pretty tough blokes and all self-sufficient but I fear there's some that got trapped early on and are holding their breath waiting for a rescue team. Especially, our older folks."

The Americans walked over to the maps spread out on the folding table. "Who do you have in charge now, Mayor Dion?"

"Please, call me Albert. In charge, you ask? Specifically, just the two of us right now. We're waiting for help but no one's rushing our way with so much damage north and east of Arrowtown." The Mayor pulled the Constable aside for a short conference.

The Constable announced, " Bill, Kate, if you accept, I officially put you in charge until we can better sort things out. The duties might change once the military arrives but who knows when that will be."

"You Yanks will get all the help we can call up." The Constable reached for his bullhorn and proceeded to activate a shrill siren bellowing throughout Arrowtown. "Anyone able will come running. Our mayor will take names and get going on identifying our first priorities. I'll give you a hand with rescue supplies over in our armory. Pretty beaten up but still standing."

"Mr. Mayor, Albert, if you would, please bring all available residents to the armory and explain our arrangements. Make that no more than ten minutes. And Chief, you have the map so please detail areas of potential casualties, hotels, restaurants any place that could hold more than 5 people." Bill, a CIA agent, was kicked into his leadership role easily and efficiently.

"I see you have a medical clinic in town." Turning to his wife, now designated his lead assistant, "Kate, how about you head down there and get help setting up a triage facility next to this tent", pointing to the open area usually used for picnics and evening concerts. "There's room along the back side". Seeing more walking wounded "and your first casualties are already lining up."

Kate left the tent and trotted towards the clinic as the first of the townspeople made their way to the temporary headquarters, following the sound of the harsh, insistent siren.

Bill placed a reassuring hand on the Constable's shoulder, "Well, Chief, after only an hour and a half since the earth moved and it looks like we're in business."

Perverse Attraction

Jeremy had gathered the remaining group and with everyone's assistance, loaded the vans with supplies, ranging from emergency medical items to packaged food and water. The trip north to the epicenter's destruction would force them to be self sufficient while helping with the rescue and administrating whatever medical care was required.

Upon Maggie Brown's insistence, Raymond and she would share a camper van. At first, Raymond was surprised at how she had suddenly gravitated towards him. He hadn't been sure she cared for his company but to share a vehicle for an undetermined length of time made him think that he had probably misread her.

As the younger members of their party loaded the supplies, Raymond, taking on a supervisory role, had time to study his new travel companion. She was much prettier than he had initially thought. Standing in the sunlight, her clothing lightly covered with dust and her face, damp from exertion, he realized that she was quite a beauty. Her dark hair framed a perfectly oval face, her lips full and lightly tinted rose and her small, delicate form accentuated full, perfect breasts, not too large. Through her linen shirt, Raymond focused on the darkened points of her nipples and he suddenly felt that strange urge come over him.

It didn't take much coaxing for him to become aroused. His groin tightened and he felt his manhood harden under the layers of khaki and flannel. He laughed to himself. "I'm not so old after all."

It took another half hour to check the road maps and decide on who would lead the rescue procession. Time was important and lives counted on their quick response.

Jeremy and his intern would drive the lead vehicle and the others would follow closely behind. They checked their cell phones and the short wave radios in case they lost phone contact. Jeremy also passed out a few Walkie Talkies to save cell phone battery power.

"Well mates, I think we're ready to move along. We have a fair piece to drive. Kate and William got a pretty good jump on us and I do hope they'll be on sound ground." Jeremy lifted his substantial frame into the passenger seat and closed the door with a might tug. "We may very well have to stop along the way. Never know what we'll run into. Keep your eyes open for stragglers. Downed trees could pose a threat. Eyes open, mates."

One by one, the caravan of 4 vehicles pulled away from Queenstown, heading towards Frankton, then Lower Shotover, to Arrow Junction, then the drive along the coast to Christchurch. There were no guarantees they'd reach their final destination, especially if they ran into impassable obstacles or more likely, small enclaves that needed their strong backs and medical supplies.

Raymond fell in line, third back from Jeremy's lead. "Well, what a way to start a tour of the South Island! Not quite what I had in mind." Raymond tried to hide his concern. "That was quite a shaker! We were damned lucky to ride it out in a solidly built structure. Felt more roller than shake, don't you think, Maggie? Quite a ride, wasn't it?"

Maggie Brown, carefully wiped her damp face with a moist towelette Reminiscent of a large cat on the prowl, she seductively stretched her legs apart then intentionally placed her free hand on Raymond's thigh. "I'm so happy we'll have this chance to get to know each other. I was getting tired of being surrounded by so many young boys. And your Kate? Or should I say, William Shepherd's Kate?"

Her remark was unnerving but the sensation of being touched. His eyes travel down to where Maggie's hand had come to rest. "You know, Maggie, I've wanted to have some time with you, too." He ignored the Kate comment. "It appears we have a lot in common."

Challenging him. "Like what, Professor Morrissey? What do we have in common?"

She seemed to be taunting him yet he let himself get caught up in her game. "Well, let's see. We're in related fields. We're both recognized archeologists. We both teach. And, let's see…"

"And what else, Professor?" Maggie put pressure on his thigh, sending a warning signal straight to his groin.

"We're both unattached?" They were both playing a sexually charged game.

"Yes, yes, Professor Morrissey! You get an A Plus! " Maggie's hand traveled further up his thigh and with no sign of embarrassment or hesitation, she unzipped his khakis and set him free. Then she firmly held him, stroking his rock hard member until he nearly burst. "An A+ Professor Morrissey!"

The camper van drifted off the road and with a sudden jolt, Raymond pulled the top-heavy vehicle back on course. The van behind him slowed while he made a correcting maneuver and checking his rear view mirror, he saw the confused look of the driver following them.

"Damn, I nearly ended up against that tree!" Raymond's voice stammered with excitement yet tinged with wariness. He was usually the aggressor and her overt act took him by surprise. "I think we should be careful." A drop of sweat formed on his brow and made its way south.

Maggie Brown laughed wickedly and kept up her sexual torment. "I heard you were well hung, but Professor, I never imagined you'd come over to my side so willingly."

Raymond was shocked by her rough, sexual suggestion. "Maggie, I guess I should say thanks. I had no idea. Sweet Jesus. What can I say? Of course I'm on your side. Shit!" He was going to burst, right in the middle of the road with a caravan of learned scholars following him.

"Well, for starters, you can say you like it." She reached over the length of the seat and planted a French kiss on him. "Then you can beg me for more." She laughed that laugh that instantly set his nerves on edge.

"Well, yes, of course, who wouldn't want more? Maggie? But we're driving. I could get us killed." He sounded like a schoolboy. "Oh, give me strength."

Maggie had accomplished her mission. She had Raymond right where she wanted him. Their little secret would remain theirs alone. No one ever mentioned these things. Perhaps she had a fetish worth exploiting. Raymond had been a bounder. Everyone familiar with him knew he was a rake. But she knew, with one evening's observation that Raymond would jump into her boat, hook, line and sinker. He was hers alone, to play her devilish game. Yes, she was brilliant in her field but she had needs like everyone else. No, not quite like anyone

Aftershock

Kate gathered a group of healthy ladies and began issuing instructions. Tents, cots and blankets were carried from the armory to the area next to the temporary headquarters. The weather was clear and expected to stay that way for the next several days, a real stroke of luck.

The armory would act, as the morgue and the local physician, Dr. Andrew Mason, would oversee it, when that time came.

"Ladies, you're doing a wonderful job!" Inspecting the double row of tents erected and furnished with two cots each, blankets and hand towels. "Can we set up an area for women and young children? The diapers, oh sorry, nappies and little blankets taken from the sundry store. Have you any idea how many children are living in town?"

A tall, lanky woman of 40, her arms loaded with infant formula, dropped her bundle on a large ground tarp. "Miss, I know of at least 10 infants and there must be at least that many visiting, staying at the different lodgings." Her face was drawn with worry. "I don't know if they're all safe or some are still buried in their homes." She held back the tears and bravely went for a second load of supplies.

Talking to whom-ever could hear her, "Well, we'll be ready for anyone that needs help." Within the hour, Kate, with the help of willing residents, had set up a functioning triage. One tent for minor injuries, stitches, burns, and scrapes and a second tent , for broken bones and other more serious injuries were set up. Critical injuries would be taken care of until skilled medical personnel rolled into town. Hopefully, that would be sooner rather than later.

The chief estimated about 1200 residents and visitors were in and around town when the quake struck. A crude count indicated about 800 men; women and children were now mingling around the triage/park area. That left approximately 400 still unaccounted for.

Using the map, Bill Shepherd divided the town into eight sections and assigned a two-person vehicle to search each area, house by house. Any walking survivors would be placed in a predetermined area in each search section for transport back to central staging. A "missing" list would be created on the large bulletin board carried over from the primary school.

The most immediate problem was sanitation and water. The town had no portable commodes but Harry Smith, a plumber and local plumbing supply owner and Jerry Blackmore, the local lumberyard owner, reduced this problem. After meeting with Bill, the men dug a trench in the far corner of the park and covered it with a wooden platform that had cutouts for brand new toilets from Harry's store. A privacy screen was erected.

A functioning water pipe with drinkable water was located in the park and several other handymen extended the pipe to the privy so pails of water could be used for flushing. "Quite ingenious, wouldn't you say?" Harry was pleased with their contribution as he volunteered to be the privy's first customer.

Another extension from the main pipe was run to the holding area where several ex Kiwi military veterans took over preparation of the rest area and the small 'tent city' for the arriving, newly homeless. In military style, each row was "dressed right and covered down." Kate watched their efficient handiwork with pride and amazement.

Then the ground shook. Another trembler, an aftershock, and Kate was knocked to the ground as dust rose and tents swayed. Women, holding their infants, still reeling from the first shaker, clung to each other while traumatized little children cried.

It lasted only seconds then it was deathly still. A swirl of dust rose and pebbles continued to slide down beside to the manmade privy.

Kate picked herself up and dusted off the loose earth that clung to her khakis. "Is everyone alright?" Kate walked from group to group, reassuring them and trying to bring a smile to their strained faces. "Should we have a contest? How big was that aftershock on the Richter scale? I say only a 5.3, what do you think?"

Before long, children were writing down numbers, the closest to win a prize, yet undetermined. They ran for the emergency radio in the main tent waiting for the official notification.

"From the Emergency Earthquake Relief Organization, at approximately 2:43PM, we experienced a large aftershock, 6.2 on the Richter scale, centered two miles south of the original epicenter site. This is not unusual but do not, we repeat, do not, return to your homes or other buildings. These aftershocks can greatly weaken structures that survived the initial shock".

Myra James and her son Wills won with an exact guess of 6.2. Kate ran to their camper van and found a soccer ball that had been left behind the seat and presented it with great fanfare! "Congratulations! You are both awarded the Grand Soccer Ball and the title of Jolly Earthquake!"

Bill Shepherd was off on his mission but phoned Kate to see how the main camp faired. "Everything OK?"

"Yes, darling, besides knocking me on my bum, I'm fine. We all seem to be fine. It was a 6.2 aftershock."

"Nice vacation, huh!" Bill had to shake his head. "I'll make it up to you, promise."

"Make up what? I've never felt so productive. And we got rid of Raymond. Now let's save some people."

"Kate, you're something else. Gotta go. Love ya." The phone went dead.

Several SUV's, still functioning, were retrofitted as ambulances and started bringing survivors to the triage area. Residents with any medical training were recruited to help with cuts and bruises. It finally came down to Moms with Band Aides.

The efficient American agent finally took a short break and hurried over to Kate's station next to triage. He took a look around and voiced his amazement. "Do you realize we've been here less than three hours and look what we've accomplished? The Kiwi's are a hearty bunch."

"The Kiwis? They're amazing! They just did what had to be done. Not one complaint. I just stood and watched."

"I doubt that but whatever, the infrastructure is set up now and we just have to locate the missing. It's pretty bad out there but it could have been a whole lot worse. The building standards prevented more damage and loss of life. Still, there are people trapped and the different teams are being careful not to set off more collapses."

One of the locals helping in the main tent approached the pair, Sir, Madam, and My name's John Lloyd. I've got a count of ninety-three still missing and unaccounted for. We've counted fifteen dead. They will be brought to the armory, the temporary morgue for identification. Sorry Sir, Madam. I guess we were all hoping against hope. This is a small town. You see, we've posted a board for those looking for family and those newly found."

"Thank you John, we're making progress. I'm sorry, too. It was too much to ask for no fatalities. One death is one too many but unavoidable under the current circumstances."

For a few moments, Shepherd looked around him assessing the progress being made. "Well, you've got things under control so I better get back and see where I can help." He gave Kate a quick squeeze and was off at a trot.

The nature of the quake gave most residents time to reach a safe place, under a stairwell or in a doorway. The unfortunate ones had difficulty leaving their beds and were crushed by falling furniture or some more fortunate, were injured from broken, flying glass. Within hours, the last of the missing were found. The final death toll: twenty-three dead, one hundred forty-seven injured, only five seriously.

By five PM, the little tent city was humming and the smell of BBQ filled the air. Food was gathered from any easily available and safe location and thrown on the "Barbie". Warm beer was brought out and passed to the hard working volunteers as well as the survivors. There would be time to mourn but right now, the families and visitors came together to share their bounty and in some cases, their luck.

Shepherd jumped up on the old wooden picnic table and, using a bullhorn, addressed the gathering. "Well, everyone, I want to thank you for everything you've done. We couldn't predict the bloody earthquake but we sure as hell gave it a kick in the ass!"

The crowd erupted, a sign of relief and exhaustion. "Hurrah Yanks, Hurrah Yanks!!"

"Hold on! It's hurrah Kiwis, hurrah Kiwis!! You're bloody terrific!" Again the group let out shouts and chants.

Bill Shepherd had no sooner made his statement than another cheer arose from the crowd. Rolling into town were fresh units of the New Zealand Army, ambulances, kitchen vehicles, bedding and portable toilets in tow.

When the Major in charge observed the preparations already made, he was astounded. The Chief introduced Bill and Kate Shepherd to the Major and detailed the couple's involvement in the rescue and visible organization. After numerous handshakes and thanks, the Major's men began to load the more seriously wounded for transport south to Queenstown's functioning hospital.

Standing with the Mayor and the Constable, the American couple felt a real sense of camaraderie. The Mayor spoke first. "We'd appreciate it if you could stay awhile. We're not in very good order but..."

"Actually, Kate and I were hoping to stay on to complete some historic research, the original reason for us coming to Arrowtown. If you wouldn't mind..."

"Of course, you're more than welcome. Of course... unfortunately, our accommodations are not what they should be."

"No problem, we are very comfortable in our rented camper van. If we can borrow a grill, we'll be just fine. May we set up camp down by the river?"

"Of course you may!" The mayor was pleased and relieved at their choice. "I'll have Harry bring a grill and charcoal and some fresh lamb steaks down. We'll pack them in ice, while we still have ice. I'm sure you'll have all sorts of food brought to you in appreciation. We're pretty generous mates."

The pair hooked arms and strolled passed the hastily constructed tent city and the severely damaged buildings, all the way down the hill to the little camper van that would serve as their home away from home. He opened the passenger door and helped Kate to her seat. "You know Kate, today has been one Hell of a week

Blood & Sweat

The coastline was pretty much as expected, the remnants of the severe quake scattered everywhere. Buildings that had withstood previous tremblers, had given up the ghost and collapsed, like giant Slinkys, lying on their sides, with glass shards and bricks fascia littering the roads. Parks, usually reserved for family picnics, became spontaneous relief camps.

The good news was Christchurch's relief efforts were well under way and the death count was less than first expected. Any life lost was too many but the feelings were one of reprieve. The lovely town would bury its dead, mourn and then set about the task of rebuilding. The old church tower would take time to reconstruct but it would be a symbol of their recovery.

Jeremy and his followers linked onto the emergency staff and rolled up their sleeves to help out as instructed. Raymond and Maggie temporarily set aside their primal urges and dug in with the rest, toiling away until the sunset and the camper van beckoned them. As darkness hit, they finally entered the confined quarters and immediately put aside the catastrophe that brought them together in the first place.

Without a word, Maggie peeled off layers of soiled clothing and proceeded to wash away the stench from digging through broken sewer pipes, crumbling homes and people's damaged lives. Raymond, painfully aware of Maggie's firm, round, naked body, sat back and took in the view. How openly erotic she was, washing herself, even the intimate portions of her body, those tender spots usually hidden from curious onlookers.

She was aware of Raymond's reaction. The thought of him watching her, but unable to touch her sent chills down her spine. The tease gave her great pleasure. She saw him shifting uncomfortably in his seat, wondering if he should make a move. Was he as comfortable with his naked body as she was? She'd put him to the test.

The blinds in the camper van were closed, sending soft beams of late day light between the narrow blinds, casting regular patterns of golden stripes over her curves, in fact resembling the markings of a wild cat. He imagined himself mounting her and riding her to the ground. The female cat could be formidable. She could leave claw marks and draw blood, even devour his flesh. He felt his muscles twitch.

"Raymond, darling, are you going to sit there or would you mind washing my back?" She seemed to purr the words and Raymond rose, like a lion possessed, to do her bidding. The camper was narrow and intimate, the small faucet delivered warm, bottled water. The sponge and fragrant soap, smooth and sensuous was in his hands.

"A little lower, would you." She slithered under his wicked touch. "Satisfy me, would you, Raymond." She fell to her knees, like the lioness, swishing her tail and waiting to feel the heat of her big, stimulated lion.

As swiftly as he could, Raymond peeled off his clothing and without a thought of his own personal bath, fell upon her rump, grinding himself deeply within her inviting thighs. The warmth of her made him gasp and his own pleasure came so quickly that he prayed to begin again, the next time, more slowly.

"Raymond, I need more of you. Be a man, and give me more." Her words were urgent and filled with disappointment. She turned on him, striking with her cat like claws, raking his chest and sending him into a heap. Maggie straddled his chest. The challenge was more than he could take and he rolled her over, plunging into her with renewed urgency and somehow he found the strength to bite and tear at her flesh until droplets of blood mingled with the sweat of their perverse passion.

Maggie dug her nails into his hindquarters, leaving a trail of red, raw flesh, stinging from his salty discharge. "Jesus, Maggie" was all he could muster. She freed a hand and slapped him with all her might, a welt rising on his backside. The slap felt like a hot whip had burned his flesh. He let out a deep, resonant moan. She was mad.

"You can't hurt me, Raymond. You're not man enough." She taunted him and he could feel the bile rise along with his sexually driven desire. "Take me and hurt me."

Raymond had initiated rough sex before but something about Maggie and her pleasure at giving and receiving punishment took him over the edge. He struck her with an open hand across her rump, creating a loud, penetrating, stinging sound and Maggie let out a loud, terrifying scream. "More hit me again." He responded until his hand burned and his body gave out, his heart pounding like a bass drum.

They lay on the floor of the tiny camper van, covered in their blood and sweat, the odor of raw, uncontrolled sex filling their heads. Maggie raised her head enough to survey the effects of Raymond's aggression. "You were a good boy and tomorrow, I'll make you a man." No one had ever spoken to him this way. He had allowed it, even encouraged it.

She fell into a sudden and deep sleep and Raymond had to carefully extricate him from her mound of spent flesh and the pile of soiled clothing. He stood with effort and tried to wipe away the remnants of Maggie's brutal assault. As sore as he was, he had to smile. This is what he had dreamed about all of those lonely nights in Peru. But it was Kate that filled his vision. Kate could never reach this level of debauchery. Perhaps, by a twist of fate, he had finally met his match.

Retreat

The Shepherds wandered back to their camper after receiving thanks from the grateful townspeople. They were humbled. Being in a location and situation that drew on their knowledge and experience at exactly the right time was stimulating and rewarding. Many people train for years and never have their training tested. The willing and able pair stepped into their roles as if they were assigned by a deity to be there at the precise moment in time and they functioned without hesitation.

Kate watched with admiration and love as her husband stepped into the town's leadership role with a sensitive ease. When the time came to relinquish that role, he did so, graciously turning over the reins to the city's mayor and the newly arrived Army Major.

In turn, the well-trained CIA agent admired the efficient, high-energy approach to Kate's organizational skills, how she managed to prepare the facilities for the injured and the comfortable, emergency housing for the hundreds of displaced residents. Robert reflected on Kate and how fortunate he was to have found, loved and married such an exceptional woman. Few men ever live in the aura of such goodness and grace. He felt that she was strong enough to survive his passing but sadly, didn't believe he could survive hers

It was early evening when they returned to the camper and happily discovered bunches of fragrant wild flowers surrounding their little retreat and the picnic table was loaded with fresh fruits and vegetables. The locals weren't about to forget the good work bestowed upon them by this selfless couple of Americans.

Sampling the delicious harvest, the exhausted couple climbed through the van's narrow doorway and fell into their cozy sleeping berth.

An hour later, their energy returned, they managed to pry their well exerted muscles from the warm sleeping berth, then hand in hand, they tiptoed to the Arrow River, a varying width of fresh, running water. Earlier, they had parked the camper at a location, they estimated to be opposite the long gone Arrowtown Bank. According to Charlie, the surveyor, his instructions placed the bank site close to where their treasure hunt would begin.

The search could wait until tomorrow. Right now, the cool water would wash away their aches and pains, the results of hard, productive labor. As they stood by the water's edge, the golden sun dipped below the tree line and the sky responded by producing brilliant hues of orange and crimson, strikingly beautiful in contrast to the earth's destructive power. Then quickly, the sky darkened and the first star of the evening, the North Star, began to glow. Within moments, the atmosphere was dotted with flecks of light, forming a Heavenly canopy over their heads.

In their solitude, stripped down to their essence, the couple took pleasure, washing their bodies in the virgin stream. All the while, their naked, glistening skin magically reflected the bursts of cosmic starlight. They held each other in the true passion of their love, feeling very small under the vast sky. Carefully, as their eyes adjusted to the natural evening light, they took turns drying each other's backs with the soft towels left as gifts at their door.

Feeling the first chill of an evening breeze, the lovers wrapped themselves in the thick towels and slowly plodded their way back to their secluded retreat. Finding contentment in the cozy quarters.

Shepherd rolled on his side and looked at the lovely face of his bride. He experienced a tenderness he'd never felt before. He smoothed away the strands of soft, blond hair and lost himself in the depths of her eyes. His love for her was exquisite. All she had gone through for him, plus the overwhelming pain of their lost son, yet here she was, with an eager willingness to help perfect strangers, the grateful people of Arrowtown.

He placed his lips over her eyes, softly kissing them and as he did, he tasted the salty tears flowing gently down her cheeks. Instinctively, she was feeling the same warmth and appreciation for her husband and lover.

Bill made love to Kate many time and each time was different. He had his soul mate and lover bonded into one, their spirits blending with each kiss and caress. Slowly at first, Kate felt her anticipation build and with no urging, she drove her body into his for the warmth and security he provided her.

As the stars made their way across the sky and the people in Arrowtown found comfort with each other, the loving pair explored their private realm until he exploded within her and Kate's own sexual energy released sparks that rivaled the heavens. This was the intimacy most dream about, but rarely find. This was love.

Heaven and Hell

Raymond woke from a dreamless, exhausted sleep and found that his limbs would not work. For a moment, panic overcame him and he struggled to comprehend. His arms ached. They were tied firmly above his head, each wrist looped with a nylon strand of rope and tied to the wooden bedpost high above the small sleeping berth.

His ankles were similarly tied, spread eagle to the invisible legs supporting the single mattress. Climbing out of a drug induced, heavy headed malaise, Raymond wanted to scream but couldn't. His mouth was covered with a soft rag and kept secure with a piece of medical tape that tugged at his cheeks.

He was alone. Trying to understand his miserable predicament, Professor Raymond Morrissey tried to take a step back and remember what had happened. And who had done this to him.

His manhood was flaccid, still asleep and apparently spent. He closed his eyes and strained towards a lost memory. His muscles hurt and he was getting anxious. If he could only scream for help.

"Well, good morning my dear!" A shadow moved through the narrow doorway. Maggie's voice sounded more pleasant than the current setting called for. "I thought you'd sleep until noon. You know, everyone else has moved on. I told Jeremy you had a bit of a hangover and we'd catch up. That's an understatement, isn't it!"? She walked over to Raymond and quickly removed the gag. "You were so noisy I thought you'd wake the camp so, I had to cover your mouth. I hope it didn't bother you."

"My God, Maggie, you could have suffocated me!" He spit out the words with the little gasp of air he could muster." Untie me. I'm dying here."

"Oh, don't be so melodramatic. It was all in the spirit of good fun. And you can't tell me you didn't have good fun."

"I don't remember a Goddamn thing. You drugged me." He was tugging at his restraints with no success.

"Here" pulling the ends of his wrist ties, "Is that better?"

"And my feet, now, dammit!" Raymond wriggled his naked body much to Maggie's delight.

She untied his restraints and let out a deep laugh. "I love to watch you struggle." She peeled off her khakis and fell on him, coaxing him back to life. "One for the road?"

"Damn, Maggie, are you crazy?" Raymond felt the full impact of her weight and the soft cushioning around her excited womanhood and he lost all resistance and let her wrap her warmth around him. Deeply, she pushed, and then rocked back and forth, slowly at first, then building in intensity. "You like that Baby?"

Raymond lay back and let him be used by this insatiable sexual being. Yes, he had been used but what the Hell. Yet, even Raymond knew that what was happening pushed the boundaries of his own sensibilities. He was a well-known scientist. A scholar. So was she. This was a very dangerous game that easily got out of control.

Penguin Claim

Yes, the uncontrolled, debasing sex was hard to justify and he had to be honest with himself. There was still work to be done and a claim to be researched and recorded.

Maggie sat in the passenger seat, going over her thick pad of notes regarding the extinct Giant Panda, recently named Icidyptes. This particular variety of penguin was a warm climate lover versus the usually cold climate adaptations preferred by many of today's penguin species.

The skeletal bones suggest that the warm climate penguins preferred deep water and had the same capacity as their later cousins, gathering fish as they traced through the water. These large, nearly five feet tall, long beaked, extinct, flightless birds, called the ocean off the shores of present day Peru home more than 30 million years ago. Interestingly, the penguins migrated in two distinct patterns. The one of particular interest, to Raymond and Maggie, moved between Peru and the southern shores of New Zealand.

There were two species originally identified. But now, Raymond claimed a third species, even larger in size had lost their battle for survival a half million years earlier. His very own penguin!

"Maggie, does anything in your notes vary from my research? I read your notes and they seem to overlook the size and weight factors of my bone fragments." He was driving at a quick pace, hoping to catch up with the remaining party.

Maggie's attitude was cool, considering all they'd done to each other. "My notes are complete. Yours don't reveal anything further than my observations."

"Anything wrong, Maggie? Sounds like you're angry at me." The air on her side of the camper van was chilling fast. "No, I'm fine. I'm just preoccupied, that's all."

"If you've got a beef with me, tell me." Raymond tried to keep his tone mild and free from accusation. He knew the power of her temper.

"Damn Raymond, just drive, will you. There's nothing to talk about." Her anger was creeping up the walls of the van.

He snapped. Feeling icicles build on his shoulders, Raymond suddenly swung the van to the right and followed a narrow, fire road, bouncing and scraping against the dense low branches. He pressed the brake, sending them both, straining against their safety harnesses. He turned off the engine, unbuckled his seat belt and faced her square on.

"OK, lady, what in the Hell is going on? Last night and this morning, you were fucking my brains out and now, you're treating me like I don't exist. What gives?" A trickle of nervous sweat ran down his brow, stinging his eye with a concentration of salt.

"Are you trying to kill me? How dare you!" Maggie could barely catch her breath. "No one talks to me that way."

"Well, Dr. Brown, I do. I don't like being treated like some sort of..." He couldn't find the words. "Pawn."

"Well, deal with it. Last night was last night and today's now." She blurted the words, a mist of spittle reaching his face.

He swiped his face with his quivering hand. "Well, that makes a hell of a lot of sense, doesn't It."? He nearly broke into laughter at her nonsensical response.

"OK, you want to know what's bothering me? I'll tell you." Maggie opened the van's door and jumped down and started to walk down the poorly maintained fire road.

Raymond jumped out of the van and tried to catch up with her. "Stop, will you. What's going on? He grabbed her arm and stopped her in her tracks.

"Don't touch me." Maggie recoiled at his touch. "I hate you."

"You must be crazy." Raymond's frustration was peaking. "Tell me what's going on or I'll leave you here and you can walk to Christchurch. Damn, I've had it."

Maggie planted her feet and set her hands on her hips. "OK, I'll tell you. You stole my find. It's mine and there's no way in Hell we're sharing it. It's mine. There, I've said it."

Raymond couldn't believe his ears. "What are you talking about? I sent you my findings months ago. You're Johnny Come Lately. It was only by the goodness of my heart that I let you in at all." He could feel his blood pressure rise and the tightness in his chest build. "You're just crazy." He thought he might succumb to a heart attack.

Maggie's face contorted as beads of sweat broke out across her cheeks. "No, no, you're the crazy one. I've done the research and I've got the necessary documentation to record my find. I'll be published and the credit will be mine like it should be." She started to turn towards the van and Raymond grabbed her arm.

"You're insane. Over my dead body." He could feel his muscles tighten. He felt Maggie struggle against his superior strength. "Now you've gone too far. I was willing to share but not anymore. I'm the only one who's going to take the credit. It's mine and the fame is going to be mine. Who the Hell do you think you are?" Raymond had never experienced such anger, never in his years on the planet.

Maggie yanked herself free from his grasp and ran back to the van. Raymond was on her heels and in time to see her reach for the small shovel resting behind the passenger door. She grabbed it and swung in his direction, missing him. Raymond jumped back avoiding the second aimed blow. When the shovel banged against the van's side panel, Raymond, with adrenaline pumping, sprung forward and grabbed the handle, dislodging Maggie's hand.

Maggie, fighting like a wild cat, recovered her footing and rushed towards him, nails slashing, only to be greeted by the heavy metal end of the digging tool. Caught soundly above her left eye, she screamed an epithet then slowly slumped to the ground.

"Oh my God, what have I done?" Breathless, Raymond stood over her unconscious body. A large welt was raising on her forehead an indication that she was still alive. He checked her pulse and it was strong. Thank God he hadn't killed her although the idea didn't seem that shocking to him.

Leaving her for a passing motorist was too heartless even for him. After all, he had made love to her this morning. Something had gone horribly wrong. He made the logical choice. Straining against her dead weight, he lifted her over his shoulder and rolled her into the back of the camper. If he were lucky, she'd stay unconscious until he located medical help.

Raymond followed the roadmap, heading further north and to the east. He was on the outskirts of Christchurch and saw the first significant structural damage since leaving Queenstown. A roadblock lay ahead with warning lights flashing and Raymond had to pull to an abrupt stop. He had an idea.

A tall, young man dressed in military attire approached his van. "G'day, mate. We have a bloody mess ahead. Where you from and where are you off to?"

"Yes, hello…. I know the damage is overwhelming. I'm a Yank, mate, here to help with the rescue but I've got a casualty in the back. My colleague, got a nasty bump on the head and I'm afraid she needs immediate medical care."

The young military man's eyebrows rose with alarm. "Bloody sorry, mate. Where is he?"

"Of no, my colleague's a woman. She's in the back, unconscious but her vitals are strong. Do you have emergency personnel here?" Raymond tried to sound urgent and more concerned that he actually was.

"Why, yes, mate, we do. As luck would have it, an emergency copter just arrived. We can transport her to the nearest hospital, if that's needed."

Raymond's heart beat, "Oh yes, I'd sure appreciate it if you could get her transported and cared for. I'll meet up with my team and we'll come for her once she's out of danger." He pulled out a card with his name and scribbled Maggie's name on the back. "Here, make sure this stays with her. She may not remember what happened to her."

"What did happen to her, mate?" The military man asked for a reasonable explanation.

"Well, let's see." Raymond tried to think of a feasible reason for Maggie's unconscious condition. "She stumbled during the last aftershock and bumped her head against the van's bumper. Pretty nasty knob on her head."

Raymond went around the back of the van and opened the van's back doors and quickly kneeled next to Maggie's prone body. He cradled her head in his lap then discretely placed a pill in her mouth, the same type of pill she had given him, promising memory loss and a very sound sleep.

The military man called for help and with Raymond's polite urging, carried her out of the van and carefully loaded her on a gurney for transport. They tucked the identification card in her breast pocket and within minutes, the young medics shuttled her to the waiting copter. "We have two other patients to transport so we'll be off immediately. No worry, mate, she'll be in good care."

Raymond extended his hand and shook the young officer's firmly. "I'm sure she will be in good hands! Thank you. I'll check in once I locate my rescue team."

Before any more questions could be asked, Raymond drove off leaving his volatile lover in the hands of the capable Kiwi military. He felt relieved yet also, remorseful. He'd hoped that their sexual dalliances would continue at least until they ran out of positions. He forced himself to put those lurid thoughts on the back burner.

Right now, Dr. Raymond Morrissey had to make sure his name was registered as the primary discoverer of the latest extinct penguin find. "What came over her?" Maggie would be madder than Hell.

The Search Continues

Bill and Kate woke in their cozy camper after a long, exhausted sleep. Yesterday had been horrendous, the earthquake destroying a large portion on the South Island, including the historic buildings of Arrowtown. The loss of life hung in the air like a heavy cloud that wouldn't drift away.

"Morning Sweetie." Bill curled a warm arm around her and drew her close to him. "How did you sleep?"

"I'm OK but it's hard not to let the events of the past two days interfere with my dreams. It seems like weeks yet it's only been a couple of days." As Kate spoke in her morning husky voice that Bill found so appealing, the small camper began to sway gently.

"These aftershocks will go on for weeks, sometimes months. I'm beginning to expect them, almost enjoy the movement. I said *almost.*"

"I know what you mean. It's like living with a ghost who shakes the lamps and rattles the windows to get our attention. As long as they stay small, I'll be OK." Kate nestled her head into the bend of Bill's arm.

"Seriously, last night, after you drifted off, I relived the emotions of being a soldier, especially how I felt after a big battle. I grieved for my buddies who were killed or wounded. But, I hate to admit it, even to you, that subconsciously, I was relieved that I had somehow survived." He squeezed her tightly, as if she could ward off the memories.

"I know many of the townspeople feel that same way. 'Why did I survive? And my neighbor's child died. As trained soldiers, we had to compartmentalize our feelings so we could keep at it again and again. For those who couldn't handle the pressure and collapsed under the strain, they had a name for it, Post Traumatic Stress Syndrome. Our commanders sent them home on medical leave and hopefully, to recover."

"Yes, they came home but unfortunately, many did not recover, especially after the Viet Nam War when sympathies ran against the war. How many drug addicts and homeless came out of that group of vets?"

"Too many, I'm afraid and it's not just that war but today, the atrocities around the world are taking their toll on our soldiers. Suicides, spousal abuse, drugs and not enough medical help. I thank God every day that I still have a head on my shoulders. Or at least, I think I do. A wonderful head on those shoulders!"

The memories rattled through his mind for a few painful minutes until his well-disciplined mind once again took firm control. He rationalized that he had seen more casualties in Afghanistan in ten minutes than Arrowtown had suffered during the high seismic earthquake. He also knew that this comparison was small conciliation to the few dead, injured and their grieving families.

Kate put her arm around him and gave him an understanding peck on the cheek. "I see it in your eyes. We did all we could to help out. No regrets. The earth moved without warning and people died. But other people survived with miraculous stories. So there were blessings and miracles among the tragedies. Just is, I guess."

Bill made his way to the edge of the small bed and shook off the past, "How about we dig out some rations and have some breakfast? I've got a few ideas for our search."

"How about finding the Mayor, if he's not too preoccupied, and also find the town's historian?" Kate sat on the edge of the tiny bed and stretched, nearly touching the van's roof.

The resolved couple threw on their khakis and large brimmed hats and left the camper, heading up the gentle incline and across the narrow bridge. They found the mayor, wearing an oversized pair of jeans, his sleeves rolled up, standing alongside a small group of relief workers. "Hi Mates!" He sounded tired but hopeful. "Feel that shaking this morning? Still causing some buildings to teeter." He wiped his face with a large, square handkerchief.

The tent city was coming to life, with children running about and their parents coming and going, each carrying salvaged items from their quake damaged properties. Little stacks of pictures frames; jewelry boxes and other precious possessions grew taller as they scavenged through the remains of their lives.

"Mayor, can you put us on to the local Historian? We have a couple of quick questions. We know he or she is probably overwhelmed and we don't want to burden him. We just have a few questions to ask." Kate's voice was apologetic.

"The last I saw him. Oh, his name's Runyon, Bill Runyon, he was going through the bed and breakfasts down that way" pointing past the tents. They're searching for reusable, undamaged heirlooms, and the products of several generations. You know, the Chinese Museum was flattened along with a few other historic buildings. Sad, very sad."

Kate thought she saw a stray tear trail down his sweat stained cheek. "We are so sorry." She had the urge to reach out and draw him to her but thought better of the idea.

"Thanks Missy. Chinese immigrants were important to this area, especially to the gold fields." She could imagine forth generation children digging with their bare hands to save family heirlooms. Kate could see how much the Kiwis were like their American cousins, tough, hard working, and resilient people.

The Mayor brushed off the dirt and headed towards the designated headquarters. " If you come with me, I'll answer some of your questions. I've been in this town nearly my whole life. There's not much I don't know about its history. Give me a chance to fill in some of those holes for you and to be quite up front, I really need a breather."

Kate and Bill marched back to the tent with the mayor and Kate spoke over the mayor's shoulder. "Well, actually, we're looking for an artifact left behind by an American born gold miner who spent some months in Arrowtown back in 1860, '61. We're not looking for gold, just information regarding their lives. Anyone who might have come in contact with them would be very helpful." Kate didn't want to sound like she and Bill were treasure hunters, especially right after the earthquake. They had built credibility with the townspeople and they didn't want to blow it.

Once inside the empty tent, Kate pulled out her sketch of the Peruvian gourd, laid it out on the camp table and explained the similarity of markings diagrammed in an old letter, written my the American miner/surveyor.

William explained that the Arrowtown Bank was the first clue but it no longer existed. "Can you tell us where it was located? And also, the second clue was a stand of old, tall trees, located, we think, several hundred yards across the Arrow River.

The mayor listened intently then finally let out a tension-reducing laugh. " I wasn't around back then, thank goodness but I think I can help with both those questions. The old Arrowtown Hotel burned down over 100 years ago. Fine old building back then. It replaced the Arrowtown Bank Building. Did its job, keeping track of the gold that came out of the local mines. Came down bit by bit when the gold dried up. No need for a fancy bank when there was no gold and no money to protect. It's been gone a long time."

He cleared his throat, enjoying the opportunity to hold the floor, "We were a rough country back then. Between battles for gold and women, the atmosphere was pretty rowdy. My grandfather, bless his soul, told me stories of the goings on. Not so different than your Wild West!"

Kate found folding chairs and they became attentive students. "Go on. This is interesting and helpful!"

In fact, some of those same characters from your Old West were here. My grandfather told me a story about two brothers who sailed here from California, stopping in Peru for supplies and such. Could be your miners or surveyors.' His eyes brightened. " You know, I think I even remember their names, why I don't know. Let's see. Charles, no, Charlie and Thomas. That's there names!"

What luck! Kate and Bill felt that his recollection of their names added credence to the old letter safely stored in Kate's pack.

"Those boys, them and others, nearly burned down the town before they left for Queenstown, the party girls and gamblers staying close on their tails. I guess they stiffed them all!" Blushing as he realized his lusty reference. "Sorry Ma'am, I guess I mean that literally as well as figuratively."

"Don't worry about it. I've heard worse and besides, that was the Old West, in America and, I imagine, here as well. Please go on." Kate gently prodded him to continue.

"In any event, the hotel was on the water at the end of Bedford Street." Pointing at his map. "Look here. You can still see its location. It was replaced by a series of rooming houses. You can tell the location because it was the last section on the street, facing the river."

Taking a moment to gather his thoughts. "I'll get back to that in a minute. The big trees you asked about were about a half a mile across the river." He was tracing his finger along the map, following the course of the river. "They were famous in their days, known as the hanging trees! Many a miscreant ended his days there."

Bill sat forward, studying the laid out trail. "So the trees are down there."

"Well, not quite. Now back to the river. That's a story in itself and will explain the trees, too. Around 1920, we had a big flood. Most of the town you see here was under water. After the crest of the river had passed us by, my grandfather and his cronies went out on an inspection tour and much to their surprise, the river had cut a new course and was now almost a half mile further from town, running right over and around those old trees! If you walk that way," pointing further down and away from town, "you can still see the roots and some old stumps sticking up."

Taking a deep breath and checking his watch, "Well, do you need any more information, my friends?"

Kate and Bill smiled. "You've told us what we need to know." Pausing as one last question came to mind. "One last thing. Was there a basement or subterranean chamber in the hotel or the bank?

"Good question. You know, to the best of my recollection, there was a storm cellar in the old hotel. Probably was a storage area for the bank as well. Not exactly sure but sounds reasonable."

Kate reached for his thick hand. "Mayor, you've been so helpful but we've kept you from the town. We'll go take a walk and see what we can see."

"Thank you so much for your time and the information." Bill extended a sincere hand and placed his left hand on the Mayor's shoulder. "We'll get out of your way and again, thanks, Mate!"

Kate followed suit with a warm hug, "We really appreciate the information."

The newly enlightened couple headed for the entryway and turned towards the river. Well, Kate, it looks like we'll have to excavate the stream. You know, it's just a small stream now and I bet, with a little luck, I could divert the flow to give us a better shot at the relic!"

Kate saw his eyes light up at the thought but all she could imagine was drawing unneeded attention to their little project. "Divert the river? Seriously? We'll see about that."

The Lie

"I can't believe that Maggie was injured. But thank God she's in good hands. But Raymond, you look worn and exhausted. Perhaps you should take some leave and grab some sleep."

Jeremy and the others in their little search and rescue party stood around Raymond because they were both curious and concerned about the blow to Maggie's head that was caused by the strong aftershock.

"And you say the shovel fell from the roof of the camper van and struck her. What a sorry situation that must have been. But that's how accidents happen. If we could predict them, well, they just would be avoidable." Jeremy rested a hand on Raymond's slumped shoulders.

"I couldn't believe it myself. It happened so fast. I wish I could have prevented it. You have no idea how much I appreciate your understanding. No one feels worse than me. It was I who left the shovel on the roof while I was organizing our supplies. I was careless." He nearly believed his version of how the injury to Maggie happened.

His self-effacing demeanor brought sympathy from the group and no one dared guess that her injury could have been the result of a flaring temper or self-defense. He hadn't shaved or bathed over the past several days and his clothing was soiled and stained with sweat, the sight of a man who had recently experienced a regrettable series of traumatic events.

Yes, he felt regret but not for Maggie's injuries but rather that he had not yet filed a claim on his discovery. He'd have to find an operational FAX line and send off the paperwork to the proper authorities. A few concerns rolled through his disheveled mind. Cutting Maggie entirely out of the discovery could come back to haunt him. He had experienced her wrath and knew what she was capable of. He'd have to give it serious thought. Both the earthquake and his mind-bending encounter with Dr. Maggie Brown had certainly thrown him a curve.

"Now go, Professor. The Christchurch Community Center still has running water and a shower to freshen up. We'll make sure you have your things brought to you. Poor man. You've come to enjoy our beautiful countryside and look," scanning the 360 degree damage, "What we give you is but a broken landscape. What timing, mate." The sad dimensions of crumbled buildings and buckling roadways genuinely affected Jeremy.

Jeremy bought Raymond's explanation without question. Morrissey seized a tension-relieving sigh of relief as he headed for the wood planked building. A warm shower would be welcomed. He'd freshen up, have something to eat then make inquiries. Sleep could wait until he had his business taken care of. He'd make a call to check on Maggie's condition once the paperwork was filed with the appropriate authorities.

If he could speak to her, he'd make sure she remembered the incident his way. Maggie wouldn't want the others, especially colleagues within her tight knit profession to know the truth no more than Raymond would. This was their little problem to solve. He was sure he had leverage over her. He couldn't imagine anyone, other than a few jilted lovers, knowing her odd fetishes. He would make sure it stayed that way unless she wouldn't cooperate. Then there was nothing sacred about her private activities. He'd expose their whole sordid episode for the world to see. Except of course, the events leading up to her injury.

Concussion

Do you know your name, miss? Can you see how many fingers I am holding up? Do you know what day it is?"

The simple questions went unanswered as Maggie drifted in and out of a drug-induced coma. Every now and then, a sliver of memory would pass before her eyes. A face. A picture flashed from her childhood. The ticking of a clock, the sound of rubber soles padding down the long tile corridors.

"We'll let her rest, nurse. Her vitals are stable. She ingested something that's kept her in a state of limbo. The medics said they gave her nothing, either by injection or orally. Strange. The toxicology reports aren't back yet so we'll have to assume she took a sleeping pill or pills, perhaps before the aftershock struck."

Dr. Jason Worthington was exhausted and needed sleep but the steady stream of airlifted patients and the walking wounded who found their way to the well-stocked clinic had kept him up for 36 straight hours. The triage was set up quickly, as all of their earlier preparedness drills gave them a leg up. Supplies were still available but his staff was running on empty. A tent was set up in the adjoining lot in case the injured kept coming.

"Dr., I'll keep an eye on her and the others in the ward. Why don't you go take a break? You look worse than some of our patients." Nurse Landers caught herself, "I didn't mean it that way. You've been here since the first quake struck sir. I just thought..."

"Don't apologize. You're right. I am rather spent. I remember those early weeks as an intern when they push you to perform your duties with no rest. I see why. But I'll take your advice and catch a short nap in the back lounge. If there's a problem, come and fetch me."

Dr. Worthington, a seasoned veteran at forty, had served his country well and now, in private practice, he served the town as well as anyone could expect. He had instructed the nursing staff to perform at high efficiency and he knew they would handle the cases unless an extreme emergency presented itself.

Maggie had been one of those emergencies. The chopper had landed, reminiscent of a segment from "Mash" and the triage team had immediately hooked up an IV drip, took her vitals and within minutes, had her stabilized. A blow to the head could lead to an aneurism, a dangerous, sometimes fatal blood clot that cuts off oxygen to the centers of the brain. The staff ran preliminary tests and once they determined that she was out of danger, she was monitored carefully. Her condition was listed as serious but stable.

After transferring her to a less frantic corner of the main ward, the nurses discretely stripped off Maggie's dusty, blood stained clothing, and hand bathed her and slipped her into a tidy blue gown. Once reattached to the monitors, they moved on to other needy patients. Maggie was pretty and peaceful, her skin, lightly tanned and blemish free, except for the large bulging knob on her forehead. Her assigned nurse regularly checked her condition and marked her chart. "Do you hear me? What is your name? Do you know what day it is,

Search Strategy

Kate and Bill sat along the bank of the Arrow River contemplating their next move. Their services weren't needed on the rescue front so they began discussing the proper procedures and legal permits to legitimately excavate the proposed site.

"If the land is public property, we can obtain the paperwork once we make a discovery. The town is in a shambles and the last thing anyone needs is more paperwork. And we haven't discovered gold. In fact, we are basing our search on a 150-year-old letter from two brothers who seem to have a tarnished image. Who knows, it could be a hoax."

"And what if it's private land? Do we have to find the owner for permission to explore the area? And would we be required to share the find?"

Gazing up and down the riverbanks, Kate assessed the area and the rusted signs along the riverbanks. "It looks like government land, either local authority or a federal easement. There are no, *No Trespassing, signs* and that sign says that fishing is permitted along the banks without a permit."

Bill washed the plastic dishes in the clear steam of cold water. "You know, we may be premature. You're right. It could be a ruse. All we have is the word of one dead surveyor."

He watched Kate bend over to rinse out the glasses and was tempted to approach her from the rear. Whatever she was wearing, even a well-worn pair of khakis, he could imagine the fine lean body beneath the cotton clothe.

He patted her on the bottom and whispered, "Stop showing off so early in the day." He felt a tightening in his groin and fought back the urge to take her along the riverbank.

Kate laughed. She read his mind. "If we weren't so involved in this project, I'd let you take me right here and now. But duty calls so we'll have to wait until tonight."

Bill pulled her towards him and held her in a loving grip. "Of course you're right but that doesn't make it easier."

She felt the solid strength of his manhood pressing against her belly, and then her own female stirrings arose. Bill, this is hard on me, too."

He laughed, finally breaking the sexual tension. "We're off. Or else you'll get your wish and so will I. Let's talk shop then. That's safe." He kissed the top of her head.

"Wonderful idea! How do we approach our little project without bringing the whole town down to the river?"

"First, we really don't know where the pipe holding the so called bone is. We have an approximate idea from the letter but the area has been altered by time, weather and of all things, a recent earthquake. I have my military grade metal detector packed in the van. I say we begin by surveying the general area and see what shows up."

Bill headed back to the van and grabbed the necessary gear while Kate remained on the riverbank, charting a workable approach to begin the search. Within minutes, he was back at her side, laden with tools and the metal detector.

"If anything shows itself, I can proceed with the formalities. I can handle that side of things.' Kate took a quick inventory of the supplies. "And how deep down does it detect metal?" She held the long handle and studied the base.

"This metal detector is pretty efficient. It can 'see' up to 20 inches below the surface, which should be enough to pick up the buried pipe, if indeed it's there. Besides ferrous material, it can also act as a magnetometer and identify masses." He took the detector from Kate and slipped the strap over his shoulder.

"We can sweep an area from the water logged roots of the Hanging Tree, back 50 yards and across another 100 yards." She stood, visually trying to get a handle on the site.

"That's a pretty good size sweep. The back section runs into that rise of earth which is probably why the flood swollen river is at its present location."

The couple gathered their wood stakes and spools of bright orange string and began the laborious task of staking out the area. It was close to noon when they tied their last knot to complete the grid.

"Let's take a break then I'll start a sweep with the detector over by the Hanging Tree." They rested next to the van for ten minutes, and then grabbed fresh bottles of water from the cooler. They were ready to begin with a new enthusiasm. The couple moved into position, Bill, holding the detector and Kate, two steps behind, preparing to extract any object spotted.

An hour quickly passed and sounding disappointed, "Outside of small objects, soda cans and miscellaneous junk, there's nothing here." Kate wiped away the steady stream of sweat from her forehead with the back of her hand.

"Honey, it takes time. We've only begun looking for the needle in the haystack. Have some faith."

Kate moved alongside him as he began to widen his sweep between the staked out areas. "I'll mark each stake as we cover it so we don't duplicate our efforts."

They had hardly gone another fifty yards when the detector's alarm went off. Bill's military training kicked into action as he viewed the cause of the sudden alarm. "Hold on. It looks like an artillery shell. Don't touch it!" The recent wash had exposed a corner of a round metal object.

"Honey, it could be live. You know, there were the Maori Wars with the Army and Constabulary. That fighting could have taken place right around here".

Bill pulled his equipment back and stood, studying the metal protrusion. "Actually, Kate, the wars were a twenty year series of battles, the Maori fighting for their civil rights."

Kate took Bill's free hand. "Ironic, isn't it? Such a beautiful land, and still, the same ugly wars being fought. We can't escape our violent past, can we?"

"And present. Sweetie, you're right, but freedom has always been a noble cause and the bloodshed has made the prize all the more cherished. It's no different here on the South Island than in other places around the globe. And back in America."

As they spoke, William carefully tried to get a handle on the size and scope of the object. Using the metal detector, he carefully traced the length, approximately three feet long, the diameter, six inches and the depth below the surface, going no deeper than fifteen inches. He got down at ground level and studied the exposed portion of the object.

"I think it's safe to excavate the pipe but we're going to take precautions. We're not exactly sure what it is. You know. It may very well be our surveyor's pipe or we might have stumbled upon some hot ordinance."

Using a small, long handled shovel, Bill carefully dug a trench next to the pipe. Soon the pipe was completely exposed. "It's not a shell and it could match the description in your old letter. Possible. Very possible."

Kate knelt next to him and visualized what the long dead surveyor had described to her. "Yes, we may have gotten lucky but please be careful just in case it turns out to be something else."

Bill, understanding the danger of old ordinance, tied two ropes around the pipe. He then ran out all the rope he had, placing them at least thirty feet away from the object. He located a depression in the earth large enough to contain both he and Kate and together, they lay flat in the concave ground. There was no need for heroics and caution was the way to go.

Keeping his head below the level of the pipe, Bill carefully kneeled up and tugged on the rope. The first pull hardly budged it. It started to dislodge on the second pull. Bill heard and felt an ominous rumble as the earth around them rose up, throwing Kate and him into the air like rag dolls. The projectile, still attached to the ropes flew over his head.

"I'll be damned, that was no ordinance. Those crazy brothers must have booby-trapped the iron pipe. It would have been nice if he told us. Kate, honey, are you OK?" He was brushing the fresh dirt out of his hair and off Kate's shoulders.

"I'm fine. Shaken but not hurt. That was quite a blast. I'm so glad you took precautions or we'd be in a world of hurt right now." Kate stood up on shaky limbs and shook off the dirt like a dog sheds water. "Oh, oh, we woke up the town."

Town's people, hearing the deep boom came running. "Are you OK? Did a propane tank explode?" Their concern was genuine as they walked around the camper, coming uncomfortably close to the detonation site, checking for damage.

Bill tried to calm their fears and still keep their little adventure a secret. "Please stay back folks. We're fine, really. We ran into an old piece of ordinance, a shell from one war or another and we intentionally detonated it. Everything is fine. But we appreciate your concern."

After being reassured, the small gathering headed back up the hill, away from the river, to report the harmless incident to the Chief of Police and the Mayor.

"Bill come look, I've got the pipe. It's still hot from the impact but I can get to it with my work gloves." She protectively knelt over the object. "Why do you suppose they booby trapped it? Especially after leaving a note. Someone might have been killed. We would have been if you hadn't taken precautions."

Bill shook his head. "Who can explain motivation? Maybe he was pissed at leaving it behind. Took it out on us a hundred and fifty years later. Who knows? I'm just glad we didn't end up with shrapnel or burns. That was quite a blast. You're sure you're OK?" He gave Kate a close up inspection.

"Really, I'm fine. Dirty but fine. Well, here we are and here it is. What's next?"

"Just wait until I give it another once over just in case the brothers planted another bomb." Kate moved back and Bill took her place, examining the object until he was satisfied that the danger had been eliminated. His eyes centered on the hollow opening and a smile formed on his ruddy face. "Well, well, what have we here?" He carefully removed the oilskin-encased object from the center of the pipe and handed it to Kate. "You can have the honor of unwrapping your find."

Kate's heart took a leap as she removed her heavy field gloves. Her hand quivered as she slowly peeled away the layers of cloth and the rabbit skin that still maintained it's soft feel after all the years. She detected the solid, smooth surface of bone. Holding it tenderly in both hands, she studied the familiar markings carved long ago on the ancient bone. Miraculously, it had remained undamaged by years of burial, raging floods and the recent explosion. " It's beautiful." She continued to study the surface and ran her hands over the sensuous curves.

Bill watched Kate lovingly caress the relic then, as if drawn by an invisible force, he ventured back to the location of the original impact. He remained silent as he studied the area's damage. Then feeling his heart skip a beat, he called to Kate. "Honey, put the bone in a safe place, will you."

"In a minute, dear. I want to hold it a little longer."

With urgency in his voice that got Kate's attention, Kate, put it down now. Come here, please."

She laid the bone on top of the soft fur nest and went to Bill's side. "What is it?" She found herself following Bill's intense gaze. Below the impact zone lay a deep crater, much deeper than expected. Kate took one step closer and caught her breath.

"Oh my Gosh, Bill." Together, they stared down at the exposed opening of a crumbling mine shaft. "Just when I thought we had seen it all."

Dilemma

Raymond couldn't get Maggie out of his mind. Was she, in fact, dead? Or had she rallied and spilled the beans about their violent encounter? Did she level blame at him? It was possible an arrest warrant could be in the works and he'd find himself a prisoner in a foreign land. He fretted over whether Maggie had it in her to pursue him.

He had learned the depth of her depravity. He also felt tingles travel up his spine at the memory of their spirited couplings. He was torn between lustful desire and his own feelings of guilt at their ruthless lovemaking, including his eager participation.

Dr. Raymond Morrissey was a respected anthropologist with a worldwide reputation for discovering and identifying ancient remains. The thought of a scandal could tarnish, not only his reputation in his field but also the memory of his well known and equally respected late wife.

He had always controlled his urges until his wife's passing, then, for whatever reason, anger, curiosity, the need to experience lust, which knows, he began to experiment with his repressed sexuality. Maybe his last hurrah, who knew or cared,

Jeremy and his team knew only what Raymond had told them about Maggie's unfortunate accident. All that could unravel with a well-documented statement by Maggie, a close personal friend of Jeremy.

His imagination was becoming his greatest enemy. He could feel the nervous sweat build. He had to go back and deal with Maggie before all Hell broke loose. He thought he could just walk away and wait until the ashes settled but a gnawing sensation in his gut told him differently. Three days had passed since he left her in the hands of Dr. Worthington. A lifetime.

"Raymond, old boy, are you ready to dig in and lend a hand?" Jeremy, his face red from exertion, stopped in mid stride and engaged Raymond. "We were hoping you'd catch up with our team."

"Sorry, old friend. I'm afraid I need to go back to check on Maggie. I know she's in good hands but I feel I must get back to the hospital and see if she's ready to come along with me." He paused and took Jeremy's arm, doing his best to hide what truly bothered him.

"I'm hoping she's made a full recovery. That bump to her head has me concerned." He was concerned…. and hoped that the date rape drug he'd given her had dulled her memory. "I'll take off in a while and be back by morning. Once she's checked on, I'll feel better then I swear I'll dig in with all my resources."

"I understand Professor." Jeremy moved his grip to Raymond's shoulder. "Maggie's a handful but deep down, a wonderful scientist. But a bump to the head, horrors. It could be serious. Go whenever you can. Be sure to have our makeshift kitchen staff pack you some rations for your drive back."

Jeremy released his grip and moved away, once again concentrating on the task at hand. Looking back over his shoulder at Raymond, "Chap, there will be plenty of work when you return. But one more aftershock like the last and we'll have to start over again."

Raymond nodded in agreement then looked around at the damage done to every structure in the once charming town. "Quite a bloody disaster, huh? I'll be back soon." He headed for the mess tent and placed an order 'to go'

Discovery

Kate carefully carried the bone artifact to the camper van and tucked it away for safekeeping. After the violent explosion, Kate and Bill faced a whole new set of problems. Bill stood at a distance and evaluated the site. "The detonation and the hole it created, are much greater than the shell involved."

"Any ideas why?" Kate moved closer to take a look. "Was it a booby trap to stop poachers or possibly an explosive device to protect this particular site?" The air smelled thick with the stench of gunpowder and wet earth.

"You know, Kate, I'm concerned about potential hazards in the hole. Look how the blown opening is raining debris. If we go down under to explore, it could collapse around us." He could tell Kate to stay away from the opening but he knew her well enough to know her reaction. She was an expert in her field and wouldn't stand for his chivalrous attitude. *'Whatever we do, we'll do it together.'*

"With your military background, you're more the explosives expert. Can you lay out a plan that we can safely follow? Needless to say, I want to get into that hole in the ground but not until we know we can get out alive. If we know the pitfalls in advance, we'll be able to get down in there sooner than later." You take the lead in this one. Kate, with little fanfare, assumed the role of professional archeologist/scientist, her voice, rational and organized. "Yes Bill, you definitely take the lead on this one."

Bill had played her just right. "Played" was a manipulative term but whatever the method, the result was to his liking. He could protect his wife from further danger.

"I'll lay out a plan as I see it. The engineer in me will make a list of potential hazards. I don't want our little adventure ending in tragedy." He handed Kate a small pad of paper and a pen. "First, let's analyze our situation. One, how big is the hole?"

Kate paced off the gaping hole. "Around eight feet by six feet, plus or minus a foot."

"Is it natural or manmade?"

Kate handed the note pad to Bill who continued to write as she edged closer to the gaping hole. "Observing the exposed edges, I'd conclude it's manmade. I notice deep, regular grooves made with some sort of metal implement. I'd suggest either a spade or an auger."

Bill strained forward. "Are there any substantial ceiling or wall supports or is there risk that the walls and overhead beams could implode?"

Kate edged closer then laid her body flat on the soft earth. "Yes, I see a portion of a beam. Wood, hand tooled. Probably local timber. It looks sturdy." Straining an inch closer. "More. I see a series of beams. If anything, they stood up to the recent blast."

"Be careful. Don't get too close." Bill reached down and instinctively took hold of her ankle, just in case.

"I'm fine. I won't take any chances, not now. What else?"

"How much loose soil entered the opening during the blast?"

"Honey, I can't see much without some source of light."

He reached in his pack and handed Kate a high-powered flashlight. "Try this."

Kate flicked on the switch and illuminated the gaping opening. "That's better. Yes, well, no, there's some but not enough rubble to interfere with our entry. A combination of loamy soil and what appears to be shale rock. The opening appears safely accessible, at least from this angle."

"OK, that's good." He scribbled notes on the small pad. "Now what about the ventilation? Can you detect airflow?"

Kate held the light up towards the surface, catching in its glow, the slight movement of dust and pollen. "Bill, the dust, and the remaining smoke residue are being drawn into the pit. I can see it in the light path." Her voice was excited and filled with hope. "There must be another opening." She edged a little closer to the opening, her head inches from the shaft. "Bill, I feel fresh air circulating around the shaft. All good signs."

She made her way onto her knees then back, away from the shaft and brushed off the layers of damp earth that coated her chest and legs. Her faced was flush with excitement. "Should we try to enter the opening? I really want to know what we stumbled upon."

Bill held her in a warm embrace, feeling her enthusiasm spread through his body. "Hold on, Darling, we need to check the van for more supplies. We'll need more than a metal detector, string and wooden stakes." He handed her the half empty water bottle then they headed up the grassy hill to the van and opened the side storage compartment.

One by one, he hauled out basic tools and she placed them on the ground. There was a good length of rope, a small winch, digging, hand tools, miners' lamps, a gas sensor, bright yellow hard hats, a bundle of flares and two heavy pair of work overalls and more gloves. "That's about it but that's enough to get started. What we need now are some strong backs and willing helpers."

Kate stood over the small assortment of excavating supplies. "I agree, we need to bring in some extra hands. There are plenty of materials and equipment around town that we could use, so pausing to make sure she was prepared for the onslaught, "I guess it's time to inform the locals, who knows what's down there. This should whet some imaginations."

After marking the area with yellow caution tape, they headed back to the town's officials. I'll keep the bone well hidden for now. As they walked they developed a feasible scenario to present to the prcoccupied officials. "You do the talking. I guess we should play it low key at first. This may be a wild goose chase. The last thing this town needs right now is false hope and a wasteful use of man power."

Bill knew what to say and before long, three strong, willing volunteers sat around the camp table discussing what was required to enter the mine shaft.

It was getting late and Bill convinced the curious inductees to meet first thing in the AM, after a hearty breakfast. Each was given a list of items that would assist in the exploration. They were warned not to enter the area because of the possible risk of collapse. He scared them sufficiently to know his instructions would be followed to the letter.

The satisfied couple headed back to the camper van, washed the dirt from their weary bodies and feasted on cold leftovers. The sun set and with it, they found comfort in their cozy quarters. Tomorrow held promise.

Journey Back

Raymond spotted the hospital, bathed in late afternoon sunshine and deep shadows. The trip back seemed shorter and the grounds were quiet, not like three days earlier when emergency vehicles clogged the roadway, and lined up helter skelter in the narrow entry.

He felt his stomach churn. Was he getting physically ill? Or was his stomach expressing how much he had missed the spirited Maggie? Mixed signals coursing through his head knocked him off his usually steady game.

A young woman saw his camper van, coated with a week's worth of grime, approach the main entry and stop. She greeted him with trepidation. Was he another "walking wounded"? "G'day, sir, can I be of assistance to you?"

Raymond returned her greeting with a smile, immediately disarming her. She was pert and pretty and trim in her nurse's uniform, a pale blue set of medical scrubs. "G'day to you." Raymond answered. I'm here to visit a patient, Dr. Maggie…"

"Oh, sir, Maggie, that's her name!" She seemed relieved to have made the connection. "Is she your wife?"

"Oh no, not my wife but an associate, my colleague. Dr. Maggie Brown's an archeologist, a scientist. So am I. We work together and she was struck on the head." He found himself rambling, devising an unnecessary explanation. Far more information than she needed.

"Please sir, if you would kindly park your camper van in that lot and I'll be happy to take you to her room." She motioned around the side of the building and Raymond found a parking space and within a few minutes, joined the young nurse inside the white, tiled entry.

"As you can see, things have settled a bit. If you were here two days ago, you would have observed our triage working at full capacity. Fortunately, we had no deaths but many broken bones and cuts. Your colleague, Dr. Maggie Brown, is in room 207. Just follow me up these stairs. You don't mind the stairs, do you?"

Raymond obediently followed the lovely young girl up the stairs enjoying the view of her well-rounded, firm bum. "I'm fine with the stairs, especially after sitting for so many hours."

"Where did you drive from, if I may ask."

"You may. After I made sure my colleague was well cared for, I headed to Christchurch to help with the relief efforts but I felt the need to come back and check on my friend." He sounded sincere and concerned and the lovely nurse turned on the stairs and gave him a sweet, understanding smile.

"How is she doing? Improving I hope."

"I'm only an attending nurse. My name is Miss Sanders, or Tillie." She seemed to blush when she gave her name. Was she too forward with the rugged appearing Dr. Morrissey? "The doctor in charge will have to give you her current condition. I can tell you she has been resting peacefully."

When they reached room 207, Tillie opened the door and Raymond brushed past her and entered the private room. "I'll be at the nurse's station if you need me. Just ring the bell on the table next to the bed. I'll try to reach her doctor. If we're in luck, he should be in the East Wing checking on his other patients."

"Thank you, my dear, Tillie, for being so gracious. I won't be too long." Raymond turned away from the nurse and made his way to the single, occupied bed. With some trepidation, Raymond pulled up a chair and sat beside his sleeping lover.

The lump on her forehead had diminished, leaving behind a large, ugly bruise. Her color was generally good and her breathing was relaxed and regular. All good signs. She still had an IV secured to her right hand. The label on the suspended bag read glucose. Nothing more potent than a dose of sugar water. another good sign.

For ten minutes, he sat and tried to recall their first encounter and how it had quickly escalated from passionate lovemaking to violent, primal coupling. To gaze at the sleeping woman would never reveal her true nature. She was a wild cat. His groin responded to the vivid memory. He adjusted himself in the rigid folding chair. Maggie's dark hair was severely combed back from her forehead then fell haphazardly across the stark white, institutional pillow. He visualized her lying on a bed of soft goose down and cool satin sheets.

Suddenly, his reverie was broken by a deep, firm voice. "So, Dr. Morrissey, you see our girl is still in one piece. I'm glad you've returned to visit. She's been quite alone."

Recovering from his shameful thoughts, Raymond rose and presented his right hand. "Dr., thank you for caring for Dr. Brown. I was so worried about her yet I had to get along to Christchurch. I knew she'd be in competent hands." He took a deep breath. "Dr, uh, Dr. Worthington?" reading his name tag, "tell me about her condition. Is it a concussion?"

"Yes, Morrissey, I'm Dr. Jason Worthington. As a neural specialist, I've been assigned to look over your friend. A concussion? Well, yes, I'd say a mild one. Fortunately, the X-rays showed no broken bone around the eye cavity and no serious internal bleeding. That's good news for her long-term prognosis and recovery. The swelling has come down since yesterday and that hematoma you see is pretty much anticipated with this sort of injury. Quite a shiner, huh! I was informed that she took a blow from a falling shovel. Is that right?"

Feeling his heart rate increase, "Yes, it was an old shovel that fell during one of the strong aftershocks. It happened like this. We were standing outside our travel van and it, the shovel, was resting on top of the van, then all of a sudden he was doing it again. Talking too much. Quite an aftershock to make it fall that way." No one could blame him for an aftershock.

"Accidents happen, don't they?"

Was the good doctor accusing him of negligence? He was letting the situation get the best of him. "Big aftershock. Hope we've seen the last of them."

Dr. Worthington deftly changed the subject. "Are you in any way related to the fine Dr. Maggie Brown?"

"Well, we're close colleagues, if that's what you're referring to." Raymond's hairs stood up on his neck. "Why?"

"Usually, only family members can receive medical details about a patient's condition but I believe, in this extraordinary situation, I can consider you family. So many victims have been brought in with injuries. It's sometimes difficult sorting things out."

Noticeably relieved, "I understand the confusion. It must be very difficult for you and your staff. I heard how busy the hospital was when Maggie was admitted. You've done a fine job keeping track of everyone." Raymond stroked the doctor's ego and got a warm smile in return.

"Thank you for the vote of confidence. And yes, we prepare for a calamity like an earthquake or severe flooding and then when it actually happens, a portion of our rehearsed protocol flies right out the window. But I'm sure we're not alone." Dr. Worthington turned back to his patient. "Strange though. Our patient, Maggie Brown, has a puzzling case of amnesia."

"Amnesia? Is that to be expected with a head injury like this?" Raymond remained calm and focused.

"Well, yes temporary amnesia can be a side effect to a blow to the head and then again, no. We don't expect memory loss as a matter of course. We hope that she will fully regain her memory but", measuring his words... "Strange thing, Dr. Morrissey, it appears she was somehow drugged. I don't believe the amnesia was brought on by the blow to her cranium."

"Really?" Morrissey felt his heart race.

The attending physician moved closer to the open window and looked down at the quiet parking area, the camper van, parked fifty feet below. " Doctor, do you know what, if any medications, she might have had on her person? We're running a second blood panel on her and the results are not yet back from our lab. Results are slow in coming with everyone working overtime." He took a minute to sort out his thoughts. "Perhaps you can shed some light on her habits in this regard. You've traveled together, in that camper van. Am I correct in that assumption?""

"Yes, Dr. we've been on the road since the quake shook Queenstown." Raymond tried to relax and think clearly. He stood with his hand under his chin, reflecting back. "You know, she had Valium in her travel bag and some other small pill bottles. Occasionally, she took a pill to sleep or after a long, taxing day. She is pretty high strung." He paused long enough to prepare a plan.

"I believe they were prescribed pills. You know, I just reacquainted myself with her a day before the quake. We hadn't spent time together in years so I'm completely unaware of what she might take in the way of medications or for that matter, who her doctor would be."

Her doctor listened carefully. "I have a thought. Is the camper van your sole means of travel? As I understand it, you and the fine doctor were sharing space the last several days.

Hesitating slightly. "Yes, why do you ask?"

"Do you think you could check her belongings in the camper van and retrieve any prescription bottles? That would certainly help us understand her predicament."

Raymond took a deep breath and found usable air. "Sure, I'll go look right now. Give me a few minutes to find her cosmetic bag. I usually don't put my hands in a woman's cosmetic bag." He tried to create a light moment but he felt he came off sounding phony and rehearsed. "I'll be right back."

Raymond took the steps two at a time, his heart pounding. He knew where the cosmetic bag was. He'd shoved it under the backbench seat for safekeeping. He'd sort through her bottles and bring back what he knew would not create further suspicion. He unlocked the back door and entered the dimly lit interior. The valium bottle was half filled and the name of the Auckland doctor with his phone number was clear and legible. There was a full bottle of hormone replacement supplements, aspirin and a prescription for arthritis, all standard medications for a woman of her age and delicate temperament.

In a white paper packet, he found three small pills resting on a cotton pad, the remainder of date drug tablets she had used on him and the same one he had given her after the tussle that caused the unfortunate blow to her head. He held the pills in his hand and envisioned the surprised reaction of the medical staff.

He removed the tiny pills from their envelope then holding them discretely in his palm, he left the van carrying the Valium bottle, pain reliever and hormones in his other hand. He exited the van on the far side, away from curious eyes. As he carefully surveyed the grounds, he carefully loosened the chrome gas cap and slipped the pills into the metal pipe that connected to the gas supply. Problem solved. Replacing the cap, he retraced his steps up the stairs to Maggie's room and to her waiting physician.

"Here doctor, the only pills I could find in her belongings. Of course, we shared this bottle of aspirin and some Alka Seltzer. Should I bring those to you as well?"

"Well, if that's all she had on her." He seemed disappointed. "Perhaps she used the last of a prescription. Is that possible?" The good doctor was prying, making Raymond feel uncomfortable.

"I guess that's possible but as I told you, we just met in Queenstown after a long absence. Then the earthquake hit and here we are." He sounded believable. Logical.

"Well, I'll send these to the lab and we'll wait and see. Maybe she ingested some sort of plant or flower. That could be it." Still searching for a logical explanation.

"That could be, too. Maggie was, is, curious about everything. It's possible she was poisoned. That's totally possible." Raymond wanted this line of questioning to end.

"Well, there's no brain damage so beyond the amnesia she'll make a reasonable recovery. Of course, with situations like this, we may never know the exact cause. I'm a neural specialist and still, the brain is a complex web of unknowns."

"Well, doctor, I think I'll just sit with her a while then maybe take some time to find a hotel room. Are there undamaged accommodations available close by?"

"Everything is pretty well uninhabitable but the hospital manages several small cottages out back Yes, we maintain them for visiting residences. The second cottage, number A-7, is open and in good form. Feel free to make yourself at home. A professional courtesy."

Raymond was pleasantly surprised. " Dr. Worthington! Thank you, I sincerely appreciate your generosity. The camper van is pretty cramped and I could use a hot shower and a good night's sleep. Perhaps, tomorrow, Maggie will recover enough to come back to Christchurch with me. Do you think that's possible?" He hoped he'd get the desired answer.

"Well, Dr. Morrissey, Raymond, let's wait and see what the test results say. If she is lucid and her vitals look good, I'll make an assessment whether she can safely travel. There are fine hospitals in Christchurch, of course, if that's needed. I can give you names of specialists. One, a psychologist, a good friend of mine has a practice in Christchurch, a very competent man. He may be of help to Dr. Brown, especially in her present state."

It was the answer he'd hoped for. He wanted to carry Maggie away and avoid further exposure. If there were any suspicions, the good doctor would have to report an intentional drugging to the authorities, especially an illegal and potent date rape drug. Once cleared of any complicity, he'd make right with Maggie. Somehow.

Mine Shaft

They would begin by laying a four by four beam across the hole and securely fastening both ends. This was easier than they originally thought. There was plenty of building materials around town after the quake.

Their volunteers showed up on time and were eager and probably just as curious about the discovery. Agent Shepherd had taken a few minutes to discuss the possibilities with the mayor and the town's acting city attorney and together, they wrote up an agreement with Arrowtown, deciding on a mutual distribution of whatever was uncovered, including the outside chance of a rich treasure trove, unlikely, but nice to think about. Both Bill and Kate were not interested in leaving the same way the brothers had.

Bill took some time sorting his equipment along with the items scavenged by his conscripted volunteers. Geoffrey, a handyman around town was able to come up with a sensor to detect poison gasses.

Normally, he would pace off a distance of say twenty feet. By breaking the ends of the tube, he could push air through the titanium oxide. If the air had any moisture, it would create a white smoke that had the same density as air. By timing how long it took the smoke to go the measured distance, he could calculate a velocity in feet per minute. By checking a corresponding chart, Bill could determine if there was enough airflow for safety. With Geoffrey's sensor, they could also determine the safety of the air.

Mason, a pharmacist assistant, dug around the museum's storage shed and retrieved some old fashioned mining safety materials made from glass tubes filled with titanium oxide that were attached to hand aspirators. Mason explained that its purpose in the old mining days was to determine the speed of airflow in the mine.

If a measurable amount of air was determined, the question was, where did it come from and where does it go? Simple questions but of great importance. The last test was using smoke bombs that Bill found among the stack of flares. The smoke was not harmful but of high volume. Therefore, dropping two smoke generating bombs into the chamber, then following the airflow into any vents down the line, would give indication of other openings down the chamber's length.

This vital information might lead them to another actual entrance to the shaft. All this assumed the shaft was manmade and of considerable length.

Bill organized his support team and assigned them their first joint task, to sling a hoist line over the beam that would allow Kate and Bill to descend into the gaping hole. A standby safetyman would be ready to pull them up as required. Kate would descend first with the sensor in hand. If the air was not foul and she could detect airflow, Bill would join her.

Both the mayor and the local sheriff showed up to watch the event. The mayor spoke up as the men lined the entrance. "What do you think you'll find Bill? His voice carried a strong hint of anticipation.

"I really don't know. It could be anything from an empty hole in the ground to a gold mine rich with ore. It could also be a smuggler's den with abandoned or stolen booty. Since we're all partners in this little hunt, let's hope for the latter!"

Everyone crowded around the cordoned off site, trying to steal a glance into the dark hole. They were disappointed. The hole was dark and divulged nothing. "Back up everyone, please." Bill Shepherd took charge of the site while Kate made sure her harness was fastened securely.

She leaned forward and threw a handful of dried grass into the air above the hole and the group watched in amazement as it was sucked into the opening. "This little test shows strong airflow into the chamber. What goes in must come out." Her voice was filled with hope.

Heads turned as they followed an imaginary path along the surface to an invisible exit point. Bill noted their trail. "I suggest that there is a vent hole of some sort in the area. The way the dried grass settled into the chamber and was drawn away, I think it is traveling away from the riverbed." All heads turned severely to the left and followed Bill's assessment.

"OK, everyone, listen up. What I'd like to do is station a few willing citizens in a perimeter within a quarter mile from this site. On cue, Kate will release the smoke bombs into the chamber and we'll look for signs of smoke coming out of the ground. Each of you has a whistle to blow when you spot something. Any questions? OK. Divide up and we'll give you fifteen minutes to pick a spot on an invisible arc. I'll blow my whistle once for ten seconds, letting you know the smoke is on the way."

The locals, whistles in hand, headed in the direction indicated by Bill. He called to a young man with a severe limp, who was lagging behind the others. "Son, yes you, why don't you position yourself about a hundred or so yards from here just in case there's a close in vent. Thanks son." The young man who had a leg damaged in the quake smiled back at Bill. He was in pain but wanted to be part of this monumental moment.

"I'm glad you asked him, Bill. Mathew was caught in the wreckage at the church. I treated him myself. He's really bruised up but no broken bones." Kate squeezed her husband's arm in appreciation of his empathetic gesture.

The locals not directly involved in the search, produced fresh scones and coffee and the morning took on a festive air. How ironic, when the town lay in partial ruin! Hope springs eternal.

Bill waited fifteen minutes then held up his hand so Kate could see it, then dropped it to indicate that it was time to release the smoke bombs. Kate lit the two fuses and one by one, dropped them into the dark hole.

Bill pressed the whistle to his lips and let out a long shrill sound that would carry from one side of town to the other. At first, the smoke looked like it was going to escape but soon it began to disappear into the bowels of the earth. Kate and Bill moved away from the opening and stood on a high point overlooking the riverbed waiting for a reaction. "The bombs have a burn life of three minutes so something should be happening soon, if at all."

Suddenly, a whistle sounded a hundred and fifty yards away from the original opening. At that signal, the entire group converged on the spot of rising smoke. Mathew, the young man with the severe limp, a smile a mile wide, stood straddling what appeared to be a grass covered wooden hatch. Smoke drifted above his head like a giant snake.

Bill reached the spot first, followed by Kate and the local officials. The others made their way back as quickly as they could over uneven ground. "Well, I'll be damned." Agent Shepherd lifted the young man off the ground and placed him alongside Kate. He was still beaming. "Good work, Mathew."

Instinctively, Bill realized the potential danger. The first entry blew with a booby-trapped wooden hatch. It could happen again. He ordered everyone away from the hatch and with the help of Geoffrey; they tied a rope to what appeared to be a rusted hatch handle. They carefully ran the length of rope over a sturdy tree limb.

With the group positioned at least one hundred feet from the hatch, Bill and the two locales lay flat on their bellies and began to tug on the rope, releasing a thick plume of trapped smoke. There was no explosion and the anxious group let out spontaneous cheers as the hatch tumbled sideways, away from the newly discovered mine shaft. Until the smoke was able to clear, the group milled around discussing what was potentially hidden beneath their little town.

Within thirty minutes, the air was deemed acceptable and Bill, then Kate descended into the original dark tunnel.

They were professionally trained and equipped to explore the shaft although the town's volunteers pleaded to be included in the treasure search. They used a roughly constructed rope ladder and carried two powerful halogen flashlights plus the poison detector. Both wore a lightweight harness with a thin, supple rope tied to their waists, the ends firmly held in the hands of their surface helpers. If there were trouble, a tug would immediately bring assistance to remove them from a dangerous collapse or built up noxious gasses.

They carried a small portable satellite radio but were uncertain if it would pick up a signal under the earth. Once their feet hit firm earth, they each gave one short tug to signal their safe descent. As agreed, Bill and Kate stood back to back, shining their flashlights ahead of them, rotating in a clockwise direction until they had examined the immediate area. Once secured, a high intensity lamp was lowered to them, illuminating the entire chamber.

What they saw surprised them. Wooden crates, three high, lined the walls as far as they could see. They moved up the tunnel, towards the second entrance, boxes still lining the rock hard walls. Twenty-five yards into the chamber, the passage descended at a seven degree grade then branched out and widened to a width of forty feet. The chiseled ceiling was ten feet above their heads. They came upon a grouping of chairs, a rustic table and the remains of primitive living quarters. A frayed, old Oriental rug was spread under the furnishings.

Kate and Bill circled the chamber, shining their flashlights in every nook and corner. What they saw shocked them. The skeletons of two fully dressed men, rested against the far wall. A ceremonial sword protruded from the chest of one poor corpse and the other appeared to have a large musket wound through his abdomen, the damaged fabric of his wool coat still speckled with blackened blood and gunshot residue.

Kate exhaled and edged closer to the dead men. "The sheriff has some very old murders to ponder. What do you think?"

Bill stood over the well-preserved corpses. Their hats still rested on their heads and wisps of hundred-year-old hair poked at unusual angles then unceremoniously fell over their boney cheekbones. Their boots were covered with dust and the leather souls were still caked with dried mud.

"One thing we know for sure. They died where they fell. But who killed them? I haven't a clue." Kate studied every detail. "They hardly look real after all of these years."

"You know, it might be your pen pal, the surveyor and his brother who did the deed then set the booby traps. Another mystery to solve, I'm afraid." Looking around, Bill was once again drawn to the wooden crates. "One thing is clear. They left empty handed."

"Should we take a look? Something's in all of those crates! And I'm dying to find out what it is."

Bill turned his attention to the long wall that was lined with the sturdy pine cartons. "I'm curious, too. These men aren't going anywhere. The sheriff will have his chance to unravel this soon enough."

Together, they approached the third tier crate and carefully tried to pull the lid away. "Well, here we go…"

Crime Scene

While Kate took inventory of the scene, Bill connected with the sheriff over his radio and informed him that there were too very old bodies deep inside the underground chamber, the obvious victims of foul play. He described the scene and the presence of stacks of pine crates that were securely nailed shut. Each much larger than a breadbox, the crates were becoming a source of curiosity.

Both Kate and Bill felt the ground shake when a bullhorn amplifying the sheriff's voice traveled through the lower chamber and struck their ears like a cannon ball. *"Can you hear me? Can you hear me? The tunnels under investigation are now a crime scene. Please do not touch the bodies. Do not touch the crates or any other items in the vicinity of the bodies!"*

The Shepherds heard the urgent message and stopped in their tracks. Bill picked up his hand held phone and called the sheriff, apparently standing directly above the main entry shaft. "What the Hell, sheriff. You nearly blew our ears drums out. We thought it was another aftershock. A phone call would have done just as well."

He listened to the sheriff's remarks. "What do you mean, the phones didn't work? We're on them right now."

Again he was silent as he listened. "Well, damn, OK. I don't like it but we'll do as you wish."

He hung up and took a deep breath to clear his head and stop the lingering, ringing caused by the bullhorn.

"Well, forget taking the lids off. The sheriff has officially entered the investigation and we're now standing in the middle of a crime scene."

"Are you kidding? We shouldn't have told him about the bodies until we had time to check things out down here. Now what?"

"We get out of here and wait until we have the court's permission to re-enter and continue our search and inspection of the crates and whatever else is down here."

The two disappointed explorers headed for the main shaft and gave a tug to their life lines and within seconds, they felt the weight of strong arms pulling them up one by one until the natural light blinded them.

The sheriff was waiting for them with a look of embarrassment written across his face. "Sorry I had to pull the plug but once I heard about the bodies and their condition, I had no choice but to phone it in and I got the word to shut things down. It's temporary, I assure you."

Kate spoke first, "Look Sheriff, exactly how long will this take? The crates are not part of your crime scene. Not really."

"I know, but technically, we have to remove the bodies and do our forensic work above ground. The crates? I have no idea who they lawfully belong to or who has the authority to remove or even open them."

Bill piped in, "That's not entirely true Sheriff. We, Kate and me and the entire town have ownership of the crates by contract. In any previous digs, all material found which were not declared antiquities, became the property of the discoverers. Similar to a ship wreck."

The sheriff assimilated the information then said, "Look, I'm as interested as you are to look inside those boxes but right now I must follow the law. I'll notify the Provincial Attorney and get a judgment. It should only take a few days. In fact, with the earthquake hitting us, he's close by. Maybe we can still explore the other end of the mine shaft, away from the crime scene."

Sheriff, you know we haven't determined the safety of the tunnel or even the main chamber. I suggest you leave that to us until we feel it's safe enough for you and your men."

Reluctantly, the sheriff shook his head in agreement. "I guess you two know what you're talking about. Last thing we need are more injuries. I just hope we can get the bodies out before dark tonight. Think that's possible?

"Well, we'll go back down and make sure the area is sound then, if your men can bring down the necessary gurneys or whatever you've got to remove the bodies…. We'll stand aside." Bill couldn't imagine a team of forensics workers taking photos and bumping into unstable walls but he'd leave the extraction up to the sheriff. He'd have to lay down the law. The last thing they needed was a collapse.

When the details were outlined, the Shepherds re-entered the mineshaft from the other end and attempted an inspection. "This tunnel must be at least a hundred and fifty years old." Kate pecked away at the support beams with a small chisel. "The beams are sturdy for their age. Not much dry rot."

They walked from the roof hatch towards the original opening exposed after the blast. The tunnel was very straight as if surveyors had laid it out. They continued cautiously in the direction of the river. The river, really a stream, was very shallow and Bill was curious why the river hadn't broken through at some point.

They approached a collapsed area completely blocking their progress. "This isn't the end of the tunnel. The river must have seeped in at this point." Pointing, "Look, over there. There are more crates under the debris." Beyond her reach, a shiny gold object could be seen. "Bill, look!"

From a distance of twenty feet, the object glowed under their fluorescent light. "I think we've got quite a find here, if we can get to it. But I wouldn't dare try to move past where we stand. We could be buried alive."

Kate's voice was high pitched with excitement. "Do you think what I think?"

"Well, I don't know what to think but I think we better keep quiet until we have a chance to roll up our sleeves and get in there. Last thing we need is everyone above ground thinking we've hit a treasure trove. They'd be down here digging around and that could cause trouble and probably lead to a serious collapse."

As they turned back, the flashlights picked up a secondary tunnel, a "Y' in the road, so to speak. Bill checked his bearings and pivoted on his heels. "Kate, this spur leads right into town. In fact, right towards the bank. I've got a feeling there's more here than meets the eye."

"What are you thinking? That the bank had access in and out of here?" Kate tried to imagine the split in the tunnel system and where the other entrance may lie.

"I think it's not as simple as we might believe. This was well engineered, not thrown together by amateurs. Look at those crates."

"Are you suggesting smuggling?" Kate couldn't believe the direction their little search for a carved bone had taken. ""But who and why?"

"Who, I don't yet have a clue but why? Money. It's always money. I think we should have the sheriff post his guards for safekeeping and we sit down and have a chat with him. Then we take a look at the bank and its foundation. This could get very interesting."

Vague Memories

"I had a full night's sleep. Thank you doctor." Raymond looked rested and eager to move along. First, he had to make certain that Maggie could be released into his care. He refused to dwell on the negative right now.

"I'm pleased and you'll be glad to know that Dr. Brown also rested soundly. She's awake and asks to see you."

A light film of sweat invaded his neck and trickled down his spine. "She knows me. She knows I'm here? The amnesia?"

"Hold on sport. She is aware of you and your name but has little knowledge of the day's past events. I questioned her myself and she barely remembers the ground rumbling under her feet. The test results showed only a slight indication of a foreign substance in her blood but to tell you the truth, our labs are running on short staff and exhaustion so I'm not entirely surprised. Her vitals are all sound so I think I can say with some clarity that she is able to travel. I've prepared a list of Christchurch contacts for you once you arrive and are settled. My administrator is preparing her release papers as we speak."

A weight lifted, Raymond shook the doctor's hand firmly and headed up the stairs to see Maggie. "Oh, Dr. Morrissey. If I were you, I'd go at her slowly. Don't expect too much too quickly. She may seem confused and she tires easily."

Raymond slowed his walk and with a slight hesitancy, pushed room 207's door open. Maggie was propped on her pillows, her eyes closed. "Maggie, do you hear me? Are you awake?"

Her eyes flickered in response to a voice and her soft lips parted slightly. Without opening her eyes, Maggie spoke succinctly. "Raymond, my head hurts." Her eyes slowly opened and she flashed him a warm smile. "I've missed you."

Raymond reached for her hand and squeezed her fingertips. Maggie, I was so worried about you. The doctor tells me you had a pretty serious knob on your forehead but luckily not a damaging concussion. Do you remember? He says you have amnesia." Perhaps he shouldn't have told her that.

Maggie covered his wrist with her free hand and held it firmly. He could feel her steady pulse. "My dear Raymond, thoughts are reality. If my good doctor believes I have amnesia, then I must. But quite honestly..." Young Nurse Tillie tapped gently on the door, silencing Maggie.

"So sorry to disturb but the paperwork is complete and I need to assist my patient, Dr. Brown, so you can be on your way to Christchurch." She carried fresh potions and a small bandage, tape and clean civilian clothing to prepare Dr. Brown for hospital dismissal.

Raymond moved away from the bed and headed towards the hallway. "I'll wait outside your room Maggie, so your delightful nurse can ready you for our departure." He smiled nervously. He had a sinking feeling that Maggie was more alert than given credit. Or, was it his twisted imagination? They'd have hours of travel to sort things out.

The Crates

By nightfall, the sheriff had overseen the removal of the two petrified corpses. He'd have his hands full solving the mystery of who they were, why they were killed and left to petrify in the underground mine shaft. Between the sheriff, the mayor, the local historians and the forensics experts, they were in for a fascinating journey back in time.

The history of New Zealand from 1810 to 1865 was a bloody series of wars between the Maori and local European settlers, along with an increasing number of new settlers. Until 1840, New Zealand was very much Maori Land. The Europeans began gathering large sections of land on the North Island, forcing conflicts to protect ancient land. Various treaties were made then broken. During the Musket Wars, a number of tribes gathered muskets to fight other tribes along with the Europeans.

By 1830, European diseases, along with the battles over land rights, caused terrible casualties on both sides. By the 1840's, migration by both Maori and Europeans began to populate the South Island. Everyone was looking for both land and peace.

It was with this added knowledge of New Zealand's past that Bill and Kate finally got permission to re-enter the mineshaft to remove and then open the crates, of course, under the supervision of the sheriff. The first crates were lifted through the blown hole in the roof of the main tunnel. After removing a dozen crates, they marked each one by number and dimension. Kate was amazed at the length of the crates, which measured over sixty inches. With the sheriff standing at their shoulder, Bill broke open the first of the sealed boxes, finding it filled with maps and locations of the entire local Pa, which was Maori for strong point or fortress. The writings were in English.

Kate contemplated its significance. "Had the locals suspected an invasion and occupation by the Maori?"

The second crate answered that question. It was filled with muskets, ammunition and powder. This find continued through the next sixty crates until they had uncovered nearly five hundred well oiled muskets.

The final, smaller ten crates added confusion and exhilaration between the sheriff and an increasing number of townspeople. Rightfully so! They were packed tight with crude bars of pure gold, roughly stamped NNZ, obviously mined and processed somewhere on the North Island. The sheriff couldn't help himself. He held a heavy, shining bar and caressed it like a precious animal pelt. The value was immense and once properly claimed, the find would help the small hamlet of Arrowtown grow and flourish.

After the final crate was prepared to open, Kate and Bill, lifted to new heights by their discovery, sat on its lid, hoping to postpone the final discovery for a few moments longer. "Well, my dear, we've done it. We found a treasure and have secured Arrowtown's good fortune and our own as well."

Bill hugged her shoulder and smiled up at the jubilant sheriff who had called the other members of his town's government to come enjoy their new found bounty. One by one, they arrived with their wives and children and dancing in the streets became a spontaneous reaction to the find.

"Bill, can we explain to our satisfaction how this treasure came to be right here?" Kate watched the jubilant gathering.

"My guess? It was buried during a flood and mudslide. The bodies may have been victims of their own greed, caught up in their anger, they died under the weight of the saturated earth."

Kate pushed the damp tendrils away from her face. "Look at everyone. We've changed their lives, haven't we?"

Bill carefully weighed her words. "We sure have but my theory sounds plausible. Still, there were no spent weapon found with the bodies, except the sword. Makes you think."

"I'm sure there will be some twists and turns. The mystery will be solved along with the murders. The sheriff can't wait to begin his formal investigation. And down the road, Arrowtown will be able to expand and improve the lives of its citizens. What an incredible, life altering find for them."

Watching the growing mass of people milling about. "But first, they need to secure the gold." Agent Shepherd spotted the sheriff shaking hands and hugging three delirious wives. "Sheriff, can I talk to you?"

The sheriff approached him, his face red as a giant rose. "Anything mate, what can I do for you?"

"Sheriff, I think it may be wise to secure this gold. The new Arrowtown Bank has a vault and it would be my suggestion that we make an accurate count and then with the help of your marshals, get this in the vault as soon as possible. Regardless of how grand the celebration, things could get ugly."

With some alarm, the sheriff eyed the gold then blew his whistle with great authority. His men approached at a run. "Listen mates, could we line this area with crime tape then bring our emergency vehicles down to the rim, right over there, then clear a path from onlookers? We need to take control of this fortune."

His men ran back towards town and returned within minutes. The area was secured, tape lining a clear path up the slight rise and an organized line formed to hand the bars up the hill an into the waiting vehicles. The bank president, responding to an urgent message, was more than willing to open the door to the giant vault that had sat nearly empty for years.

The final count was one thousand and five gold bars, each currently valued at over seventeen hundred American dollars per ounce. The bank president immediately called in an armored guard service to stand at the entrance to his fine granite building, still standing after the quake. With his chest puffed out to its full extent, the bank president exemplified what the entire town felt. Newly discovered wealth had expanded their vision and brightened their future.

Once all the gold was safely packed away in the vault, the muskets and maps taken to the museum's storage area, the citizenry slowly dispersed. Finally, Kate and Bill walked back to their camper van. It had been an exhilarating, exhausting day. Stripped naked and standing together under a drizzle of warm water, the pair held each other in their private celebration. "Well, we're back to the bone, aren't we?"

Washing her smooth, tired back, Kate's accomplished husband paused to compile a worthwhile thought. "I think our work is done here. I feel a longing to go home. I miss the states and I'm tired. The mystery of the bone won't go away and I'm sure a once we clear our heads; the pieces will begin to fall together. The sheriff will keep us in the loop regarding the murdered men. They have quite a town project ahead. They don't need us any longer. And there's more I need to tell you, but not now."

Agent Bill Shepherd thought of Manuel and Conchita and their darling twins who had taken residence as political refugees in their DC home. Kate would be surprised, maybe angry that he hadn't shared that information sooner.

"It's been a whirlwind, hasn't it? The earthquake and now the gold. All this in less than a fortnight. We need to tell the others. Jeremy, and even Raymond and Dr. Brown. But to tell the truth, I'm so relieved they weren't here to complicate issues."

"Good choice of words, Darling." She wrapped her arms around his neck. "Trust me. Word will travel faster than the seismic waves we felt. We'll need to write a brief press release and get it in the papers. I don't want a new gold rush to begin over gold that was mined years ago."

"It could get out of control." Bill held Kate warmly. "Tonight we'll put something together and you can run a proof. We'll fax it off ASAP."

"There's still an operational computer at the mayor's office. We can e-mail it out to every news organization. It will be on the front pages tomorrow on five continents. Unfortunately, our phone will be busy for a while."

They turned on the small showerhead and stood under the warm stream of water. Responding to the pleasure of Kate's soft, lathered hands, Bill decided they had even more to discover.

The Press

Within twenty-four hours, the world was aware of a spectacular find on the South Island of New Zealand. The little gold town, in fact, the discovery of the gold, was a worldwide phenomenon. Gold cast in such crude form indicated that the miners probably had cast each bar themselves. The local assay office tested a few bars and indicated a high level of purity, probably close to 22 carats. With each bar weighing a kilo, or 22 pounds, converted to 352 ounces each, the find came to a total of 353,760 ounces. A conservative estimate, if the purity held at 22 carats, put the value at $1700 US per ounce or almost $601 million US dollars!

It was decided that this incredible find's worth be kept secret to avoid all sorts of problems. The primary characters were noted and the value underestimated to save the town from greedy investors and unscrupulous carpetbaggers. Regardless, as expected, every local citizen became reacquainted with distant relatives and long lost school chums. Life would never be quite the same for the fine people of Arrowtown.

Bill and Kate's agreed share was 20% or $120 million US before NZ taxes, refining and sale at somewhat less than $1700 US per ounce. That amount was retail, not wholesale.

Kate laughed, "Poor us. We'd only be left with $60 million US." The great good fortune would accrue to the devastated residents of Arrowtown. With their share of $480 million US, they would be able to rebuild the whole town to their exact liking.

The local committee, overjoyed by the find, was happy to transfer the Shepherd's meager share to the nearest provincial bank. The remainder would be apportioned to projects decided by the committee, starting with water works, power and the homes most sorely needed to replace those damaged or destroyed by the high magnitude quake.

Kate and Bill went with the flow and said their goodbyes to Arrowtown, then Jeremy, Raymond and Maggie along with their young assistants. They also learned for the first time of Maggie's strange injury. Little time was given to delve into their Arrowtown experiences. The less said the better. They would read the outcome in the local newspapers.

It was time to go home and put their tired feet back on American soil. The details had been ironed out, the papers signed and notarized and bank account numbers recorded. Home beckoned.

Kate still had the primitive bone safely tucked away but with all of the excitement, they were no closer to discovering it's meaning than when they had first arrived. But they were much richer. And a portion of that windfall would help them pursue the answers to the puzzle.

During one of their few quiet moments, Bill broached the subject of Manuel and Conchita and their toddler twins and how and why they were forced out of their home in Peru. He also told her of Conchita's father, Ramon's brave sacrifice. She was noticeably saddened; annoyed that he hadn't shared the truth earlier but finally, after reminiscing back to the events in Peru and the wonderful friendship they shared, Kate was excited and pleased that they were now both safe and secure in their Washington DC home.

What Bill hadn't discussed with Kate was the real possibility of mounting an aggressive search in Peru, for the other gold treasure tied to their original discovery, the ancient carved gourd. Money could buy influence and perhaps that is what they needed. They could organize a well-funded search of the rainforest and with their new celebrity; they would have no trouble finding supporters for their research.

Would they include Dr. Raymond Morrissey and Dr. Maggie Smith in their quest? Secretly, Kate feared the greed and jealousy of both Raymond and Maggie. In some convoluted way, they would feel they were entitled to a portion of the reward of gold and create more problems down the road. Even though the actual amount was a well-guarded secret, rumors in the press would run rampant.

Peace

"You haven't said more than five words the last two days." Raymond felt like Maggie had fallen into a silent world where simple conversation was set aside for the sound of tires beating thick tread against the bumpy road.

"Is it your injury? Are you feeling ill?" He was sincere in his concerns.

After her discharge from the hospital, Raymond took great care not to bring up sensitive issues. Out of guilt, he had finally added her name to the paper he had composed explaining the unique penguin discovery. Once published in scientific journals, they would equally share responsibility even though he knew he alone should be awarded the recognition. That was a major concession on his part.

Maggie lifted her head and managed to focus her eyes on Raymond's profile. She shifted in her seat and wet her lips. Her tongue lingered on the rough, chapped surface of her lips, parched by her time in the hospital, her liquid consumption restricted to occasional chips of ice. Her memory was blurred. She remembered the earth moving and the rush to leave Queenstown. Then the black spaces swamped her mind. She squeezed her eyes shut then opened them wide, hoping the cobwebs would fall away.

"Raymond?" A raspy voice arose from her small frame. "Raymond?" She took her time forming the word.

"Yes, Maggie, it's me. Raymond. Do you remember? We've been traveling from the hospital into Christchurch." He didn't wait for a reply. "Do you remember? We spent some time with Kate, and Bill before they left for the airport.

Do you remember?" He felt excitement build and hoped it would crack Maggie's memory bank. "They found the mine and bars of gold. It's in all the papers. Quite a find." He ached from being excluded from their discovery. "Do you remember, Maggie? They've gone back to the States.

Maggie was deep in thought, holding onto his words, sorting through the fragments of familiar and forgotten moments. "Raymond, I remember Bill and I think, Kate, too." The fog was slowly lifting. "Jeremy? Where is Jeremy?" She lifted her head and slightly arched her slumped back. "Was Jeremy there?"

"Jeremy, he was there with us. He spoke to you and told you about their rescue efforts. Do you remember?" Raymond felt a breakthrough coming and pressed on. "He kissed you on the cheek. Do you remember? Maggie?"

"Where are we?" Her voice, slowly regained an even tone, "Tell me, please."

"We're on our way back to Queenstown. Our business in Christchurch is finished. We'll take a day or two to rest and then we'll be off, you to Auckland and me, back to Peru. To Lima or," Raymond paused then mouthed his irrational wish, or, maybe you'd like to come to Peru with me." Immediately, he regretted voicing this invitation. But it hadn't mattered. It was a simple series of coming events but to Maggie, it appeared to overwhelm her senses.

"Peru? Oh, must we go? We have to find the penguin, the giant penguin." The thought sent a flush to her cheeks.

"Peru was forgotten. Honey, it's been done. We've located the evidence we needed and it's all taken care of." His voice reached out and stroked her softly. Then catching himself, he found himself regretting his generosity. Guilt can be costly.

"Maggie, both our names have been attached to the find. While you were in the hospital I managed to officially register the necessary descriptions. Our find is protected under New Zealand and International law. I was told we should be hearing from the scientific community within days."

"I can't remember. Only..." she paused and rubbed her eyes. "Only that we argued over something." her words trailed off.

Raymond felt his body turn rigid in the driver's seat. Taking a deep, controlled breath, Raymond answered, "Yes, we had a minor disagreement but it's all settled now. We both have our names on the discovery. Yours and mine." He'd hope the equanimity would put the issue to rest.

"I don't remember how I hurt myself." Maggie laid a cool hand over his. "Tell me please so I understand better. My face is so discolored." She tipped the mirror down and studied her face for answers

Searching for a tepid approach, Raymond stuck to his original story. "There was a large after shock. We'd emptied out the camper van and I stupidly left the shovel on the roof. It fell and struck you. I am sorry I was careless."

She seemed to weigh the explanation then removed her hand. "I suppose it could have happened that way. Strange, I can't remember."

"You went down so quickly, it's no wonder you can't remember. People have accidents all the time and can't pinpoint the moment. Perhaps it's meant to be that way to lessen the trauma." He sounded truthful and hoped it would satisfy her need to know. "And now you're getting better and before long, it will be a minor blip in time. You've got a life to live Maggie and I'm so grateful you weren't badly hurt."

"I'm tired." Maggie's eyes closed involuntarily and another mile down the road, she lapsed into a sound sleep.

Raymond gently stroked her cheek and felt the warmth enter through his finger- tips. She was quite beautiful when asleep, when her erratic personality was tucked neatly away. He wished she could discard the painful past. He could deal with portions of Maggie, including her uninhibited lovemaking. What he couldn't deal with was her flashes of temper and her need to control his every move. If events went her way, life was a breeze but if she was crossed or made unhappy, all Hell could rain down.

He had been crushed under the weight of her anger, yet not surprisingly, he relished her searing passion. With little prodding, the memory of their last physical encounter forced its way into his head and sent his pulse racing. His body responded in kind. She was indeed dangerous.

"Sleep tight, my dear." He spoke the words softly, not to wake her, probably more for his own benefit. "Sleep tight." In another hour they'd be back in Queenstown, a hotel room, undamaged by the initial quake, waited for his tired body. Maggie would have her own adjoining room. As much as he'd like to sleep beside her peaceful body, he thought it unwise to tempt Pandora's Box, at least not yet.

Homecoming

As the plane touched down at Dulles, the Shepherds, exhausted from the trying yet thrilling weeks in South Island, gathered their meager belongings and exited the massive plane. The tools of their trade had been flown out on a commercial freight carrier, to be delivered to Kate's Smithsonian research office later in the week. Bill patted his jacket's inner pocket, feeling the thin bank folder, the reward earned for researching and carrying out a successful mission during a very difficult and destructive natural event. An 8.2.

For all the pain and suffering, the small enclave of Arrowtown, would rise from the rubble. They would eagerly await the outcome of the Nineteenth Century murders beneath the placid Arrow River. The final report on the crimes would close the book on one portion of their discovery. The other, the heavily engraved gourd and the smooth animal bone with similar markings would have to wait.

His longevity, in this mad world was far more questionable than Kate's. As beautiful and sensuous as she was, she had even greater physical and emotional strength. His lifestyle, both past and probably into the future produced seeds of doubt regarding his chances of survival. Kate could continue her archeological exploits on safer ground. They certainly had the money and connections.

The gourd, and now the carved bone, hung over their heads, crying out for answers. He was sure Kate would never let it go. Peru had a hold on them. That's where the answers could be found. But could they ever return to a new dig site without jeopardizing their lives? Between revolutionaries, corrupt politicians, both Peruvian and Columbian, brutal drug lords and other hazards, the trip would be fraught with danger.

The clearest avenue was to help Manuel organize a popular uprising. With Manuel, now in Washington, moving among the power brokers, a democratic Peru would be an obtainable benefit for the good people of Peru, a lasting peace and a fortified ally of the USA.

As the facts and options took form, Shepherd decided that upon landing, he'd have to determine whether Manuel was willing to pursue such a monumental undertaking. He could become the next President of Peru. Manuel's courageous efforts on behalf of his homeland made him ideally suited for the position of power. From his comfortable seat in Washington, the former Commandant and Bill could arrange to move the military pieces on the chessboard without exposure to immediate danger.

And Kate could be left in peace to research and plan her return to the Rainforest. He found himself grinning like a stricken teenager. "Oh, the Rainforest." Would they ever find Kate's waterfall in that dense jungle? Would they once again make love all night long under the warm mist? He let out an imperceptible shudder. He feared that time might have passed never to return.

That was then. This was now. As the jet prepared for landing, Bill Shepherd woke his wife with a soft kiss and a light caress over her thigh. Again he smiled, "Well, I'll be damned. Everything is still working!"

The drive back to the Georgian colonial was pleasant. The trees were beginning to come into spring bloom, the air sweet with Cherry blossoms. Daffodils and tulips, in lush, colorful bunches, lined the private gardens and manicured public parks. "I'd nearly forgotten how pretty spring in Washington DC can be." Kate rested her head on the rich leather headrest, her eyes floating along with the movement of the car. "We're home."

Manuel and Conchita, with their toddler twins in hand, smiled expectantly as the couple edged their way through the throng of arriving passengers. Kate was caught in the warm grasp of her friend. Manuel leveled a strong hand towards Bill, gripping his hand in a genuine show of male affection. The twins, overwhelmed by the sights and sounds around them, held onto Conchita's skirts, shyly peaking up at the vaguely familiar faces of the new arrivals.

"Conchita, Manuel, the twins, how they've grown! I am so happy, *we* are so happy to see you." Kate, caught in the young woman's soft grasp, took a step back only to be welcomed by the strong male scent of Manuel. He had taken a liking to Bill's after-shave, a woodsy, masculine scent, heady, yet a bit strong in such close contact. "Manuel, you look good, both you and your family. America agrees with you!"

It seemed strange to be welcomed back home by their Peruvian friends. It was out of context. Slowly, the reality took center stage. Their friends, political fugitives, were now virtual citizens of this country and their homeland, Peru, was a place of their turbulent past.

Ramon, Conchita's father, became a tragic victim of a corrupt government seeking revenge for Manuel's efforts to stand up to both government corruption and the dangerous drug trade.

Manuel had a choice to stay and risk the lives of his young family or leave for America, accept political asylum and fight his battles another day. He chose the latter and occasionally second-guessed his decision. Then he'd tuck his babies into their beds and deep down, he'd know he made the right choice.

His country took enough of his blood. It was time for others to fight the battles. When he thought honestly about his country, he had to embrace the idea that there may never be a positive conclusion to the violence and corruption. The drug trade was too lucrative. Virtually everyone had a price. If not, with a wave of the hand, a bounty could be placed on their heads for defying the drug lords and scores of corrupt officials. Heads often rolled in gruesome displays of cruelty.

As the jet had cruised back towards Washington, Shepherd contemplated their wildly wonderful yet jarringly dangerous escapades. His attitude regarding adventure was strongly modified by his marriage and love for Kate. Whatever the future brought, nothing would replace in his heart, Kate's position. He could visualize them aging together, still very much in love.

Raymond & Maggie

"If only we had stayed with them. All this wouldn't have happened." Maggie was boiling mad. First, Raymond and she had taken off on a God awful mission and now, word had spread like wildfire that Dr. Kate and William Shepherd had hit the Mother load. "Dammit, Raymond, you bloody Hell better figure out how we can get our share."

"It had been nearly a week since the Shepherds had flown off for the states and the papers and news channels were relentless. "They're bloody heroes, you hear me Raymond, the great professor who ruined everything for me." The throwing of barbs was more than Raymond could bare but he kept quiet and let her vent. He didn't need another blow to the head, either for Dr. Brown or for himself. She had little recollection of what had transpired between them and he wanted to keep it that way, so he placated her.

"Don't worry. It will blow over soon enough. I believe that after the quake, any good news had to be reported to lift spirits. They've made a much larger issue than it really is." Raymond lied.

Maggie's face turned beet red with disbelief. "Are you insane? This is the largest find of gold bullion in recorded history. Millions, I say millions of pounds, Euro, American currency, however you want to convert it to. They will never have to dig another hole or write another bloody paper as long as they breathe. Where does that leave us?" She looked at Raymond, his elbows propped on the dusty, crooked picnic table. All he could do was pick up his bottle of ale and gulp down the warm liquid.

"I'll think of something. The game's not over until it's over." He sounded defeated, not at all convincing. And he was getting tired of hearing Maggie go off on him. He hadn't imagined an educated woman with her credentials could scrape the gutter with the filthy language and vile hand gestures. She was Jekyll and Hyde, one moment, pleasant and the next, climbing out of a rat's hole with her foul mouth and terrible thoughts.

"You bloody Hell will think of a way to line our pockets or," Maggie paused as if to choose her words carefully, "or the whole world will know what happened to me."

Raymond, his eyes suddenly the size of saucers, raised his head and tried not to react to the threat. He didn't want to question her. He really didn't want to know what she was thinking. "I need to take a shower and freshen up." Before Maggie could come up with a retort, he quickly rose and headed in the direction of the Arrowtown Manor.

Trouble Building

It was three weeks before the Shepherds' homecoming. Manuel received a troubling phone call from an old fellow officer in the Federales. He shook his head as he listened.

"Manuel, my dear friend", the voice of Hector Gonzales was guarded, "it has been a long while but I know you remember my name. Many things have changed at home and I feel we must talk in person. The phone may not be a safe way to discuss these topics." Hector paused then continued. "Manuel, old friend, I need your full attention. Say we meet in Georgetown."

Manuel picked up the tension in his voice and felt his skin turn damp. "What is this about Hector? I now have a growing family and my devoted wife. It appears you want me to come back to help resolve some problem." He chose his words carefully. " You know old friend, I am no longer interested in putting my life in jeopardy."

"But please grant me this favor, Manuel." Hector's voice rose as he continued. "The security of our country depends on us working together. Please old friend. If you choose not to..."

"I'll meet you at the Georgetown Bistro near the park but, Hector, only to hear what you have to tell me. Please expect no more of me."

"Yes, yes, I am close to you now and I promise, I will only share my story. You have no gun to your head, my friend." Hector's tone was one of relief. "One hour my friend. And... there is no need to share our conversation with your wife. It may only worry her needlessly."

"One hour but I must not linger. Conchita will become suspicious and ask too many questions. I care not to make her concerned."

An hour later, Manuel sat across the small table listening to his old right hand man. Memories of this courageous soldier flashed back in a series of powerful visions. How many raids and fights did they share? How many times did they come to the aid of the other?

How many times did he save Manuel's life? He'd save Hector's more than he could count. He was a loyal and brave soldier.

"Yes, we would like a cold drink. "A Corona for me. and one for my friend." Together, they quenched their thirsts. "My throat is dry, old friend. The circumstances have brought worry to my life once more." Hector leveled a stare at Manuel, his eyes ringed with dark circles.

"What brings you so much worry and lack of sleep?" Manuel anticipated his dire reply.

Hector scanned the immediate area with wary eyes. "Manuel, the Shining Path, the Sendero Luminesco, is coming back, in great strength. It was not so long ago. Remember, thirty thousand Peruvians, our countrymen and women, were slaughtered by them and another thirty thousand more by the government during the twenty years of their uprising." He paused to gather his thoughts. "The Maoist philosophy is gaining strength because of the economic failures. Sendero is working closely with as many as three hundred thousand cocoa growers and drug traffickers. Once we thought they were reduced to as little as six hundred members. But it is not the case now."

Manuel closed his eyes and imagined such numbers occupying his home -land. "This is bad news, my friend. Worse than I imagined. I understand now why your eyes are so red. You carry a huge burden. There is much to worry about."

"Now you see why we had to talk. Unfortunately, President Fujimora was incompetent and corrupt. It never ends, my friend. This US State Department makes foolish statements. They say our country does not work so well. Any woman on the streets of Lima would say the same. My friend, eighty-five percent of our people live in the most rudimentary conditions. And everything has gotten so much worse than when we cleared out Sendero." Hector wiped a nervous hand across his forehead then held the bottle of Corona in a death grip.

"I despise hearing such news. I've been away from my country for only a short while and so much has taken place that displeases me. I cry for our country and our people." Manuel felt fatigue as heavy as a stone gripping his soul. "So much effort for nothing. Would there ever be peace in our homeland?"

"There is more, my friend. FARC is pushing at our borders once more. We can expect no help from America after 9/11. They are occupied by the radical Islamists."

"Yes, I understand that our people feel little hope and are ripe for the Maoists. Are they centered in the universities? That always seems the way." Manuel answered his own question. Youth was always vulnerable to radical movements and violent upheaval.

"Dear friend, that brings me to my point. Your friend, William Shepherd, his wife, the Doctor Kate, has several acquaintances amongst the students and the professors at the University. They have become the leaders of Sendero."

"I feared it would be so but hoped that it would not be. Such fine minds wasted. They could make our country a better place but they choose to follow the wrong path, the Shining Path."

"My trusted contacts understand that many of their ideas are truly valid, especially considering how the government, in conjunction with the drug lords and terrorists, continue to exploit the good people of Peru. But their solutions only harm us more. Manuel, it is critical that we get inside the universities and determine the best way to eliminate the leadership. For our country's future."

"But I don't see how Senor William Shepherd would be involved, or his wife. They are just to return from a successful though frightening trip to New Zealand where the earthquake nearly killed them. We stay at their home and plan to welcome them back any time soon."

Tightening his jaw as he came to the reason for their meeting. "Manuel, my trusted friends want to cut off the head of Sendero and give democracy a chance to grow. We can't get close to the university without raising suspicion. We have already lost our young people who tried and were sadly discovered."

"So, let me understand you. You want the Shepherds or at least Kate, to return to the university and mount an assassination." Manuel's' words escaped his lips but didn't quite reach comprehension. "Kate Shepherd, an assassin?"

"No, no, not that way. Yes, we want your friends to return to Peru and make contact with the Shaman's son and his new associates. We have heard that he feels cheated out of the gold discovery found in New Zealand. After all, he supplied the miner's letter from his father's only possessions."

"You know about the letter?" Manuel sat up and felt a noose closing over his throat. "How?"

"That kind of news travels very quickly, my friend. The Shaman's son is greedy and desires the possessions of the rich not like his pious father. Perhaps, a few letters and a visit to see him, to do more research at the original site, perhaps entice him with a handsome reward may very well whet his appetite and then he lets down his guard." A small grin appeared on Hector's face, exposing a gold tooth that caught the light.

"But Senora Kate, Dr. Kate, she may not want to go back into such danger and with such a plan. She is an educator, not a spy or an assassin. She is grateful that the young student gave her the letter. She would not want to end his life." Manuel grappled with the plan. It was hard to grasp.

Hector continued, "and after your friends have an opportunity of further research, we can collect the leadership and your friends would be free to return to their comfortable lives." He made the plan sound so easy and painless. "My group is not a size-able force so we must act like commandos to cut off the serpent's head. I see you don't like that I say 'commandos' but I must be honest with you. You know my loyalty to my country and to the welfare of my people." Hector leaned back in his chair and took the last gulp of his Corona.

"I agree something must be done but I know nothing of how Senor and Senora Shepherd would react to your plan. They are

Americans and don't feel the same pain, as we do. " Manuel couldn't imagine himself approaching them.

"Please, my friend, give it your serious attention and think how to approach your friends and ask for their cooperation. We only have thirty days to mount our efforts and save our country. After that, we may never have another opportunity. Too much is at risk."

Turmoil

The two couples, along with the scampering children, entered the lovely Georgian home. Bill and Manuel hauled the heavy suitcases up the tiled stairs and dropped them in a corner of the large entryway. Like many homes of this design, the columns that supported the front portico led to beautifully etched glass and heavy carved wood double doors and a two-story foyer, tiled in marble and lavishly furnished in period pieces. Brilliantly polished hardwood banisters curved upward along the twin sweeping staircases to an upper mezzanine that led to the spacious bedrooms and Kate's well-appointed study.

The moldings were richly enameled, substantial yet delicately carved, the light fixtures simple yet refined and the paintings that decorated the walls appeared to be of local landscapes plus equine portraits, presumably rendered in the early 1800's. They were the real thing, not copies and most likely, lesser artists' work purchased at auction or from the occasional premier estate sale. Regardless, the home was inviting, comfortable and casually elegant.

This particular red brick home had been built within the past fifty years yet it had the feel of a classic Eighteenth Century estate. They had been fortunate to lease it furnished. The owners had accepted an ambassadorial position oversees yet they did not want to part with their home in case the assignment was not to their liking or, more likely, if they were forced to return to the states due to dangerous political unrest in the Middle East.

Conchita had made certain that the home was maintained exactly as before their journey to New Zealand. With the help of a small staff, the grounds were manicured and the interior was spotless. Kate smiled as she stepped inside. "Conchita, Manuel, it's good to be home and it's even better that you are here with us." Kate's voice carried real emotion.

The loss of Conchita's father was disturbing yet the quick decision by William Shepherd to arrange political asylum for the Peruvian family had worked to everyone's advantage. Yet, the murder of Ramon brought to the fore how dangerous Peru still remained. Kate would take time to spend with Conchita. The young woman had just reconnected with her father after a difficult period of time and then, suddenly; he was taken from her forever.

Bill and Manuel picked up the heavy cases and carried them up the stairs while the women took a short tour of the lower floor. The men came down the stairs laughing and pleased to be together. A slightly off color story had struck Manuel as funny.

"Ladies, while you take the children up to their rooms and unpack, Manuel and I are going to have a splash of that bottle of Brandy I've been waiting to open." He had his hand on Manuel's shoulder, guiding him in the direction of the comfortable library that also served as his male enclave. "We promise not to smoke our Cuban cigars!"

Kate knew he was only joking because the small sign on the vestibule read, *Please No Smoking!* The owners of the lovely home would be very upset if the smell of stale smoke permeated the upholstered furnishing and the freshly dry cleaned window coverings. "We're on our way, gentlemen but after we're all unpacked, save a sip of your Brandy for us!" Kate wasn't inclined to imbibe but a sip and welcoming toast from Shepherd's prize bottle would punctuate their arrival home.

It took longer than expected to settle the children in their room and unload and sort the bags. They had washed their dirty clothing when they could but dust and bits of debris from the earthquake and their successful excavation still filled the pockets of her jeans and denim shirts. Kate had a list of stories. The earthquake, the group assisting them in the rescue. Jeremy. Dr. Maggie Brown. Dr. Morrissey. It would take days to sort it all out.

"Well, Conchita, I've dominated the conversation. I know you have a lot to tell me as well." Her voice dropped to a whisper. " Senior Bill didn't tell me about your father's murder until a few days ago. He knew there was nothing I could do but worry. But I'm so sorry. It's hard to imagine that people can be so cruel. Your father was doing so much to better his country, he was a hero in so many ways."

The tears welled in Conchita's eyes as she struggled to find the right words. "I miss him so much, Kate. The children miss their Grandpapa" She reached for the box of tissues on the bedside table. "He was a good man and became a good father to me. Now I have only Manuel."

"Oh, you have more than that." Kate moved closer to Conchita and stared into her dark eyes. "You have your children and you have us. We'll do anything to help you through this. And Manuel, he's a very fine man. And very handsome!" Kate winked at Conchita as she tried to lighten the mood. Conchita blushed. "You're so right Kate. Manuel loves me and I love him and he loves our children. I am lucky to have you as well. Still, I miss my father. I think that is only natural."

Kate hugged Conchita warmly then put her at arm's length. "We are both very lucky women to have strong men in our lives."

"And, you let us stay in your beautiful home and Senor William did so much to help us leave Peru. I wonder if I ever go back. It is a beautiful place but so dangerous now. I still sorry it came to that." Looking into Kate's eyes. "And they murdered my father. I can not forgive that so easily."

"Let's go take a sip of that fine Brandy and be grateful for all we do have, beautiful, healthy children, men that love us and a home to share in a safe country." Kate led the way out of the master bedroom, past the happily playing children, through the wide hallway to the balcony overlooking the perfectly arranged foyer. Then together, they walked down the winding staircase. Conchita was a half step behind, her mood gradually turning from sadness to joy. Kate was right. She should be grateful for her blessings.

"William, Manuel, do I need to get two more brandy snifters from the bar?" She had forgotten whether the glasses were kept in the library 's small drink cart. "Bill?"

The doors to the library were slightly ajar and a soft light curled under the heavy wood panel like a sunburst. "Bill?" Kate tapped on the door then pushed it open. The room was empty. The bottle of Brandy sat on the broad reading desk, the lid off. Two snifters, still holding a swallow of the amber liquid sat on the delicately inlaid Chippendale table that rested between the large, leather wingback chairs. The back door, leading to a small garden and slate patio was opened slightly

"Bill?" Kate pushed the patio doors open and walked outside. The smell of spring flowers and freshly cut grass was so pleasant to her sense of smell, she wanted to take it in and enjoy the moment but she dreaded the reality. She knew deep in her being that something was terribly wrong. She called Bill's name, then Manuel's. There was no answer. Together, the women walked around the foundation of the large colonial.

Conchita's breathing became labored. "Manuel, Senor William, where are you?" She hugged herself, her nails digging into her palms. "Kate, something is happened. Where are they?" There was panic rising in her voice. She carried too many unpleasant memories to be optimistic

"There must be a logical explanation. Two strong men don't just disappear into thin air." They rounded the house and made their way down the small pathway back to the secluded library terrace. From another angle, Kate saw a familiar object lying under the iron chair, partially obscured by freshly fallen petals. She got down on her knees and picked it up, turning the object over in her hands. For a moment, she tried to make sense of it but sometimes things just don't make sense.

It was William Shepherd's compact leather wallet, the one he always had on his person unless he was sleeping. Then it sat next to the bed. She didn't question him about it. Maybe she should have. He was CIA. There were always some unanswered questions. She unfolded the soft leather and found a business card that was badly worn on the edges with a dark stain, perhaps from spilled coffee. The printing was faint but still legible. She didn't recognize the name but obviously, it was someone important to her husband or else, he would have discarded it long ago. He had never been a saver of irrelevant items. She placed it back in the wallet and tucked it in her pocket.

It still didn't explain where Bill and Manuel had gone. Maybe it was something as simple and harmless as a stroll down the lovely street to get rid of the kinks caused by the long flight. She couldn't think of another reason for them walking away.

The flustered women went back inside the library and just stared at each other. Should they wait a while to see if the men returned? Should they call the police? Two hysterical women reporting their men missing for only half an hour? They'd be told to wait awhile longer and most likely, they would return under their own power.

So they sat down and fidgeted. Their imaginations were running wild. They had experienced so much between the two of them that they automatically gravitated to the dramatic. Bill was CIA, invisible to the world. Manuel was formerly living in a corrupt country with enemies everywhere. They were both survivors.

Kate tried to take a deep, reassuring breath while her eyes perused every square inch of the comfortable library. Three walls were strikingly designed to hold as many as a thousand leather-bound books and journals of every size. The ten-foot ceiling provided ample room for an attractive and practical brass and cherry wood ladder, with wheels riding on a track that swept around the shelves.

The room smelled like parchment and leather bindings and sweet brandy. The wingbacks were situated away from the grass-clothed wall and the deep pained window seat. A large Queen Anne reading desk, with a banker's lamp and a neat writing pad, filled the center of the room. The mahogany drink cart stood next to the desk,

It all looked so neat and tidy. Kate could imagine the men entering the room, poring themselves a couple of her husband's premium brandies, swirling the rich liquid in the snifters, making a toast, taking a taste, then something happened. They didn't take the time to sit and enjoy their drinks. The glasses were barely touched.

Kate's heart suddenly lurched out of her chest. On the top bookshelf, there was an empty space, the other books leaning lightly together. Something was missing and she gasped at the realization. The Bible. The Shepherd's family Bible, the one that she had placed the invaluable clues, the symbols from the gourd was gone!

"Conchita, they've taken the Bible, the Shepherd's Bible!"

Conchita's eyes widened and her breathing was raspy. She followed Kate's eyes uncertain exactly how she should react. So she stood and watched Kate. Under her breath she whispered, "Who took the Bible? Why the Bible?"

Kate, nimble as ever, climbed up the steps of the ladder to make certain. In its place was a dusty smudge. It had been recently removed. No stolen! And the men? It was no coincidence that they were also missing! On instinct, she reached into her pocket and fingered the small leather wallet. The worn card slipped into her hand and she read the name, Cory Danielson, Special Consultant. Without thinking further, she grabbed her cell phone and dialed the number.

Compatriot

"But Senora Kate, should we not call the police? I feel so scared for Manuel and Senor William. and the Bible. Why the Bible? Who would take such a thing?" Kate had a lot of explaining to do.

"William's CIA, Conchita and Manuel, his connections to Peru are suspect. We can't treat this like most crimes. We don't want the police involved. We'd have too much explaining to do and my husband has always lived a covert life. They can't help us and it would only make things worse.

Conchita listened, not fully understanding the brevity of their situation. "I trust you Kate to do the right thing for us and for our men." She wiped a stray tear from her cheek and tried to part a smile. It was better than nothing.

Her skin had grown thicker since the first time they had met and Kate was relieved that she could count on the young woman in what appeared to be a growing crisis. "Why don't you check on the children while I wait for Senor William's friend to arrive." Conchita was grateful to leave the library to be with her children. She'd have to rely on Kate's judgment. After all, Senor William was missing along with Manuel.

The library was quiet as death. She strained to hear Conchita's footsteps advance up the stairs. Kate's racing heartbeat suddenly reached her ears. They had barely arrived home and now this. "My dear husband." She tried to make sense of what had just taken place.

First, someone must have known when they were returning from New Zealand and that Manuel and Conchita, along with the children, would be picking them up at the airport. They knew the home would be empty so they could set a trap.

Second, Bill Shepherd and Manuel are both powerfully built men. It would take an act of surprise to subdue them. There were no signs of a struggle so they must have been taken some other way. A laser gun could silently knock them to the ground but both men could probably ward off an attack and turn the weapon to their own advantage.

Or, they could have been drugged somehow. Kate looked at the bottle of brandy then to the nearly empty brandy snifters. The most logical and risk free way to subdue the men was by drugging them. A chill came over her. Had they been killed, and then carried away? Poison, especially the ones used by assassination teams were potent and could bring instantaneous death. But why take them away? Why not leave the bodies and make it look like a robbery gone badly? "No, they're being kept alive for some reason." Kate had to remain positive.

Then, there was the Bible. No one knew about the symbols and notes that she had placed between its pages, no one except Bill and her. She had placed them there when they were evacuating Peru, hoping that if something happened down the road, they wouldn't fall into the wrong hands. But someone knew. She had sent a brief note to their private attorney just in case but Daniel Goldman new nothing else. And her husband would have no reason to make mention of it. Someone knew or it would still be sitting on the top shelf.

And why? The whole plot seemed ludicrous. They had found a tremendous stash of gold in Arrowtown. A thought raced into her head. It may be as simple as kidnapping for ransom. The international press was filled with stories about their discovery, but nothing about the Bible. Yet, kidnapping the men would be dangerous. If they had snatched Kate and Conchita, William Shepherd, CIA operative, would have taken after them and torn them limb-by-limb.

Yes, Kate and Conchita would be at a disadvantage. They didn't have the same brutal force and skill packages. They'd have to rely on their wits and whatever help they could get from Cory Danielson.

The phone conversation had been brief. He wasn't surprised when she introduced herself. He was on his way over to fill in the blanks. He thought the phone might be bugged. CIA agents were suspicious of everything. Kate looked at her watch. It was 2:15PM. It had been nearly an hour since the men vanished. She jumped at the sound of the heavy brass doorknocker.

As Kate opened the door, she gathered her emotions and set them aside for another private moment. Cory Danielson dressed in a pair of faded Levi jeans and a Dartmouth sweatshirt greeted her with strikingly dark eyes and a slight smile that exposed two perfectly straight rows of white teeth. His salt and pepper hair was still damp from his shower and he smelled vaguely like citrus.

"So you're Kate. Shep's told me a lot about you. So even though we haven't met before, I feel like I know you." He extended his hand her way and she grabbed it like a lifeline. "Hold on Kate, it's going to be OK. Trust me."

Kate thought she was under control but all of a sudden the realization that her husband was really gone hit her between the eyes and she couldn't hold back the tears. "I can't believe this. We just walked in the house and Bill's gone and Manuel is gone and the Bible, the old family Bible." She turned around, embarrassed at her emotional outburst and Cory followed her through the foyer. He walked behind her, trying to grasp the flow of her thoughts. She walked him into the library then turned to face him. Her eyes were red but the tears were subsiding.

"Bill would want me to keep my head together. This is the scene of the crime." She pointed around the room and up to where the Bible had formerly been. "I think they were drugged. Maybe the brandy they were drinking. Bill and Manuel would have fought off just about anyone if they'd been confronted by whoever came into our home."

Cory kept quiet and let Kate talk. "And they stole a family Bible that had hidden ancient symbols that we found on our first trip to Peru. They were similar to the symbols that were given to us in an old miner's letter that eventually led us to the gold find in Arrowtown."

"I read about it. You hit the mother load, and the earthquake. Quite a holiday you two had! I'm to assume that all of this has a direct connection to the abductions. Until we prove differently, we'll follow that premise."

"Whoever planned this had brass balls. Sorry for my crude language but what kind of fool goes after two highly skilled men? If it went wrong, Bill and Manuel would have ripped them to pieces."

You ask what kind of men? Two kinds. Either very stupid ones or very motivated ones willing to lay it all on the line." Cory walked around the library's rich interior. He pulled a clean cloth out of his packet and carefully picked up the one of the brandy snifters and gave it a whiff. "Damn."

"What is it?" Kate hated to be right.

"It smells a little too sweet. But we'll have it tested so we know exactly what was used and how much they ingested." He placed the glass back where it had been and moved towards the terrace door. "Were there any signs of forced entry? This door is untouched."

"We looked when we walked around the house but didn't check all the windows. But a pro could force a lock with no problem, right."

"With the right tools, you can break into Fort Knox. Any alarm?"

"Conchita told me that Manuel set it before they left to pick us up but to think about it, we didn't have to punch in the code when we got home. It was already green. I didn't question it. We were so pleased to be home with good friends."

Cory walked out on the terrace and Kate was on his heals. "This is where you found my card? Under that table?"

"Yes and no. I found it out here but under the iron chair, not the table. I don't know how it ended up there unless Bill was sitting in the chair and somehow it came loose."

"Or he was still conscious enough to place it out of sight of his abductors knowing you would find it and call the name on the card. Shep knew I would come if the call came in"

Kate looked at him quizzically, "if the call came in? It sounds like you expected something to happen."

"Well, Shep and I had a pact. We both live on pretty shaky ground." Cory pulled out the identical leather wallet and handed it to Kate. "Here, open this."

She took the familiar bi-fold and opened it to find her husband's card, nearly as threadbare as Cory's. "So you watched each other's backs from a distance." She was surprised but not unduly so. "You come to the rescue in case Bill's in trouble and he does the same for you. I envy that kind of loyalty." Kate was sincere and relieved that her man had such a close friend to count on. That she could count on. She handed him back the wallet. "Put it someplace safe"

"Now it's time to get down to business." He pulled out his cell phone and called for reinforcements. "Hold on a minute. Fred. how about a favor. I need your help identifying a foreign substance in my brandy, and fingerprints, maybe some fibers to check out. Bring the package. Yea, right now. We're in a nice neighborhood so make like you're coming to call on friends. Yea, the Jeep will do."

He turned towards Kate and a glimpse of a smile appeared. "We're going to be on his trail in no time. Trust me." Then he finished up with Fred, giving him the address. "A half hour is good. Thanks pal

Love, Hate

Raymond decided it was better to wave the white flag than to keep up the constant barrage of vitriol. Maggie was a controller and if she felt threatened, she would immediately go on the attack. And there was no compromise for her. She'd draw a line in the sand and there was Hell to pay if you stepped over it.

Raymond had dealt with a lot of different women but never had he experienced the tremendous highs and the debilitating lows that she could create. One moment, she'd be fawning over him and the next; the poison would ooze out of her pores. She was like a beautiful plant in the woods that devoirs its prey, luring the timid insect into her warm center then enveloping the hapless creature in a sticky though sweet mixture of love, hate, hunger and savagery.

Fortunately, her memory of past events remained vague. She had occasional headaches and experienced a few episodes of vertigo but an aspirin seemed to take care of things. There was no immediate need to seek further medical care. Raymond preferred it that way, in case some ambitious head doctor extracted the missing pieces and caused a firestorm.

Christchurch residents were pulling themselves up slowly. The aftershocks continued to rattle nerves and the estimation of damage was immense. Time would heal all, except those who lost loved ones. The scars would linger forever.

Their time with Jeremy and his team had come to an end. They had flown up to the North Island, to Auckland and Maggie's home turf. The city was involved with charity drives and volunteers gathering supplies and money to help their southern cousins. The University was a welcoming peaceful reprieve from the frantic pace and pressure they had been subjected to during and after the quake.

Maggie's office was small and cluttered with books, maps and cabinets filled with fossils and small treasures. The bookshelves were bulging with well-used volumes of academic literature,

National Geographic Magazines and framed photos of Maggie, standing alongside a number of prominent archeologists and paleontologists, Lewis Leaky the most prominent, recognizable personage to grace her walls.

"Sit down, Raymond." Maggie settled behind her desk in an old leather office chair that had seen better days.

Raymond found the overstuffed armchair next to the floor to ceiling window to his liking and leaned back into the deep, soft cushions. He liked the feel and the smell of her study. It reminded him of his own comfortable space where he met with students and discussed theories with his late wife and fellow archeologist. A pang of longing ran through him. He hadn't allowed himself to think about Helen in a long time. Heat seemed to rise from his trunk up his neck and explode on his face.

"Are you OK? Raymond, you look flushed. Are you too warm?" Maggie noticed the change in his complexion and surprised Raymond. She was so self-consumed, he didn't think she'd notice if his blood was running onto the floor, unless it saturated her rare Oriental.

"It's nothing, just a sign of fatigue. It's been a hectic couple of weeks." He hated to admit it but did anyway. "I'm not as young as I used to be."

Maggie laughed, an odd reaction to his explanation. "You lit up once before like that but it had nothing to do with fatigue."

Raymond would have blushed if he hadn't already sent all the available blood to his face. At least she was light hearted and not on the attack. "I vaguely remember something like that." He figured this was as good a time as any to figure our where they were going. Was this a relationship worth nurturing or should he run as fast as possible in the opposite direction? "What now, Maggie?"

She was expecting the question and swiveled in her chair. "Do you like Auckland?"

"Sure. It's a nice city. Clean, friendly and the weather's not bad. The University is well respected. What's not to like?" He wasn't sure why she posed the question. "Why?"

"I've outgrown it." She had been stewing over this for a while and Raymond was probably the first one who heard her vocalize her displeasure. "I want to go to America."

So that was it. How was he to facilitate that desire? Marry her? Find her a spot as a guest professor? "I always thought you loved it here. You certainly were successful here, having a fine time teaching, researching and publishing a stack of noteworthy papers. Your name is passed around in the best circles. Why now?" He didn't know whether he wanted to hear the answer.

"Simple as can be. I need a change and I'm hoping you can make it happen. I want to go to Washington DC. I'm tired of living among the sheep and the simple people." An elitist tone welled from deep within her and made Raymond uncomfortable. More than that, something else, even more personal hung around the edges of her sudden declaration.

Bill and Kate Shepherd made their home in Washington's comfortable suburbs and he was sure Maggie knew that. He hoped their presence in the city wasn't a motivating factor. He kept it to himself. Raymond kept his voice clear and interested. "Do you want to teach there? Perhaps at Georgetown? I have connections there but everyone has cut staff. They may not pay you much for the privilege to teach."

"I'm not concerned about that. I just want a change of scenery. I live a pretty simple life so I have enough socked away to last a while." She took a long pause and studied Raymond's demeanor before she continued. "Of course, I wouldn't mind adding to it." She smiled at Raymond and he knew his suspicions were right on the money.

"Like how?" He tried to sound off handed but it came out just like he thought. She knew what he was thinking. She had to know. "Planning on playing the stock market?"

Dr. Maggie Brown took a long, thoughtful look out the window, the view pleasant with Eucalyptus trees, shading the cool grass, forming a wide path to the heart of the campus. "No, I want to add gold to my portfolio."

Trepidation

Kate sat on the edge of their bed. Cory was downstairs making phone calls, lining up his support crew. She needed a moment to herself to think and understand what had just occurred. Bill had simply vanished along with Manuel. Conchita found comfort in the twins but all Kate could do was hug her pillow and reach out to her dear husband's lingering scent.

They hadn't had time to make love or even kiss since they returned home. The bed was crisply made, the pillows placed in perfect order. She wished, no prayed, that it had all been a bad dream and any moment, she'd awake and find her husband lying next to her under the cool sheets. His skilled hands would reach out for her and she'd respond in the early morning hours and together, they'd find peace, warmth and passion.

Tears welled in her eyes and burned as they escaped down her cheeks. He was so capable of taking care of her it seemed impossible, unbelievable, that anyone could carry him away. And Manuel. The poison must have been very potent. She shuddered to think they could be dead. Then why carry away their lifeless bodies? Nothing made sense. Kate reached deep inside herself and stifled the lingering cries. Bill would want her to stay strong and keep her head.

And thank God for Cory. He had taken the time to explain their relationship that went back more than two decades. Cory had dual citizenship, his mother from the states and his father, a former Canadian Mounted Police official, originally from Calgary. He had spent his childhood in the cold Northwest until his mother tired of the long winter nights and the family moved south and took up residence in Bethesda, Maryland. The move was possible because his father, still a relatively young man and well respected around the Beltway, took a job at the Canadian Embassy in Washington. Years later, his father encouraged his son to serve the country they now called their permanent home.

So he graduated Georgetown with a degree in political science and applied for his first government assignment. After that, his record was sealed and even his immediate family knew little of his work.

Bill Shepherd and Cory Danielson had been drawn together by circumstances and their personalities meshed. They had been partners on a number of oversees assignments and over time, became more like brothers, than colleagues, guarding the other's secret identities in the field and coming to the other's aid when called upon.

Cory carried Shep's weathered name card in his pocket in a similar wallet. He explained why they decided to make the purchase while on assignment in Hong Kong shortly before the Mainland Chinese takeover. Cory had been 'ousted' and Shep brazenly planned his extraction before Tieneman Square blew into absolute chaos. On the flight back to safety, they had made a solemn pact and respected the oath. Now Cory was at her side and would do whatever it took to get Shep safely back home.

In appearance, he was the exact opposite from Shep, one with thinning, blond hair, of average height and weight and the other, displaying thick, dark hair, standing over six feet tall and impressively muscular. Although Cory wasn't as physically impressive as Shep, his demeanor was confident and persuasive. They made a good team. Kate could recognize strong traits in men, both comforting and assertive. Right now, she didn't want to call the shots. Her husband's abduction was too personal.

"Senora Kate?" Conchita stood in the door of the master suite. "Senora, is there any word? I am so worried." Her hands shook slightly and her beautiful face still had damp smudges from her tears. "Does Senor Cory know who kidnapped our husbands?" Her voice was strained and showed signs of mental fatigue. "I pray to God above he helps us."

"He's downstairs right now making calls. Pretty soon we'll know more. The only thing we can do for now is keeping our wits about us and rely on Cory. He's Senor William's best friend and they've worked together for years. He's our best hope right now." Kate had to convince herself that things would turn out the way she wanted them to but doubts crept into her thoughts no matter how hard she tried to keep them at bay.

They made their way down the stairs to find Cory sitting in the big wingback, the cell phone to his ear. He saw them enter and raised his hand as if asking for quiet. "OK, I see. I guess that's good news. Anything else I need to know?" He looked at the women and a slight smile appeared on his attractive face. "Well, call me or text me if there's anything else. And keep this under your belt. Talk later." He closed his cell phone and stood to greet the two concerned women.

"Is there news?" Kate's heart was beating like a drum and her hands were moist. She held Conchita's hand and squeezed her fingers until they turned white. "Please, Cory, any news at all?"

"Some, not all bad. He gestured for the women to take a seat across from him. "They were drugged not poisoned. Sounds the same but we know the same drug administered to Michael Jackson was used. Anesthesia used in surgical procedures. Usually not fatal."

"But Senor, Michael Jackson died." Conchita felt tears well up.

Yes, but he was already very weak and in bad shape. Shep and Manuel, I know to be fit and strong. That's a plus. And because it was anesthesia, chances are they didn't mean to kill them but rather to take them alive for some purpose, like holding them for ransom."

Kate was relieved with the revelation and sat back to listen to what else Cory learned

"The gold you discovered in New Zealand was on all the news networks. It is possible that the motive is a huge ransom against the value of your take."

It makes perfect sense. They came back to the states without discussing such risks. Surprisingly, he didn't broach the subject. So unlike him. But perhaps he figured they had been through enough over the past year and they were in for smooth sailing. Still, not like him. He was too worldly, too savvy to let this slip past. "Bill was always on guard. What went wrong?"

"Shep's human. We all slip up now and then. We just hope it isn't a big slip up and if heaven forbid it is, we have each other to rely on." Cory sounded rational. His partner was flesh and blood, not invincible. Shit happened.

"So, where do we go from here? Kate took a few deep breaths and drew in as much air as she could to clear her foggy brain. "Do we just wait?"

"Well, that's part of it, I'm afraid. But I've got feelers out. You'd be surprised how Homeland Security has added resources to my bag of tricks. Of course, none of this will hit the papers or local law enforcement. We've gone covert. We'll have wiretaps out there and satellite surveillance if we need it. The big guns are on this. Shep's important to a lot of higher ups so I had no trouble pushing the envelope. Every rock will be turned over. The only thing I ask of you is to remain positive. We'll need you to help out, primarily with information and names of anyone who had you worried, for any reason. The more heads we put together, the better."

Cory stood up and brushed his fingers through his thinning hair. "I'm your legs, ladies. I just met you but I know you Kate." He stopped talking and let a smile cover his face, exhibiting a fine set of even, white teeth. "Shep told me what happened, with the Professor the drug lords, and the Peruvian government officials. I know you have a machete of sizeable proportions in your suit case and I'm also aware that you know how to use it."

Kate couldn't help but grimace at the reminder. "Yes, I used it but it was justified. I was kidnapped." The memories came back in a wave and momentarily swept her away. "And I'd use it again, in a heartbeat." Her tone was filled with resolve. "You better understand that I'm not very good at sitting on the sidelines."

Cory couldn't help but admire her spunk but he feared her bravado. "I'd really appreciate it if you'd let me do my job. When the time comes and I need you to produce your machete, I'll let you know." He hoped that time would never come.

Deception

Manuel thought deeply about what had transpired with Hector. How could he explain the situation to his close friend and ally, William Shepherd? Could he risk his friend's life for a cause that was not his own? Like most men, Manuel appreciated that the best method was the most direct method. He would speak with his friend at the first opportunity.

On the flight back from New Zealand, Bill couldn't stop thinking about how he could reengage Manuel in the salvation of Peru. Shepherd had contacts at CIA who advised him that time was coming for a dramatic resolution to the crisis and the urgency to short circuit Sendero. Manuel and Conchita had been relocated to America and were living a comfortable, stress free life away from the dangers of their homeland. Could he be persuaded to give up the comforts of their exile?

On the ride from the airport, the conversation was light. The women and the children added to the mood. When the men were finally alone in the library, the women upstairs with the children, the talk turned to the seriousness of the situation.

Pouring a brandy for Manuel and himself, they sat down and finally spoke with passion and sincerity. "I don't understand why but the future of Peru is falling on our shoulders." Bill swirled the brandy around the glass and stared into its amber color. "Whether we like it or not, I'm afraid we are all, including Kate and Conchita, caught in the middle of this courageous struggle."

"Senor William, I believed that only I understood what is at risk. But now you, you my dearest friend, understand and share my concerns. You have come to love my country and want to see democracy come to its people." Manuel followed Bill's lead and let the cool liquid flow down his throat. "The brandy is very good. It helps ease my worry."

"Everything comes with a price, my friend. My country has a stake in the outcome and we have a personal stake as well. By innocently investigating the old miner's letter that was given to Kate by Carlos Minoro, the old Shaman's son, we discovered a great storehouse of gold that opened the doors to both greed and hatred."

"I understand how greed can get the best of people.... but for one with a cause, like Carlos, the Serpent, well, there are no boundaries. He is so young yet so filled with personal ambition."

" Very true. Unfortunately, the treasure's value also generated jealously from former friends, like Professor Raymond Morrissey and Dr. Maggie Brown, not to mention Maoist leaders like Minoro and innumerable thieves and dishonest politicians. Money brings out the worst in so many. We just wanted to follow our clues..." Shepherd took a long pause, "It was a game. But it became a serious pursuit, no longer a game and a means to stay close to the woman I fell in love with."

"But Senor William, the value of the gold did much good for the poor people who lost so much in the earthquakes. You were not greedy. You didn't bring on such hatred. It is just human nature. Greed."

As the two close compatriots sat in the study and as more facts exposed, they both were disturbed by the threat to their families. Bill offered some suggestions. The first solution was to eliminate the heads of the Sendero with a quick surgical hit. This would require Kate to make contact with Carlos Monuro, probably using the guise of further research and a little guilt trip, raising the possibility of providing some of the New Zealand gold to him for his help and as a reward for providing the original old letter.

Could Kate be party to such a deception? She was a scientist, not a spook. She'd have to falsely confide in Carlos Monuro, that the find in New Zealand led them to believe that much more gold was hidden in the Peruvian rainforest.

No self-indulgent Maoist, trying to enrich himself and finance his revolution, could let this opportunity slide by. But was Kate up to such a task? She had befriended the old Shaman and later, his son. It would take some effort to convince her of his growing deceit.

"Senor William, any activity on our part will draw greater interest to our plans. Hector Gonzales, my former military strong man came to visit me last month with a warning and to ask for my help."

"I know of your meeting. You were being observed by one of my trusted men, Cory Danielson."

Nothing is as it seems, is it my friend." Manuel lowered his voice as if someone might be listening.

"Don't worry. The home's interior is secure. We can speak freely. But your friend Hector has his men watching the activity around our home. He's kept a strong, protective cordon around my home and not surprisingly, Cory Danielson has kept an eye on them. You were living under a protective blanket. Fortunately, the two opposing parties never met. Who knows where that would have gone."

"How do we move forward, Senor? I worry for the safety of my wife and children yet I must help my people. I need your advice. This weighs heavily on me."

"Conchita and your twins must be put into protective custody." Shepherd stated the obvious. "They cannot help you and they could fall into the wrong hands and be used against you."

Kate will have to be convinced to contact Carlos Monuro a soon as possible, pouring a second glass of brandy, "but for a few days, I need to have her out of the picture. We need some time to set up the preliminaries without involving the women."

"That may be not so easy. If we try to relocate them, then Hector will see something is happening that is different than normal or your friend Cory Danielson. Have you a plan, my friend?"

"Well, Manuel, this may sound a bit extreme but it may work to our advantage although it will make the women madder than hell when they discover we've deceived them. But it would be for their own good." Bill's plan sounded crazy, even as he outlined it.

"Tell me what you have in mind." Manuel had no idea where Shepherd was heading.

"I'm thinking of staging our own kidnapping."

"Kidnapping? Are you serious senor?"

"Yes, very. Here, let me show you something, something that is for your eyes only. Not even Kate is aware of this." Bill got up from his wingback chair and headed towards the bookcase. He removed a novel of Sherlock Holmes Greatest Mysteries from the lower shelf then firmly pressed his hand against the cherry panel. The wall miraculously opened, exposing a steep set of wooden stairs that led to a secret, subterranean room.

"I had no idea. What is this place?" Manuel stood up and stared into the blackness.

"One of the reasons I leased this larger than practical home in Georgetown was because of this fully ventilated, fully furnished safe room built into the basement. My office recommended it to me and I've kept it from everyone including Kate. Just in case I needed to go underground, literally."

Inside the twenty by twenty foot room, not including the shower and toilet facilities, was the latest computer system, satellite and a state of the art conferencing network designed by Cisco Systems. Fully equipped with a full kitchenette, comfortable beds, additional clothing in various sizes and fully stocked with a year's worth of foodstuffs and beverages; the CIA had concocted a perfect war room.

"In a minute, we will go down but before we do, we must set the stage."

"Set the stage? What do you mean, set the stage?"

"If we want to have the women believe we've been kidnapped we have to make a few changes." Bill took out his billfold with Corey Danielson's card prominently displayed inside. He opened the terrace door and placed the small brown wallet under the chair, in sight as if he had tossed it there while being carried away by his abductors.

Manuel heard a noise and cautiously headed for the library door. He opened the door an inch and after hearing the children laughing upstairs with Kate and Conchita, he closed the door and returned to Bill's side. "They are still upstairs but we must hurry."

Shepherd took a small paper envelope out of his locked desk drawer. "From now on we drink no more brandy." He emptied the powder into the carafe and gave it a light shake, then poured an inch in each of their glasses. "Nothing deadly but a good, quick sleeping agent. How else could we have been kidnapped?"

He continued to look around the room. "I don't want the women to think we've been killed or injured, only taken away. No blood or signs of a struggle. They'll expect a kidnapping for "ransom". Maybe involving the wealth of the well publicized gold strike. We don't want them to panic any more than what I think they can handle. Kate knows I can take care of myself. Conchita feels the same about you. Kate will discover my billfold and call Cory. I'll contact him again once we're secured below ground. He'll ease their concerns and help when we need him. I trust him like I trust you, Manuel."

Manuel's head was spinning. "You think this all up in a few minutes, Senor? You amaze my senses."

"Well, to be honest, this has been on my mind for a while. I just didn't know when I'd have to activate a plan. The safe room makes it all come together." He spotted his family Bible, the book that Kate had carefully placed the symbols found on the original Peruvian gourd. He took the ladder and reached the top shelf and tucked it under his arm. "Security. She'll see it's missing and it will give her pause for thought."

"I feel we must hurry. We must go soon before the women return. I trust your judgment but I am still with worry for my wife and children."

"OK! I'm ready if you are. Do a last minute assessment. Let's see, the door to the terrace is unlocked, the wallet, the brandy and the Bible. Everything else is undisturbed. We'll have time to plan and when we are ready to bring Kate and Conchita into our confidence, well, we'll have to see how they handle our deception and staged kidnapping. We have many challenges ahead of us, my friend."

"Then what, Senor William?" Manuel looked around the comfortable room for the last time.

"Well, in the event we have to leave the safe house, for any reason, we have an armored door that leads to a lighted tunnel. A two passenger electric car will take us from the basement through the half-mile long tunnel to a second safe house. For security purposes, they've supplied me with a hand held remote control that will release various gasses that would disable but not kill any interlopers. My people are thorough."

The men heard footsteps making their way down the main staircase and reacted. William Shepherd led the way. The heavy bookcase closed behind them.

The Hen House

As they descended the staircase, motion detectors turned on lights. At the bottom of the stairs, the lights illuminated the great room. Bill had never before entered the secure room. He had heard about it but was stunned to see it in reality. As they walked to the center of the room, a sixty-inch video screen came to life.

"Welcome guests", a comely young lady said. *"Since you are here as guests of the United States Government, allow me to give you a virtual tour of our facility. Please, sit down and make yourself comfortable."*

Shepherd and Manuel took a seat in the high back leather executive chairs then swiveled them around to face the smiling young woman on the flat screen.

"You'll have noticed as you entered, the ventilation system has turned on, evacuating the existing atmosphere and bringing in fresh air. The interior atmosphere is maintained at 72 degrees Fahrenheit and 65 RH. When the space is unoccupied, the secure room is still conditioned to protect the sophisticated electronics."

The two men carefully scanned the room, paying attention to the rows of small red lights along the ceiling, leading in the direction of the escape tunnel.

"My program does not allow me to know why you are here. All I know, if you'll pardon the electronic poetic license, is that you are very important to us. No one, other than the head of the CIA knows your true identities and that you are here. You have access to a large variety of advanced communication systems."

The virtual tour began by moving slowly around the secure space.

"The red phones are secure communication. No one can intercept your calls. The black phones are secure in the sense that they cannot be traced to this facility. The rest of the world thinks you are calling from Florida."

The tour continued.

"The secure space has been stocked with an assortment of pre packaged balanced meals and beverages, snacks and fortified protein products providing healthy nutrition. Also, please notice the apparatus, provided to help you stay physically fit while in residence."

Shepherd was pleased to see the thought put into their comfort as well as their security.

"If you wish to access my data banks, simply dial zero on the black phone. Now before I leave you, the Director wishes to speak with you. When I vacate the screen, he will appear visually with secure audio. No one knows about this call as the Director is in another secure room somewhere in Washington. Good day gentlemen and have a safe activity."

Momentarily, the screen went dark, and then a CIA shield appeared followed by the life size visage of the Director.

"Good afternoon Bill and Manuel. I trust your virtual tour was educational. I'm sorry to disturb your quiet life Bill, but during our last conversation we requested you meet privately with Manuel and see if he would be interested in leading a reform government in Peru."

Manuel shifted uneasily in his chair. The gravity of the moment was suddenly upon him.

"Initially unknown to us, his group was attempting to recruit us, well, you in particular, to strike at the Sendero. Their self imposed leader, Carlos, has been radicalized in the last year and is actively recruiting other intellectuals at the university, sadly, to join with the drug lords and growers. I don't have to tell you but I will anyway, just so we are talking the same language. FARC stands for Revolutionary Armed Forces of Colombia. Founded in Colombia, they still closely follow the Maoist dictates and are still very active as is Sendero. In fact, recent news indicates leadership in Sendero has been captured in Peru and the current Presidente is trying to associate with FARC."

Manuel leaned closer to the screen, carefully following the Director's overview.

"The drug lords, with the vast amount of resources available to them have been able to corrupt the legal government but fortunately, so far, they have not been able to capture the hearts of the people. That is why the unholy alliance with Carlos and Sendero. The Peruvian people have a long history of surviving despots, so we have a repository of freedom minded people."

"Director", Bill needed to respond. "Manuel and I are on the same page. Your conversation only strengthens our resolve."

"I'm glad to hear that Bill, Manuel, because as we speak, our agents, under the command of your colleague Cory Danielson, are gathering up both your families and taking them to a safe house in Virginia. Kate, as planned, discovered your billfold and placed a call to Agent Danielson. He arrived within an hour's time and did his best to calm the women's fears. They are handling your supposed kidnapping better than expected."

"Senor Director, if you please, my children and wife, they are also out of harm's way?" Manuel tried to sound calm even though his stomach was churning.

"Yes, Manuel, they are secure and comfortable for now. There is no need to worry about their safety. The entire American CIA is looking over them. I've assigned a female agent to help with their transition."

Manuel allowed a smile to leak through. "Thank you, Director, now I am fully at your disposal."

"Gentlemen, we expect that your residence is under surveillance by others, besides Hector's group, possibly mercenaries paid by the drug cartels. Make no mistake, these are cold blooded killers and they want you and Manuel dead."

"When will the women and children be removed?" Shepherd's voice concealed his anxiety.

"Your women and children are being secretly relocated as we speak. I cannot share how that will happen but I will tell you that as soon as they are secreted, they will be replaced along with you by body doubles, only to confuse those watching your home."

Bill had no idea that the CIA would go to that extent. Obviously, the threat was a clear and present danger. The Farm took very good care of its own.

The Director continued, *"Manuel, the children who will replace yours are not at cute as yours nor are the women as beautiful as your wives."* For the first time, the Director allowed a smile and a soft laugh to escape his controlled demeanor. *"Rest assured. We will guarantee their safety as best we can gentlemen."*

"Then what?" Reinforced by the safety of their families, Bill pressed further.

"Within the next five hours, we will deliver Cory Danielson and his team of agents to your secure room for a formal meeting on our plan of attack. Since we are using only a small group, we must plan diligently. We have organized six Navy Seals, fluent in Spanish and the Peruvian dialect to stand by for possible activity."

The Director paused a moment to drink a bottle of water and clear his throat. *"Your visitors, including Cory, will enter through the underground tunnel. Bill, only you can admit them after identifying them by outside surveillance video. If there is any identity question, remember, the electric transport only holds two people. Press the button number, five, on your remote keyboard. This will release a non-lethal gas into the tunnel side of the door. This will knock out any intruders for an hour, giving you ample time to positively ID them.*

"Gas masks are in the cabinet to the right of the inner tunnel door. Make certain your guests are not equipped with gas masks. If they are, you may have a security breach. Unlikely but never say never. Cory should be the lead man so you should be able to identify him and his crew." The Director took another swig of water and relaxed back in his black leather chair.

Manuel and Bill followed his lead as he relaxed in his chair. The explanations and direction of the mission were spelled out to their satisfaction. They would have an active hand in the planning and implementation.

"Thank you Director, you have put our minds at ease. We're ready to lock and load." Bill's confidence rose to the surface and the Director picked up on it.

"Good! I'm gratified by your response. We are sorry for the pain we are causing your families but we agreed in advance that their safety was of paramount importance. They will be advised of your survival as soon as possible. No more than three days."

"And Kate? Her roll in all this?"

"Well Bill, she'll be raging mad when she finds out what we've orchestrated but we can handle that. Trust me. She's a bright woman. Kate will be brought in as soon as possible. Then she will fully understand the importance of her role in this operation. Her contact with Carlos, from an educational perspective, is vital and we will make sure she fully appreciates the value of her participation in Peru's and Manuel's future."

"Thanks, Director. You're right on. She'll be madder than hell at me for being involved in this ruse. But she will come around and cooperate. This should be interesting." He shook his head as he visualized her reaction. "Is there anything else we should know about while we've got your full attention?"

"Yes, but first, Manuel I know this is a daunting operation and we are aware of how it will impact your life. I assure you that we at the Agency we have the greatest confidence in your ability to lead your country into a democratic world. None of this would be on the planning table if it wasn't for our confidence in you and your vision for your country."

"Senor Director, I say this with all sincerity. I will not disappoint you. I will lead my country and never allow myself, or my people, to forget how you supported my efforts. The country of Peru will be forever in your debt."

Manuel tightened his jaw and straightened his back before he continued. "But rest assured, Senor Director, I will not allow myself to become a figurehead or, what you say, an American puppet. I do this for my country, for no other reason."

"Manuel, we'll be rewarded adequately when your strong, democratic government supports human rights, a lucrative free trade agreement and probably, just as important, the elimination of the drug cartel culture".

"I will do whatever it takes, Senor Director." Manuel felt the weight of his country's challenges on his broad shoulders as he took them on as his own.

"Now, one more thing before I let you go. Agent Shepherd, to answer your question, you need to get some rest. There will be no night and day for the next three days. You will get rest periods of up to five hours during each fifteen hours. That's how it is if we are to accomplish our goals and come out of this mission alive".

The Director checked his notes and made a few key entries. *"You will be happy to know that you won't have to lay eggs every time the lights go on! A bit of an inside joke. We call your little facility "The Hen House" and now you know why! There are sedatives on the nightstand to assist you. We need you rested in case we require a halo dive over Peru. Are you still qualified, Bill? Oh, I'm just kidding. Good night and sweet dreams."*

The screen went dark then the Director's face was replaced with a panoramic mural, soft, environmental music, a cooling waterfall and light thunder followed by a spring shower.

"Well, Presidente, shall we get some sleep? Since both of our minds are racing at one hundred miles an hour, I suggest we take the good Director's pills.

Fessing Up

The shutters were closed emitting narrow slivers of light through the horizontal boards. The furniture was small in scale, new and in neutral earth tones. Ikea, most likely. A wall clock ticked the hours. It was 6PM as the women sat, partly distracted by a documentary on global warming playing on the wall mounted big screen TV. Yes, the massive glacier was slowly but surely disintegrating.

Cory had left them on their own, promising to return in time to share a large pizza and a bottle of red table wine. His explanation was vague and his instructions simple and to the point. *"Sit tight."* There was no reason to call his bluff. Cory Danielson was Bill Shepherd's closest associate and comrade in arms. If there was one person to trust, it was Cory.

The children were asleep in the back bedroom that was remarkably equipped with two identical youth beds. The two other bedrooms were furnished and comfortable, the wardrobes recently filled with women's clothing, in various sizes and styles.

Kate walked into the small kitchen and found the fridge well stocked with quality cheeses, fresh fruit and a wide assortment of juices and soft drinks. By all appearances, it looked like they were expected houseguests.

There was a light tap on the door and Cory entered, followed by a young woman who was carrying a bag filled with children's toys. Small hangars in her other hand displayed toddler size clothing recently purchased from Target, the price tags still attached to the miniature garments.

"Kate, Conchita, this is Marcie Clemens, an agent with the department. She's been assigned to help out with the children and anything else you may need." Cory was relaxed and in perfect control. There was no sense of urgency or signs of tension in his demeanor.

Agent Clemens walked forward and handed the items to the women. "I'm at your service ladies! I have a slew of nieces and nephews and I love kids. I hope to have a few rug rats myself one day. Just let me know what you'd like me to do." The female agent was pleasant and her eagerness was genuine.

"Senora Clemens, I think I hear the children waking from their naps. I'll introduce them to you so they are not frightened by a strange face." Conchita motioned to Agent Clemens to follow her into the hallway leading to the children's room and together they carried the recently purchased clothing and toys. "The twins will love the new toys!"

When they had disappeared around the corner, Kate moved into the kitchen and leaned against the center island. "Cory, any news? We've done our best to remain calm but waiting is a killer."

Cory's big moment had arrived and he wasn't sure how to handle it. He admired Kate and he didn't want the established trust between them to evaporate. "We've got to talk."

"You have news? Tell me. Are the men OK? Or has something happened to them?" Kate's blood pressure rose. "Please, tell me what's happening."

"It's OK but you'd better sit down."

"No, I prefer standing up. "Is it bad news? I need to know, please." She held her breath and braced herself for something terrible.

Cory cleared his throat and moved to the other side of the island. "I don't want you to be upset but," he took a deep breath, "but we've involved you both in a ruse. Bill and Manuel are under protective custody by the CIA in a secure setting. The kidnapping was staged and carried out by the Agency not by our enemies." There, he had said it.

Kate's face reddened and Cory could tell she was on the verge of imploding. She held on to the counter top until her knuckles turned white and ached. "Are you insane? Why, why would you subject us to all of this? Conchita, the twins, we've been sitting on pins and needles thinking the worse and now you tell me you did all this on purpose. My God, why?"

"I'm sorry Kate but it's complicated. Peru is on the verge of collapse and upon your return from New Zealand, the atmosphere was heating up and we had to find a feasible ploy to remove you, and secret the men away from a likely assassination attempt. We had solid intelligence telling us that Manuel and Bill's lives were threatened. You could have easily become collateral damage. We did what was expedient and decided to deal with the fallout later. This, I guess, is later."

"Where are Bill and Manuel?" Her heart was racing. "Can we go to them now?" She wasn't sure how to react.

"All in due time. I can't compromise the mission by telling you their whereabouts. But I can say they are close by, within the city limits. And yes, you will be reunited with Bill but not until all the details are taken care of and the situation becomes more stable."

"And Conchita and her children. Are you also going to tell her the truth?"

"Not yet. I can't do that. We are planning on securing her in this safe house for the duration. Manuel is a primary figure in this operation and if his wife fell into the wrong hands, the operation could be severely compromised. I ask that you keep any information I give you to yourself. It's better for her if knows as little as possible, for her safety as well as Manuel's."

"How can I lie to Conchita? She is so worried about her husband." Kate took a soft drink out of the fridge and handed a cold beer to Cory.

"Thanks, Kate." He pulled off the cap and took a long, cool swig. "I know this is a pisser but we have no choice. I'll let Bill explain the details when you're reunited. But you've got to sit tight for a day or two more. It's essential that you proceed as usual until I get the word that's it's safe for you to travel away from this location."

"Gosh, Cory, we just got back from New Zealand. How could all this happen in such a short time?"

"Trouble has been brewing for the past six months and lately, the intercepts have shown that the threat level has risen." Cory placed the empty bottle in the sink. "Remember why Manuel and Conchita took up residence in your place? It was getting hot even then. I'm sorry that I can't tell you more right now. Rest assured that you will be thoroughly briefed shortly and any questions you have will be answered to your satisfaction."

"I guess I tried to forget about that. You know, about Conchita and Manuel and Raul's murder. Bill didn't tell me anything until we were half way back from New Zealand. No wonder they took shelter in our American home."

"Listen Kate, Shep wanted you to enjoy the trip South and you couldn't have done a thing about what happened."

But Cory, can you tell me how and who kidnapped Bill and Manuel? Were they actually drugged and carried away? I need to know the truth." Her voice turned soft and resigned to the unseemly facts handed to her.

"Well, at this time I can only tell you they were not drugged, manhandled or injured in any way. They were both aware of the situation and were involved in their disappearance. That's all I can tell you."

"So, you knew when I called you. You already knew. Cory, you are quite an actor! The billfold, your phone number, everything was staged. What a good performer you are!" She forced a laugh. "And just when I thought we had smooth sailing." She rubbed her eyes and shook her head. "Smooth sailing? I feel like I have a permanent berth on the Titanic!"

"Kate, I'm truly sorry for the set-up but it had to look like the real thing. I can assure you that your life will eventually sail on but unfortunately, right now, there's going to be some rough seas to ride out." If he allowed her to believe the next weeks would be a cakewalk, he wouldn't be doing her any favors. This was a very dangerous mission and there were no guarantees of success.

There likely would be casualties. Bill would be directly in the line of fire. So would Kate, once she accepted her part in the operation. "The details are being worked out and soon, I trust you'll understand. I'm sorry to be so vague but I've been instructed to give you only a brief outline of events."

"I understand, Agent Danielson. The CIA is secretive and I promise I won't ask any more questions. As long as I know Bill and Manuel are out of harms way, I'll keep quiet. Can I say anything to Conchita?"

"Just encourage her to think positively. I wish you could tell her more but believe me, it is not the prudent thing to do."

Cory and Kate retrieved another cold beverage and sat down on the leather sofa to watch the final scenes of the global warming documentary. "Are the ice caps really melting or is that a CIA ploy, too?"

Cory laughed. "Kate, how did old Shep get so lucky?"

The Visit

"I told you we should have called them in advance. No one's home and I feel foolish standing here ringing the bell." Dr. Maggie Brown leaned against the pillar supporting them, and now we're stranded here." The cab had driven away, in a hurry to pick up another fare and head back to the airport.

"I'm sorry. I just thought." Raymond looked sheepishly at the front door. "Well, I'll call for another cab and we'll stay in town. It was presumptuous of us to barge in and expect an invitation for room and board. I'll call for a suite at the Mayflower." Ray connected with information and was about to ask for assistance when two men, dressed in dark, well cut suits, came around the corner of the property and approached them, their faces stern.

"Would you mind coming with us." In unison, the men flashed ID's. "Please, don't cause a scene." The two men stood shoulder to shoulder and skillfully herded the couple around the property down the service drive to a black SUV with tinted windows, covertly parked around a blind corner.

"Who the hell are you? We just came to visit our friends, the Shepherds. You have no right," Maggie didn't like being manhandled. "Don't touch me or I'll make sure you lose your badge, whoever you are."

"Ma'am, I apologize but we have our orders. Please come with us willingly and once we sort out who you are and the reason for your unscheduled visit, we will release you." Maggie struggled to look behind their dark sunglasses, part of the dress code of Federal Agents.

"Gentlemen, has something happened to the Shepherds? We were just with them in New Zealand and stopped by to inquire about their return trip. We're friends as well as colleagues." Raymond was curious as well as concerned. Why the special attention? What event had taken place since the Shepherds landed on American soil?

Raymond and Maggie were ushered into the back seat of the Government Issue SUV. The doors were slammed shut. The sudden silence hit them. "What is this all about? They have no right."

"Maggie, we'll have to wait and see. Obviously, something has happened to the Shepherds, maybe they've been killed or perhaps there was an accident."

"What kind of accident could attract these government agents? It has to be foul play, with everything that's taken place. What you told me of your experiences in Peru and then the gold strike in Arrowtown. All that money. Who knows how many enemies they have."

While they discussed options, the two agents opened the front doors and got into the vehicle. "Sorry for the inconvenience. We've checked out your identities and we are sorry we had to detain you. Where can we take you? Are you staying in town?"

"Wait. Hold on." Raymond was dumbfounded and had to voice his confusion. "How do you know who we are? You didn't ask for our identifications or passports."

"Sir, I can only tell you we are equipped with some pretty sophisticated facial recognition technology. You were both on the short list of acquaintances. You've been cleared. You are no threat and now we will deliver you to your lodging with the understanding that you will not discuss this encounter with any of your friends or associates. It's a serious matter of national security. I hope you understand." The firm set of the G-man's jaw spoke volumes.

"That's it? No explanation? How are the Shepherds? Or are they dead?" Raymond wanted to know what had happened and pressed the stoic government agents.

"Sir, we are not at liberty to discuss the conditions of the Shepherds other than to say that the situation is being diffused as we speak. And we request your cooperation at this time." Conversation over.

"Understood. Please, I was just making room reservations at the Mayflower Hotel. If you would be so kind. The airline will deliver our bags to our suite later today." Maggie leaned back against the headrest and closed her eyes. Raymond took her hand and gave it an encouraging squeeze. "Well, welcome to Washington DC."

Back from the Missing

Kate had spent the third evening in the safe house with Cory while Conchita and Agent Clemens entertained the children with their new toys. Once she had been given clearance, he had done his best to explain what had taken place in Peru and what her role was to be. At first, she protested. The Shaman, Moochica's son, Carlos, had been a key player in leading her from Peru to New Zealand and the massive gold strike. And he'd also allowed her to do her research undisturbed at the Universite de Truijillo. Coming to terms with Carlos' dark side took some convincing. But Cory answered all of her concerns and after three days of indoctrination, Kate gave in to the logic of the facts as Cory described them.

"When can we leave for the secure room? The Hen House?" Kate didn't want to plead but she missed seeing her husband and wanted to get going, especially since they had come to some sort of agreement regarding her contribution to the mission. "I've completed the letter to Carlos and I don't think it says enough to raise red flags. But if he is as greedy and driven as you say, this will definitely get his attention." Kate had carefully folded the hand written letter and slid it into the envelope. "Here, Cory, the beginning of my assignment as a spy."

"Listen Kate, it will be over before you know it and we'll all go home like nothing ever happened." He was kidding himself but he didn't fool Kate.

"I hope you're right but I think you're just trying to keep me from backing down. Don't worry, Cory, I won't. Once committed, that's it."

"I think I know you well enough," Cory had to smile. This woman caused his blood to boil. If only she wasn't in love with his best friend, he'd sweep her off her feet in a heartbeat. "You'll do just fine. Of course, after the Agency's unexpected contact with Dr. Morrissey and Dr. Brown..."

"I can't believe the nerve of them showing up at our doorstep unannounced like that. Under the circumstances, they could have been killed or worse."

Cory laughed. "What could be worse than being killed?"

Kate returned his laugh, "Well, I guess there's not much worse than being killed other than Bill banging heads with Professor Morrissey, who's made continuous indecent proposals to bed me."

"Yes, that's worse than death. Anyone who fools around with Bill's woman would wish he were dead." Cory thought of himself and knew he'd keep his thoughts and actions to himself. He was no cad and would never move in on his best friend's wife, even though she was so tempting.

"Agent Clemens will take good care of Conchita and the twins, so if you're ready."

"Kate was startled, "Right now? We're going right now?"

Cory touched the small earpiece. "Right now. The SUV is parked around back with another decoy out front. Our driver has instructions to take evasive action just in case they pick up our movements."

"Who is the 'they'? Any ideas?" Kate walked towards the front window and peaked out between the narrow wood shutters. "There's a very official black SUV out front."

"The 'they' is any of a number of interested parties who want to keep Peru in chaos." We'll let the Director and his team of strategic planners sort that out. My responsibility is to deliver you safe and sound to the secure room, hopefully, without detection."

Kate gathered her few belongings, gave Conchita a quick hug and left the safe house through the back door.

The second safe house was nondescript, a small bungalow on a quiet street with large, well-kept lawns. They were quickly ushered in the back door and down into the unfinished basement, to a utility closet, complete with a water heater, cement lined sink and a rusted sump pump. To their right, behind the door, Cory carefully pulled a flimsy wooden cupboard, its shelves filled with cleaning supplies, away from the wall, exposing a narrow passageway. He took out his flashlight and motioned to Kate to follow him.

"This is the tunnel that leads to the secure room? How did they set this up without anyone else knowing about it?" Kate brushed away a few cobwebs that stuck to her hair.

"The CIA works in mysterious ways." That seemed enough of an answer and was accurate.

After proceeding about twenty-five yards, the tunnel widened and faint red lights mounted to the ceiling guided them forward. Cory held up his hand and pointed his flashlight to the right where a small vehicle, no larger than a golf cart, stood at the ready. He put Kate's belongings in the rear compartment, and then they took their seats and buckled themselves in.

With a press of a button, the dashboard was illuminated in the same dim red light. The instrumentation was easily read and pretty basic, a mileage indicator, a GPS and directional indicators, forward, reverse, on and off. The small vehicle moved slowly and silently forward on a narrow gauge track, the cement pathway, as smooth as the kitchen floor.

"We'll be at the other location in a couple of minutes. In the meantime, we are being observed by close circuit cameras so don't do anything foolish, like kiss me!" That would be as close as Cory would dare get to flirting with Bill's beautiful wife.

"Well, Cory, I'll try to control myself! But after what Bill put me through, he'd have it coming." She wondered how their first glimpse of each other would go. Her anger had replaced fear and now her anger was trumped by understanding. The CIA could be very harsh and insensitive. Just deal with it.

"When we arrive, I'm going to leave you alone with Shep, well Shep wanted some time one on one with you before the meeting begins." He hated parting company with Kate but his time as escort was coming to a close.

"It could be a little awkward." Kate wasn't sure how she'd react. Right now, she was sitting in a tunnel that ran underneath their beautiful Georgian home, that connected to a passageway that opened into a CIA secure room known as the Hen House. How ludicrous was that? If it wasn't so serious, she's been tempted to laugh about it. Did Bill Shepherd harbor other secrets? So much for Kate always being in control.

The small electric car came to a stop and Cory hopped out and pressed a six-digit code into a digital keypad mounted on the wall. *"Password."*

"Jeremiah."

"Please stand twelve inches from the retina scanner." Cory did as he was instructed. *"You are clear to enter Agent Danielson."* The heavy, metal reinforced door opened automatically and Cory walked through.

Before it closed behind him, Cory looked back at Kate and winked, a boyish grin on his finely chiseled face, "He'll be here in a minute or two. See you inside the Hen House."

Kate sat in the small vehicle. Suddenly, with Cory gone, deafening silence surrounded her. She was at least twenty feet below the ground, surrounded by gray cement walls randomly illuminated by red lights that danced on the rough surfaces. Her heart was racing. Her breathing was too shallow as she tried to calm herself. Claustrophobia and hyperventilation came to mind.

The heavy door finally opened and Bill Shepherd stood in the entry, looking tall, handsome and very sheepish. He wasn't sure whether to smile or beg for forgiveness. They made eye contact and magically, the ice melted.

Kate unhooked her safety belt and launched herself into his arms. She kissed him like she meant it. "You bastard!" She pulled back and prepared to slap his face, thought better of it and instead, took aim at his mouth with her soft, eager lips. His arms enfolded her and they remained in a passionate embrace until they both needed to breathe.

"Kate, my love, I am so sorry I put you through this but I had no choice." He kissed her again and ran his hands down her back. "You feel so good to me. I can't believe how much I missed you."

"I thought you were kidnapped, maybe even dead" A tear escaped and washed her cheek. "And Conchita was frantic. Couldn't you have found another way?" It was water under the bridge but she had to say it anyway. "What would I have done, if you really had been kidnapped? Or killed? My God, Bill."

Bill Shepherd released Kate from his tender grip then looked deeply into her eyes, "Everything is good. My darling. You did just what you were supposed to do. You called Cory Danielson and got the ball rolling. Forget everything else."

"But." Kate wrapped her arms around his solid waist.

"But, nothing. You are one hell of a woman under duress and I'm proud of you. The Agency's proud of you."

"Don't patronize me, Bill. That was hell. Believing you, of all people, were taken against your will? That was pretty cold of the Agency to set me up that way."

"Darling, what can I say? Yes, I'm guilty but I have to tell you there's still no guarantee of an easy outcome. We're both involved in this until the bitter end."

Bill led her back to the small vehicle and they sat side by side. "I think I know your feelings toward the Shaman's son, Carlos, but with the facts we've gathered, he's not what he portrayed himself to be. He's a very dangerous young man and he may destroy the Peruvian people if he's not stopped."

Bill drew her close to him and she could feel his heartbeat merge with hers. "We better go inside. I asked them for a few minutes without the surveillance cameras on and, yep, there goes the light. We're on the screen again." A flashing green light lit the panel.

Kate withdrew from Bill's embrace and stared at the small camera lens. "Must we?"

That same voice came over the hidden speaker. *"Yes, you must, Dr. Shepherd. If you would be so kind to stand twelve inches from the retina scanner."*

Kate did as instructed and the secure door opened. B

Operation Goldrush

Present in the Hen House, sitting around the table were Cory, Hector, Manuel and two representatives from the CIA, Harry Smith and Charles Bascom. As Bill led Kate into the small space, the men rose and introduced themselves.

"Senora Dr. Shepherd", Manuel Sanchez reached out and took Kate's hand. I am sorry we have done this to you and Conchita. My sincere apologies."

Kate flashed him an understanding smile. Senor Manuel, I'm sure everything will be fine. And your wife and children are handling things well." She let her hand return to her side and smiled at the serious faces standing awkwardly around the table. "Please, gentlemen, sit down. Thank you for the warm welcome." She took a seat next to Bill and across the table from Cory.

"Now that we're all here, it's time to get down to business." Bill was taking the lead and called the meeting to order. "The first task we have is to confirm the present situation. Hector, you are the closest to the situation, followed by our CIA guests who will bring us up to date on our latest intelligence."

Bill turned to face Hector Gonzales. "Please begin and also, tell us why you think Manuel Sanchez can be of service."

Hector rose from his chair and as he began to speak, he picked up his marking pen. "Gentlemen, Madam, a little background first. The Sendero started over twenty years ago, causing the deaths of thousands of Peruvians. Guzman, the leader at that time, was captured after several years. President Fujimora, in his first term, was sensitive to the people's needs and fortunately, the core belief of Sendero was greatly weakened."

Hector nervously walked around the table and stopped behind Kate. "Unfortunately, his second term was a disaster, leading to turmoil at the universities as well as in the streets. Fujimora was finally removed but not until after the Shaman's son, Carlos Minuro began recruiting supporters for a new but modified Maoist regime."

Hector continued to walk around the table, nervously tapping his pen against his palm. "His group of twenty intellectuals has become radicalized and is using the press and radio to spread Maoist doctrine. Of course, the Peruvian people are practical and most realize that this form of communism failed before and will probably fail again." He took his seat again and opened his bottle of water and took a swallow.

"Failure, my friends always means that they, the people, die." Hector waited until the strength of his message hit home. "The greatest threat? Their overtures to FARC. President Chavez of Venezuela desiring to start a new campaign to take over Peru and then Colombia has recently approached FARC. As much trouble as Colombia has had, it still has experience as a functional democracy. But Chavez is very persuasive."

The group sat around the table, taking mental notes. "As you can see and understand, with the core at only twenty people, perhaps a few more, we have an excellent chance of cutting off the head of this serpent. As you learned, unfortunately, some of our younger supporters tried to take action on their own and attacked the Universite de Truijillo. Sadly, they were all killed."

Hector paused and took a drink of water. "The net result, my friends, this university has become a fortress with the majority of its student body acting as protectors. Youthful idealism!"

Hector took another swallow. "We have only ten students who remain loyal to a democratic government. They feed us information. But we worry for their safety."

The group had a few questions that were deftly answered. Hector completed his presentation. "Our group is comprised of forty legislators who feel they must return Peru to a representative democracy, with a well respected and intelligent leader." Hector's voice lowered an octave, "Of course, as a prerequisite, the threat of revolution must be resolved."

He nervously vacated his chair, walked behind the dark, muscular military leader and laid a hand on his shoulder. "This brings us to Manuel Sanchez."

Bill cleared his throat and signaled that he had something to add. "Hector, you have described the current situation clearly. My concern? I've never met forty politicians who wish to serve their country without personal gain."

There was mutual agreement throughout the secure room. "Are you sure that your group has not been infiltrated by Sendero?"

Harry Smith, one of the CIA Agents got the attention of the group. "I think I can address that situation. Our intelligence has data on five members that are closely suspect as sympathizers. Rather than blow their cover, we have not exposed them. Our friends in the press could do that easily. I believe that somewhere in the development of our situation, we can use their greed and betrayal to our advantage."

Bill spoke in response to the disclosure. "Pretty predicable. One of our deficiencies is that Hector cannot recruit support until we eliminate Sendero. To do so will be tricky and very risky."

"Agent Bascom sir." The agent identified himself. "The reason I am here is to give a profile of the twenty leaders of Sendero, at the Universite de Truijillo. As is the case with many universities, particularly in poorer environments, the professors are paid poorly. With the pending political action, their side income has dropped off. The approach, therefore, should be a combination of self interest and greed."

"Agent Bascom, enlighten us. How do we handle this situation, to the best of your knowledge?" Bill voiced what the others were thinking.

Bascom continued. "Exactly. Well, that brings us to your role, Dr. Shepherd." The table of men turned towards Kate. "We begin with dropping your name and a few well constructed letters. Or better yet, with your direct participation in the activity. Agent William Shepherd, why don't you take over from here?"

"OK. Thank you for your comments, Agent Bascum. Well, the whole world knows about Kate, rather, Dr. Shepherd and my discovery of a large quantity of gold in Arrowtown, South Island,

New Zealand. However, very few know that it was connected to another location deep in the rainforest of Peru."

He took a breath and stood in front of the interested group. "Let me explain. This connection came about through a letter, a very old letter, found by Carlos Monuro among the personal effects of his deceased father, the reclusive Shaman, Moochica. The content of this letter was the motivation behind our trip to New Zealand, ultimately leading us to the discovery of a large cache of gold bars."

"We suspect that Carlos believes that he is rightfully entitled to some of the uncovered millions. A finder's fee, should I say? We wish to exploit that possibility. I have asked Kate, Dr. Shepherd, to construct a letter to Carlos Monuro, to be delivered by Hector to the Monika Post Office. In it, she will thank him for the gift of the original letter and then she will suggest that the discovery in New Zealand indicates that there are still great riches to be found in the Peruvian rainforest. Kate would explain that Carlos would receive, not only the finders' fee but also, the potential of undiscovered gold."

"Do you believe he would cooperate without becoming suspicious?" Agent Smith was skeptical.

"Well, Agent Smith, all Dr. Shepherd would ask of him is to support an expedition to the rainforest, personally participating in it through a substantial grant from Kate's, Dr. Shepherd's own foundation. A pre-negotiated sum will be set aside to tempt him further." A smile took shape as he looked over at Kate, "I hear that the young Carlos has an eye for beautiful women." He hated to think that Kate would be bait but it lessened the odds against failure.

"Further, my representative would also include Dr. Raymond Morrissey, a world renowned archeologist, who's very familiar with a particular Peruvian dig site. Possibly, Dr. Maggie Brown, his colleague would be included in the party. Both are familiar with Dr. Shepherds' earlier excavations and research in the country."

Bill took a drink of his water. "We're almost finished with our summation. I hear that we have had unexpected luck contacting

Drs. Morrissey and Brown. They were at our doorstep, not a hundred feet from where we sit!" For effect, Shepherd looked up at the ceiling over their heads. "Quite by accident, they came calling and unfortunately, we weren't home at the time but our surveillance team was. They are now comfortably housed in town at the Mayflower, awaiting our instructions."

Kate nearly fell out of her chair. By boldly coming for an unannounced visit, the pair had been drawn into a new drama. She handed over her drafted letter meant for Carlos and smiled, speaking for the first time. "I'm sure you'll want to check out the content and make any changes your psychologist would like to see." Agent Smith nodded politely, took the letter and deposited it in his leather folio.

"Cory, I want you to lead our Seal team when it's decided to launch a raid. I suggest you and the men take a one-week vacation to Peru and reconnoiter the university and anything of interest. When the group heads for the rainforest, you can provide security, either as part of the team or covertly. Your call."

Bill was tying the last loose ends before the group did their final due diligence. "Kate, Dr. Shepherd, we'll have to meet separately with Drs. Morrissey and Brown to arrange for their trip down to our staging site. We'll discuss Dr. Brown's role in the plan. To make sure they are totally committed, we can suggest a trust of say, one million dollars, be set up for him and possibly one for Dr. Brown as well. Any actual finds would be allocated in the standard way."

"A million dollars?" Kate was taken aback by the sum.

"We can discuss the details of funding later." Bill dismissed the objection.

"Gentlemen, we'll meet back here in six hours to iron out any sticking points. Hector, Cory and our team will be ready to fly out in less than twelve hours."

Everyone rose from the table and headed towards the heavy exit door leading to the connecting tunnel. "You'll all be resting comfortably at the adjoining safe house. Dr. Shepherd and I will remain safely secured in the Hen House. We have some catching up to do." A smile formed across his face.

Within minutes, they were alone.

The Mayflower

Drs. Morrissey and Brown had been confined to their suite for the better part of three days. Room service brought them an assortment of house specialties and the duel master bedrooms gave them the privacy they requested. So far, sex hadn't become an issue.

Agent Dunlap had paid them a visit the morning after they had been removed from the Shepherd's doorstep and had explained in clear English, the peril they had been in by trying to visit their friends and what likely lay ahead of them. Raymond was painfully aware of Peru's political condition and, when they were left alone, he explained the facts he had amassed on his last expedition to that volatile country.

They were being drawn into the turmoil and regardless of their objections, the Agency held power over them. Then Cory Danielson had paid them a visit. He introduced himself as William Shepherd's representative. He mentioned a fee for services rendered and that changed the tone of their discussion. No specific amounts were discussed but it would be lucrative. Shepherd would be meeting with them soon to iron out the final details.

Raymond wasn't sure whether Maggie Brown should be included. She could go off on one of her tangents and upset the expedition. She was rash; bull headed and had a temper to rival a drug lord. But she was sitting in the suite, listening to the options and it would be difficult to dismiss her, unless of course, she backed out on her own.

Since moving into the Mayflower, they had remained cordial. With a guard standing nearby and the prospect of a South American expedition waiting in the wings, they had lost interest in arguing over past indiscretions. Water under the bridge, like a fortune in gold. Water under the bridge, like a violent encounter with a shovel. Maggie still complained about headaches and her memory was clouded. Her recollections of their physical relationship were lurking around the edges of her mind. That could change.

Raymond chose to look upon their early clashes like unfortunate growing pains. He hoped their volatile relationship would mature and eventually evolve into something palatable. He had doubts whether they could stay together for the long haul. His memory was clearer than Maggie's. She was terribly self-serving. Regardless, the foreplay was satisfying and she managed to fulfill nearly every boyhood fantasy.

But Raymond wasn't stupid. He had to face reality. He was a mature man and was showing signs of silver in his hair. Perhaps it was up to him to advance the relationship in a careful, more civilized direction. Ever since his wife died, he felt he was on a mission to hold onto his youth. He was running from death. Much to his dismay, he continually found himself confronted by dangerous, near death scenarios. Raymond felt the ravages time was taking on him and knew he had to change. A process of uncomfortable, painful soul searching, finally led him to admit that he didn't want to be the victim of a self-fulfilling prophesy.

For years, he had lusted after Kate, ever since she was his bright and beautiful student. He nearly had her then but because of his stupidity, he lost Kate's heart to William Shepherd. He needed to be more patient. He chased her like a stallion after heat. In the end, she chose Shepherd and left him to lick his wounds. The regrets and recriminations were hard to shake.

And now there was Maggie. He was playing the same wild games that got him in trouble with Kate. Perhaps Dr. Brown would return to earth and would willingly share his life. Raymond thought they were a good match, both were passionate in their fields. They were both strong willed, sexually charged beings. Could he disregard the old adage, "opposites attract"? Were they too much alike? Would they always bump horns? Bumping horns at twenty-five was a far cry different from bumping horns at fifty. Yes, even Raymond occasionally wore down and craved a good book and a comforting fireplace. Growing older was hell.

Raymond and Maggie spent their sequestered time talking, something he hadn't done with a woman since Helen, his wife, was at his side. They discussed their career fields and their greatest accomplishments. Maggie was more interested in talking about herself than in listening to Raymond. Helen used to listen and really care. He couldn't expect the world from Maggie but at his age, maybe a little was enough.

Room Service knocked on the door and delivered their dinners. Two prime filets, medium rare, baked potatoes piled high with sour cream and butter and a side of crisp, fresh asparagus. The bottle of California Merlot had already been opened and was nearly empty. They seated themselves at the small dining table, toasted their fate and waited for the phone to ring.

Turning Point

When the door to the underground chamber closed, Bill turned to Kate, "Darling, we have six hours until the team returns." He toyed with her hair, "You don't suppose we'd have enough time to make mad, passionate love, do you?"

Kate scanned the secure room, "Only if you're an exhibitionist!" He followed her gaze. " As you can see, the Hen House is wired to hear a pin drop and I wouldn't be at all surprised if the cameras are also up and operational."

Bill was impressed by her astute observations. "You must personally know a CIA agent to be so aware of your surroundings, my dear. But as far as I'm concerned, I don't care who knows how much I love you and my willingness to demonstrate it to the world!" He planted a long, lingering kiss on her lips.

Out of the corner of Kate's eye, she saw the small red lights turn off. "Look, we embarrassed them. At last, they've left us alone." Kate returned the kiss and held his warm body close to her as they worked their way towards the small, corner alcove.

"I'm so happy I have you back in one piece but Husband, that was a hell of a homecoming." Kate rested against her husband's bare chest and soon they shared the government issued bed. "Our life isn't meant to be normal, is it?"

Bill had to snicker, "What's normal? Since day one, we've lived on the edge. Normal? We met in the midst of a crisis and since then, we've faced a series of threats that would have most couples running for the hills!" He stroked her head and twisted her silky hair through his fingers. "You're beautiful."

"Oh, you're just saying that. Tell me more!"

"Sweet Kate, I close my eyes and see you standing next to me, discovering the world's darkest secrets and defying evil." He let go a boyish chuckle. "Sort of comic bookish but that's how I see you."

"Darling, we ran for the hills, only we were chasing the enemy instead of the other way around. I guess we have a calling." She closed her eyes and purred. "That feels so good.

Don't stop." He was rocked back on his heals. "I won't. When the plan to get you involved again surfaced, I couldn't bear the thought of it. As tough, rugged and smart as you are, my dear, I cringed to think of you exposed to such risks again. I'm a man who still wants to protect my woman."

"Must be love and, sweetheart, I feel the same about you. If anything happened and I lost you, I'd be devastated." Kate nuzzled closer and felt the warmth of his manhood.

"This Peruvian crisis crept up on us and I guess we should be flattered that the powers that be have put trust in us to help unravel a very dangerous situation." He nibbled on her neck and tickled her ear with his tongue. "It will be over quickly. Does that feel good?"

" It feels wonderful. Do you actually believe that young Carlos can be silenced and Manuel will regain a position of leadership?" She answered her own question. "I guess that's the way it was meant to be from the very beginning. It just took a little longer to come to a head."

Bill Shepherd shifted his weight to relieve the bulge in his trousers. "Speaking of heads." A mischievous smile crept across his face. Slowly he unbuttoned Kate's silk blouse and let his hand play upon her breasts."

"I'm tired of talking." She was struck by a sudden case of gooseflesh. They traveled from her husband's warm hand massaging her breast, down her smooth belly to the center of her sex. "Don't stop."

"I have no intention on stopping." He could feel his heart rate increase as he loosened her clothing and skillfully slipped out of his duds. With familiar ceremony, they merged together until she felt him fill her completely.

"Just hold me. Hold me. Please make the outside world go away for a little while." Kate pressed her palms into his back, pulling him deeper into her until she felt a gentle quiver, then a powerful spasm, a streak of lightening that heated her core" Oh, yes. Oh, yes. Oh..." She let out a small cry as Bill released his seed. They lay perfectly still. The familiar quiet and warmth of their lovemaking enveloped them.

"Kate? Are you asleep?" Bill lightly rubbed her bare back, her head buried beneath the down pillow. "Darling, we need to talk before our team arrives." He checked the small wall clock. In another hour, Cory and the others would make their way from one safe house back to the Hen House.

Slowly, Kate rolled onto her back and opened her eyes. "Where are we? Oh, that's right, we're underground! How quickly one forgets." She smiled and braced herself into a sitting position.

"Listen Kate, before we get company, I have a few things to run past you. I just want you to listen, so lean back on your pillows and hear me out."

"Is something wrong?"

"No, not at all, it's just I've been doing some research and have a few facts and observations for you to digest. It may be nothing but then again, it could be something." Bill sat down on the edge of the bed, a government supplied bathrobe exposing his muscled legs.

"OK! I'll be quiet and let you talk." Kate pulled herself into a comfortable position, covered herself with the cotton sheet and nodded. "I'm ready. Shoot."

"Well, where do I begin? First, your letter to Carlos Monuro is on its way by special courier. I honestly don't know if we can turn him against the revolution he supports. History is not on our side. I did some research. You probably already know a lot of what I'm going to say."

"Go on. I'm listening."

"A little ancient history. Pissarro landed in what is now Peru. He only had two hundred men. But because of his steel swords, lances and rifles, he was able to push back the vast Inca tribes."

"It was more than just the weapons." Kate couldn't resist.

"You're right, my dear. Pestilence reduced the total population of the tribes and of course, not all of the people were in favor of the Inca. In many ways, like all despots, they alienated the people. They built great monuments, but on the backs of their enslaved people."

"Unfortunately, the monuments we most admire around the planet came about at a horrific price. The price of immortality was slavery and death to the enslaved workers." Kate felt a pang of guilt to admire those lasting monuments.

" You're right. And the great battles against the Inca were fought between both indigenous tribes and the Conquistadors. It took the support of the tribes to help the Spanish conquer Cuzco and even earlier, Lima. And Kate, remember, the Inca and tribes fought their battles with clubs. No guns or sophisticated weaponry."

"Yes, it was bloody and very messy. I hate to think how many have died fighting for their right to survive as a people. Just think how many people would be on this planet today if it wasn't for the wars that have plagued the world population. Our Civil War is a prime example."

"Yes, you're right but if it wasn't war, another form of population control would have arisen, other black plagues or natural disasters, like volcanoes and earthquakes, even another tsunami to wipe out thousands." Bill paused to get back on track and looked at the clock. "We're running low on time. Where was I?"

The Conquistadors

Cuzco. After Cuzco, the Spaniards chased the remaining Inca into the dense rainforest and to the south." He stopped to make his point. "That is why I believe there is much treasure below the earth cover, not in concentrated stores. The Inca fled and were forced to deposit their gold and other trinkets as they ran to save themselves."

Kate sat up a little straighter. "So you think."

"Remember the graves we found in the rainforest? They were not traditional Inca graves. The Inca buried their dead sitting up in deep graves. The bodies we found were laid out flat as if buried in a hurry. I doubt if the Inca had much time for ceremony."

"I buy that." Kate rose from the bed and began to dress. "Go on."

"When and if we go back to that part of the rainforest, we should examine the bodies more closely to determine if they died from bludgeoning or from natural causes. I did some reading and there's quite a bit of research on the subject. We may as well take advantage of the existing research."

"You know, Dr. Raymond Morrissey did much of that research. He considers himself to be a front-runner in understanding the fate of the Inca. But do we really want him involved to that extent?

"He's going to be whether we want him to or not. He's waiting over at the Mayflower as we speak. So is Dr. Brown."

"I have also asked the CIA research lab to collect the most current history and theory of the Inca conquest, not from the Spanish writers whom I've been told, wrote a very biased account. Knowledge is power. "

Kate finished applying her lipstick, " I can only imagine the "early" CIA, snooping around the Inca camps way back then!"

"That would be something, wouldn't it?" Bill began to dress and ready himself for their guests. "By the time we reach Lima, we had better be expert because this is the approach we will use with Carlos."

"So that's the reason for the long dissertation! Now I get it." We'll tempt Carlos with a vast wealth of gold." I like it.

"Kate, it's hard for me to believe that a gentle scholar would turn into a killer so quickly. I'm betting that there is something of the old Shaman in the young Carlos that may lead him to a peaceful resolution. It's only a theory. And a wish."

"For Carlos' sake, I hope you're right. I remember him as bright and inquisitive and kind. After all, he gave me the miner's letter rather than exploiting or worse yet, destroying it." Kate brushed out her blond hair and tied it back from her face.

"Kate, that's Plan "A". Plan "B" is to locate, with the help of the Seals, his associates, identify and mark them for capture. We must also search for FARC infiltrators both overt and covert. They may not trust Carlos either and may even mark him for death as a martyr. You know, *"Young professor, son of honored Shaman, killed by government soldiers"*.

The lights indicating activity in the connecting tunnel turned on and a low pitch alarm was sounded. Bill turned on the big flat screen to confirm identities. Manuel, Cory and his team would arrive in five minutes.

"Kate, before they enter, I want to finish my explanation. We have to clearly define our roll in this episode. So this is where Manuel comes into the picture. His duty is to collect as many previous followers as he can to form an ad hoc government. He must particularly get the army on his side. His record is so good that he may get the top brass to join him. They are sure to remember his patriotic activities during the aborted revolution. And last but not least, we must neutralize the Sendero, find the Columbian FARC infiltrators, subvert the existing government and do it all in thirty days!"

Bill headed for the passage door and quickly lifted the compression lock. "Welcome Gentlemen. Kate and I have been waiting for you. Let's get started."

Hector and Cory entered quickly, shook hands with Shepherd and Kate then immediately seated themselves in the high back chairs. "I think I'll enjoy this luxury for a few minutes", Cory said understanding full well that the field would supply him with little more than a wooden bench and hard ground.

"Hector, have you been able to contact your friends in the current government and secure their cooperation? That's the first step in forcing transition." Bill took a seat after Kate had settled into her chair across the table.

"Yes, Senor Shepherd, please remember that Peru, is imperfect but Senor Shepherd, it is still a constitutional democracy. Our Presidente, no matter how incompetent, was elected. My point, Senor, Senorita, Senor Cory. And once they accept, that they must act to protect the existing government when a coup attempt is made."

Hector took his seat next to Kate and continued. "After we destroy the coup attempt by Shining Path and also FARC, it is essential we get the government to resign."

He paused, regained his line of thought, "This action will allow us to appoint an interim government that will include Manuel. Of course, elections will be held within six months and that will give Manuel enough time to explain his favorable programs and of course, allow him ample time to gain support among my Peruvian people."

Shepherd listened intently, formulating details to their plan as Hector spoke. "Please, Hector, continue."

"Manuel Sanchez is well respected by the people but Senor" looking at Cory, he must still win their votes. My group cannot hold together this collision if the result is only another dictator." Turning his gaze to Shepherd, Senor, this I have promised to the politicians and also the military. We must honor it."

Agent Shepherd leaned back in his chair and stretched his arms over his head, then brought them down firmly on the table. "Well thought out Hector. You bring an important perspective to the culture of your countrymen." Shepherd tuned his attention towards, Manuel. Will you agree to such terms?"

Understand me please. I would never leave my family and risk my life and the lives of my people if there was a chance that we end with another dictator. We must succeed." Manuel firmed his jaw as his eyes traveled from Cory to Kate to Hector and finally settled on Bill Shepherd. "Yes, I am agreeable to such terms."

Cory took a deep breath then slowly exhaled. "Now that we are reading from the same script, when do we begin?"

"We've already begun!" Shepherd stood and walked around the table to relieve the tightness in his muscles. He could feel the tide of inactivity turning to a full force plan. "With the cooperation of the CIA and a friendly press, a series of provocative press releases have been prepared explaining that Dr. Kate Shepherd is organizing an archeological expedition back into the rainforest to follow up on the astounding discoveries uncovered in New Zealand."

Kate raised her hand to speak. "Gentlemen, I've been notified over our secure communication system that the first was placed today. And this, in conjunction with my letter sent to Carlos, the Shaman's son, at the University should get the ball rolling pretty quickly."

Shepherd followed her statement, "Yes Kate, gentlemen, there's more. The articles are so placed to appear to stir interest with our old associates, Dr. Raymond Morrissey and Mr. Maggie Brown. They will lead the site selection for the deed without raising concerns with either FARC or other opposition groups. Raymond, Dr. Morrissey is a professor of great stature and has quite a reputation in Peru. Not all good, of course, but nothing that would raise red flags within the government."

Cory added, "They are in transit as we speak to meet us in the Hen House. They will participate. They really have no choice." Maggie and Raymond had stumbled upon an escalating situation and a choice to either contribute to the outcome or be placed in protective custody until the mission was completed.

"You trust them Senor Shepherd?" Hector was skeptical of newcomers joining the mission.

"Yes, Hector. They are professionals in their field and they will not be directly involved in other aspects of the operation. Let's just say, they'll create a diversion while we go about our business."

"I will trust your judgment, Senor." Hector leaned back in his chair for the first time.

"Cory, you and your team should prepare to leave for Peru, ASAP. You've been given a supply list, including two Land Rovers, stored in a Lima warehouse."

"We're secured and ready to move out. We've had our scout check out the facility and the condition of the vehicles along with the GPS systems and the satellite coordinates. We're good to go."

"Good news. And you are aware, Cory, your handsome, young SEALS are pre registered for courses and you can immediately integrate into the student body.

To answer your question in advance, yes, we have hacked into the university computer system and your fictitious names have been added to the roster." Shepherd pulled out a large envelope and handed it to Cory. "Here are the assumed names and other information your men will need. Read and memorize."

Cory took the envelope and tucked it into his field jacket. "Good as done."

"To eliminate any questions about the SEALS' appearance, please make sure they downplay their physical attributes, if that's possible. I want them to come across as bright, academically involved students. Hector has made sure they appear to be exchange students from other Spanish speaking countries."

"They were selected because of their fluency in the language and will take heed not to socialize until they feel comfortable with their integration. These guys are pros. The best of the best."

Shepherd tried not to laugh, "Yes, I know they're pros but make sure they take it easy with the coeds. They should be prepared to use leftist tinged language." Shepherd stopped speaking and cleared his throat. "They are also healthy, young men. Make sure they keep it in their pants. We have enough politicians that come off as so-called pros and end up letting the little head do their thinking. An indiscretion could unravel all of our efforts."

"Damn, Shepherd, we are a wrung or two above politicians. There will be no screwing around on Uncle Sam's dollar." He was flustered at the assumption that his men could be corrupted so easily but then, he looked at Kate and felt his own loins tighten. So much for the little head.

"I didn't mean to offend. I just want everything to be crystal clear so we have no misunderstandings down the road."

"I understand and I'm not offended. Just proud of our men, Sir," Heads around the table nodded in agreement. "We're good to go."

"Good, in your packet is also information to make their transition easier, a short history of the country and information on local idiosyncrasies. Study and discard. Good luck."

"Manuel, your orders are the nicest!" Shepherd walked behind Manuel and laid hands on his shoulders. He could feel him tense. "Relax, my friend. It will take at least a week to get this all going. Once we depart, you, Conchita and your children will return to the Hen House. We'll accommodate the children so don't worry. Kate and I will remain a few more days before we join the others in Peru. Manuel, you will be able to communicate on secure lines to any of your associates and keep up to the minute with their progress."

"Thank you, Senor Shepherd. I will follow every move you make until the time comes for me to return to Peru. As long as you understand that I want to be included in every movement within my country. I repeat that I will not be a figurehead but a true leader with authority to lay out my country's future direction."

"We want it no other way. Peru, without a strong, competent leader is a Peru that is destined for failure." Hector stood and walked to where Manuel sat. "My friend, you are the one man to put our country onto the path to prosperity."

"Gentlemen, gentlemen, we have a long way to go. Let's hold our congratulations until we have a positive outcome." Agent Shepherd understood that failure was not discussed but remained an unpleasant option. Unknown variables could turn the tide.

"Manuel, until we vacate the Hen House, you will be escorted to another secure house where your children and wife are being kept. Enjoy your time with them." Shepherd knew it would be a while before they could once again live as a family in their Peruvian homeland.

The meeting was ended when the red light signaled a military escort and Drs. Morrissey and Brown's arrival through the tunnel entrance. "Good, you'll have a chance to meet our expedition leaders before you head off. Dr. Shepherd and I will give them an overview before we send them back to the Mayflower to await our Peruvian departure. They will be briefed and sworn to secrecy."

Bill Shepherd ran a thorough security check on the academic couple. The flashing red light turned green before he could slip the latch on the secure door to the Hen House and admit them to their hidden war room.

Final Instructions

Dr. Maggie Brown with Raymond on her heels, entered the secure space and looked around in amazement. The high technology and the practicality of the space, left them slack jawed. Agent Shepherd pointed to the tall chairs around the table and on cue, they lowered themselves and waited for someone to speak.

"Welcome, both of you. I know this must seem pretty bizarre to you but it's our new reality. And, now yours, too." Shepherd sat across the table from them and Kate joined them, a tray of bottled water in hand.

"Hello Dr. Brown, Raymond. Glad you could join us." Kate didn't know what else to say so she gave the floor to her husband.

"I understand Agent Cory Danielson briefed you in advance. The fact remains. Even if you hadn't come calling, chances are the CIA would have brought you in, partly because of Raymond's history in Peru and the nature of this mission."

"I had no idea." Raymond opened his bottle of water and drank it down.

"And me, what about me? I'm a citizen of Great Britain and also a citizen of New Zealand."

"Dr. Brown, unfortunately, you were in the wrong place at the wrong time but as a trusted colleague of Dr. Morrissey's and in some respects, my wife Kate, your cooperation is now expected. Of course, you could be deported but that would be a last resort. Not very friendly of my government, I'm afraid." He opened a bottle of water and paused so the couple could mull over what he'd said.

Raymond spoke first. "So Peru is on the brink of revolution? Our small group can turn that around? I find that hard to believe."

"Well. Raymond, it sounds ambitious and it is but we have a small window to cut off the head of this serpent. In another month, you're right, we may not have the opportunity to turn history around." Bob paused for greater effect. "But the fact remains. Your responsibility or should I say your role in this, is more smoke and mirrors"

"Smoke and mirrors? Please explain." Dr. Brown was subdued.

"We don't expect you to become involved in the removal of certain key figures but rather, we expect you to lead an unrelated trek into the Peruvian rainforest, back to Conchita's father, Raul's original dig site." Bill Shepherd took a few minutes and described his theory on the gravesites and reasons for the gold stashes.

"So you think the temptation of gold might sway the Shaman's son, Carlos, the head of the serpent?" Maggie Brown sounded skeptical. "What you're saying is, well, let's see if I've got this correctly, you don't believe he is as committed to the cause as his followers believe him to be."

"Dr. Brown, precisely. In fact, I'm counting on it. But if we're wrong, Carlos will be neutralized. Kate had dealings with him and she found him to be a decent, pure intellectual not the fanatical and driven tyrant being discussed in the streets of Lima who's feared for his brutality."

"Carlos was helpful when I was conducting research and he cared deeply for his father although he did admit to me that father and son were from different worlds. I liked him. I hope he can be turned around before it's too late for him." Raymond's met Kate's gaze. She smiled then diverted her attention back to her husband.

"Kate's pretty astute. Until a few months ago, Carlos seemed content to remain on the sidelines, until the highly publicized gold discovery in New Zealand and other pressing events in his homeland stirred new passions. Suddenly we're looking at a potential national threat."

Raymond tried to clarify the time line leading up to the current crisis. "Did I hear you correctly? Peru is looking for alternatives to their present state of affairs and suddenly, a relatively unknown is chosen and placed on a pedestal and overnight he's elevated in stature. And you say we need to knock down that pedestal."

"In a nutshell, yes." Shepherd had said all he cared to about the political climate. "Hopefully, you won't be involved in any of that.

We need you to go about your business as scientists. Kate and I have put together a pretty comprehensive plan. All you have to do is follow it and, if we're lucky, you'll hit pay dirt."

"When do we leave? What about our supplies?" Dr. Brown jumped ahead. "If we're going on a treasure hunt, I'd like to get on with it." She was becoming bored with the talk of a coup. She wasn't particularly interested in the fate of Peru. The gold interested her. She didn't appreciate the heavy-handed approach but she kept quiet. They hadn't scored in New Zealand and perhaps; this would be her golden moment.

"Maggie, if I may call you that, supplies are being transported as we speak. You and Raymond will be transported within twenty-four hours to a staging area and finally, taken into the designated site by armored chopper. That's all I am at liberty to discuss with you until you are in the air."

Shepherd did not like this woman and would have preferred if she had been stricken from the team but it was too late. Hopefully, Raymond Morrissey could deal with her snappish attitude. And, he'd have to keep her within the CIA's strict guidelines.

"Raymond, Dr. Brown, trust me. This is the last thing we expected upon our return to the states. We are sitting under our home! How strange is that?" Kate broke the tension and laughed at the absurdity of their situation. "Right over my head is a very comfortable sofa and a fireplace. Look around you. We're living in a bomb shelter!"

"Oh honey!" Bill Shepherd joined in. "It could be so much worse. I don't know how but it could be." He broke the tension with a halfhearted laugh.

The group rose from their chairs and Kate conducted a brief tour of their close quarters.

"How in the world did the CIA build this?" Maggie Brown was incredulous.

"It was in place before we ever leased the house. Makes you wonder, doesn't it?" Kate left it at that.

"Bill led them to the exit door, "Maggie, Raymond, once you leave us, your escort will make sure you are safely returned to the Mayflower. A phone call will set the wheels in motion. From now on, just go with the flow. Any objections or unnecessary questions will be met with silence."

The red light turned green and they were gone. Kate and Bill Shepherd were alone in the Hen House.

"I don't like that woman." Kate turned towards the little kitchen area. "She will be trouble. She wouldn't even look at me. She may be a brilliant scientist but I wouldn't work with her for all the gold in, in Peru."

"Relax darling. She's Raymond's responsibility, not yours. I rather dislike her myself but for the good of the mission, I'll turn a blind eye to her." Bill took Kate in his arms and gave her a comforting hug. "Now, we have some down time and I'm going to take full advantage." He guided Kate towards the sleeping alcove, punched the Privacy Request button and together, they sunk into the cool sheets.

Desire

"I'm British. Why should I have to listen to the bloody CIA?" Maggie Brown was back at the Mayflower and a throbbing headache, probably the after effects from her earlier head injury made her temper inexplicitly rise. "If it wasn't for the money, I'd purchase a ticket and travel to New Zealand or better yet, to London. I despise being told what to do and how to do it." She was irrational and her arguments were pointless. She threw herself on the bed and dramatically hid her face with her forearm.

"Listen Maggie, I know this is a little bit out of the ordinary..."

"Out of the ordinary? Ordinary? This is way beyond that."

"Maggie, I agree we got roped into something unusual..."

"You call this unusual? You're as bloody insane as the rest of them."

Raymond's voice broke with frustration. "My dear Dr. Brown, think of the reward, the gold, the financial gain. A little inconvenience and you can buy that house that caught your eye." Perhaps he had said too much.

"You are referring to the Shepherd's home?" She sat up and straightened the simple and tasteful Anne Klein dress she had chosen to wear to the meeting. "Is it for sale?"

"I might have spoken out of turn but my experience tells me that everything has its price." Raymond had succeeded in diverting her interest and dampening her anger.

"But the Hen House. Isn't it accessible from their library?"

"Yes, but I'm sure they'll have to seal it up now that we know it's there. The CIA is so secretive that the Hen House will never be used again. Trust me." Raymond spoke before he gave it much thought but it made sense. "The CIA will build themselves another tunnel under some other estate."

"I'd like that."

"Like what?"

"The Shepherd house. Isn't that what we were just discussing?" Maggie shook her head at Raymond." "Oh Raymond, come here, will you?"

Raymond did a double take. One minute she's reading him the riot act then she's patting a spot next to her on the bed in her private suite. "Are you sure?" Raymond didn't want to fall into a trap, if he misread her intentions.

"I'm sorry I've been so difficult Raymond but, you're right. I despise admitting that to you. We should make amends." Maggie began unbuttoning her pretty Anne Klein. "If we go along with the CIA and the Shepherds and you can promise me the Shepherd house. She slipped out of her dress and smiled up at Raymond.

He was weakening. It had been a long while since he had engaged in a sexual encounter and memories of her uninhibited lovemaking came rushing back. He felt a familiar tightening in his loins. He stood over her, slowly removing his outer layers of clothing. "You're sure, are you?"

"Come to me, Raymond. Make me happy." The woman was shameless. She opened herself to him and his will power crumbled.

Carlos

An uneventful day of waiting had passed. The wheels were put into motion but the Shepherds had another few days to wait until they were put in place.

Kate and Bill took the off time to recharge their batteries and reconnect on a number of different levels. The time alone helped strengthen their commitment and for a couple who lived so close to the edge, time, with no outside distractions, allowed them reflective moments to retrace their journey and to count their blessings. Yes, they lived on the edge but they lived on the edge together and each understood the strengths of their partnership. They both were alive because of the other's heroic efforts in the field. Facing death brought about introspection.

"Darling, our break is about over. By now, your letter to Carlos has been delivered and Hector promised we'd have Carlos' response post haste." Bill finished his exercise regimen and dabbed himself with the Government Issue towel. "I want a quick shower and then we'll see what comes through."

Kate had finished her shower and threw on a comfortable pair of jeans and a sweater. "Go ahead, shower. I'll keep an eye on the screen. We've waited this long, haven't we?" She brushed up against him as he headed to the small bathroom. "I'll miss this, you know."

"Honey, me, too. It's been a long while since we had so much time together without interruption. But it's about to come to an end." Bill dropped his towel, exposing a well-shaped pair of buns!

Kate couldn't help but notice. "And I'll miss *that!*"

"What?" Bill looked over his shoulder and smiled. "Oh, *that!*"

A brief, incoming e-mail brought information they had waited for. Hector manned a mail watch at the university post office and they had just intercepted the correspondence from Carlos Minoro, meant for Dr. Kate Shepherd. The letter would be opened with her permission, translated and transmitted within the hour.

Kate responded and gave them consent to open the confidential, stamped letter. "Well, now we'll see if Carlos is as greedy as everyone believes him to be."

"Darling, the letter is being translated as we speak. It will be e-mailed soon."

Bill ran a brush through his damp hair, threw the brush on the bed then put on his Dartmouth sweats. "Good. Want to make a bet?"

"A Bet? About what?" Kate was sitting in front of the blank screen. "Oh, you think Carlos is getting excited about the prospect of gold?"

"Yes, that and well, I bet he's very interested in seeing you. I think he'd love to get you alone, the older, beautiful scientist meets the young, virile, brilliant young professor…"

"You're serious? He's a kid." Kate shook her head. "You've got quite an imagination."

"Laugh if you want but I understand the power an older, more experienced beauty holds. And he's no kid. He's leading a revolution, for pity's sake."

"If you say 'older' one more time." She wasn't that old. Kate wasn't a schoolgirl anymore. She had grown into her beauty with confidence and style. I'm thirty something. I'm in my prime. At least I think so."

"Kate, you are the most beautiful woman I've ever met. The idea of sharing you with a young upstart is not to my liking. But they've set you up as bait and I have to live with it. Regardless, whatever takes place, I will be close by. Trust me. I'll have you under very close scrutiny." He came up behind his wife and hugged her as she sat in front of the large flat screen and next to the compact fax machine.

"I'm sure you will. I know how you work." She turned in her chair and put her arms around his neck and whispered in his ear, I do love you."

"Ditto. But, no need to whisper. We are still in privacy mode. No one's eavesdropping on us, at least not now." He gently freed himself then sat down in the chair next to hers. Over the secured fax machine, the translated message came through. "Well, Kate" handing it to her, "It's meant for you. Why don't you read it to me?"

"If you insist, here goes." *Dear Dr. Kate Shepherd, It was a pleasant surprise to hear from you. You are correct in thinking of me. I am very curious of your trip to New Zealand and particularly what role my deceased father's letter, the one from the old miner, played in your success. The newspapers and current magazines were filled with articles about the method of your gold discovery.*

Your mention of a reward was most welcomed because the salary of a novice Peruvian university professor is quite modest. I'm sure you understand and sympathize that intellectual excitement tastes better on a full stomach.

I will gladly welcome you at my university office. When you arrive, we can discuss our mutual interests.

Your willing Servant, Carlos Monuro, Professor, Universite de Trijuillo

"Well, that's an invitation if I ever heard one." Kate set the fax down and swung her chair towards her husband.

"Yes. Problem one. We received his translated letter barely minutes after he wrote it. Under normal circumstances, we'd have to wait two weeks to receive his reply."

"How do we get around that?"

I've got a bright idea! Tomorrow, we have the US Embassy notify Carlos that they have been requested to contact him on your behalf to arrange an appointment for next week. They can stress that you are on your way to Peru, accompanied by your husband, to discuss the letter you recently mailed to him. Maybe we should not mention my name. There's an urgency that may get his curiosity aroused. Maybe more than that."

"That would take care of the time discrepancy. And what do you mean by *'maybe more than that'?*

"Nothing, really. Well, yes, I still believe Carlos would love a roll in the hay with you. It's not going to happen but he's going to fanaticize about you."

"My dear, I'm flattered, I think, but I believe you're reading too much into Carlos' behavior. He never laid a hand on me and he had ample opportunity when I was doing research in those isolated archives."

"Yes, but he's had time to think about you and the gold and I guarantee he's imagined some pretty outrageous scenarios. I know because I've done the same thing." He hadn't planned on confessing but it hit home.

"Bill Shepherd, are you telling me you had erotic dreams about me when I was under the control of the Peruvian drug lords?"

"I guess you could call it erotic dreaming. Actually, it was more kinky than that."

"Enough. I'll let my imagination fill in the pieces. You dog you." She laughed and ran her hand up his thigh. "You bad dog."

"OK! Let's get serious or we'll be back in bed again. Not that I wouldn't mind." Shepherd couldn't help but enjoy his wife's flirtatious teasing. "What about your young rebel, Carlos? How do you handle him? Seriously."

"As you can see, I know how to handle men, not only my very sexy husband. I'm capable of handling a young buck, educated or not. He's educated and he's smart. He's also hungry for wealth. I have an irresistible carrot to dangle before him."

Bill was tantalized by Kate's beauty and brains and he had to force him to keep on track. "Darling, you have the historical data on the period of Peruvian history that is relevant and after describing the find and the nature of it, you can then guide Carlos from the New Zealand gold right back to the original point of origin, in the Peruvian rainforest."

"I agree. Most likely he has gotten wind of the burial site and its relevance to the disposition of Inca gold. But the exact location is known to only a few, one being Raymond Morrissey."

"Carlos is a bright young man and we should do whatever it takes not to put him into a position to challenge you."

"I'm not sure I understand you."

"Well Kate, he will realistically want to know why he is being solicited. You'll have to tread lightly. I see it playing out this way:" Bill sat on the edge of the desk and continued to paint a picture.

'Carlos, you sent me the miner's letter and I accepted it with no expectation of reward. By circumstance, the accidental discovery delivered great wealth. We returned the majority of the gold to the people of Arrowtown.' Bill took a moment to arrange his thoughts.

"Let's see, where was I? OK, the lions' share of the gold was returned to New Zealand." *'My husband and I decided we must return to Peru to revisit the rainforest and confirm our suspicions. Of course, in archeology, we are wrong more than right but we felt we could accomplish two things at one time.'*

Kate commented, "I better explain the ethics involved. Something like this:" *'Carlos, in our scientific field, there are definite procedures for sharing discoveries, both academically and monetarily. Carlos, anything we find will be shared per our agreement. And furthermore, any new treasures uncovered from your country's illustrious past will be returned to the Bureau of Antiquities, in your name. Carlos, you must recognize this will give you tremendous recognition both academically and politically, while making you a very wealthy young man.'*

"Reinforcing his personal wealth is a good hook and your short dissertation should feed his political and academic desires. We can also offer him an annuity just in case we find nothing of value."

"Pretty persuasive, I'd say. If someone made me the same offer, I'd have a difficult time turning it down. Of course, the ticklish part ,he has to guide us into the, center of their pending revolution. That could be tricky and might tip our hand."

"You're spot on, darling but I'm sure, with your feminine persuasion, Carlos will choose the perfect time to help turn the tide our way. Our SEALS will be in place and we'll be able to stand back and observe, out of harm's way. At least that's my plan."

Kate stood, stretched her stiff back and headed to their sleeping quarters. "We can discuss this some more but right now, I'm going to pack my bag. Look at the flat screen."

Bill read the message that flashed across the screen. "They're sending a vehicle in one hour. Darling, the time for action has arrived."

Operation Gold Fever

Kate packed her trusty machete. She insisted that their escort retrieve it from under the master bed in their Georgian home above their heads. "I hope I never have to use it on another human being but I don't feel right heading back to Peru without it by my side. Maybe I'm just superstitious."

The Embassy car was maneuvering through traffic on the way to Andrew Air Force Base to the awaiting small supply plane that was leaving shortly for Lima, Peru. The plane was equipped with luxury seating for VIPs with pending business in the South American city.

"Our Embassy in Lima will accommodate us." Agent Shepherd rested against the comfortable interior. "This is unusual for me to travel without cover. If anyone is curious, we're simply the good Dr. Kate Shepherd, archeologist and her husband, what's *his name!*"? He enjoyed the irony. "In fact, Dr. Shepherd, you may want to put on your bush hat when we land in the event someone wants to take your picture or get you autograph. You're quite a celebrity."

Kate wasn't accustomed to being in the spotlight. "I doubt that, dear *anonymous husband.* The only people who are aware of our arrival are Embassy staff, Peruvian Immigration and Customs. I don't think any of them will want my picture, unless immigration collars me. Don't worry, that's a joke."

"You're squeaky clean. But with a little luck, Cory will be around to greet us. If he shows up, I suggest you wear a Burka."

"Why on Earth would I do that?" Kate looked at him, her eyes like saucers. "A Burka, of all things."

"Kate, you must understand the effect you have on other men, Cory is intrigued by you. He's my best friend and would never cross the line but it's there and I can't blame him. You put out some special pheromones." Shepherd intentionally rubbed shoulders. "You're irresistible and I have to live with that."

"Darling, you have nothing to worry about. You're my horse and I'm sticking with you until the very end." The conversation was light and teasing but her response came from the heart.

Kate gently smacked her handsome husband across the arm. "You're the only one that I allow under my Burka." She felt his hand wander. "Which is where your hand is right now! Darling, our ride to Andrews is almost over so just relax. Another two inches and you're in trouble." She wanted to giggle but contained herself. "Stop it Bill. Act like a grown up."

"Damn Kate, I am." He removed his hand and let go a hearty laugh. The driver, curious, caught Bill's eye in the rear view mirror then quickly turned his attention to the road. "We'll finish this discussion later, in the privacy of our embassy suite."

Kate kissed him on the cheek. "I comply." As she lightly bantered with her husband, Kate carefully stroked the Maori carved bone that she carried in her pocket. The smooth surface was somehow calming. Across the seat from where they sat, her well-traveled machete rested in its custom made sleeve. It resurrected powerful memories, not all pleasant.

They were driven out on the tarmac, straight to the sleek plane. The flight would be lengthy but comfortable. The CIA had graciously assigned a steward to the Lear Jet. With extended tanks they could reach Lima non-stop.

Once on board, the couple opened and reviewed the relevant documents they found on their seats. They tucked the packets away as the plane reached cruising speed.

"I'm still a little unsure how this is going to play out. Who makes a decision on Carlos' fate? Will we be forced to kill or capture him?"

"Well, Kate, that final recourse is not our concern. We will only set up the situation. Hector and his group will make that decision. Remember, this is a local problem. We don't want to get imbedded in nation building. I hate that term."

"So my job is to entice Carlos into guiding us on a trip into the rainforest then try to solicit his attitude on the Sendero uprising. without raising suspicions. That's pretty dicey."

Bill interrupted her, "Chancy, I'm sure you can weave the dicey subject into your general conversation. *You're just curious*, that's all. Whatever comes out of those casual interchanges will give us a sense of whether the threat is overstated or possibly, the intel was wrong and he is not leading a revolutionary group."

"And if that's the case? What then?"

"Well my dear Kate, we join Raymond and Maggie and see what gold we can discover!"

"Just like that? And do we recover the gourd we so carefully reburied?" She had been thinking about retrieving it but hadn't had the opportunity to broach the subject. "I'd really like to have it in my possession, even if I have to pull strings with Antiquities."

" The gourd? I almost forgot about it. Yes, we'll figure out a way to take it with us. Returning to the dig site may not be quite that simple but once we share our Intel; it will be up to Hector to find the real leadership of the revolutionaries. And remember, Cory has his men imbedded. His Intel will count as much, if not more than ours. One way or another, we eventually wipe our hands and go away."

"Bill, I have one other question. Where's your family Bible? Someone took it from the library when you were supposedly kidnapped and I hope it was you." The original rubbings from the gourd were carefully stored between the yellowed pages.

"Oh, I'm sorry I forgot to tell you. I'm guilty. I didn't want it to fall into anyone else's hands so I locked it away in the Hen House for safekeeping. I should have told you, darling. I apologize for the oversight."

"As long as you took it. I saw it missing and that really threw me for a loss. No one, other than you and me knew about its contents." She rested much easier. "That's a relief."

The steward came down the aisle, offered them a glass of white wine and handed Bill a sealed envelope addressed to him from Cory Danielson.

"I expected this. This is good. He may answer a few of your questions. He tore open the envelope and found two neatly transcribed pages. "Hold on. I'll read this to you."

Dear Bill:

We had our men pre-registered at the Universite de Trujuillo. It was hilarious. These buff, young men, as much as we disguised them, started a female stampede into their classes. I think the Peruvian girls, from birth, have been trained in the art of attracting men. The men are trained to resist while on assignment but it was a struggle for them.

Another time, wow! These highly disciplined SEALS are seriously considering taking courses after their assignment is completed!

Time to get serious. After the initial culture shock, the men started to attend the more politically charged classes that we believe might attract revolutionaries. There were a few macho challenges then with some subtle diplomacy, the Peruvian students adjusted to our men. Politics came up almost immediately.

As instructed, two of our men pitched some Maoist doctrine. They also initiated discussion on fighting alongside Venezuelan forces in Africa, a situation that was not well known. They debated the slaughter of innocent civilians, women and children by both sides and how it changed their minds about the justice of revolutions. It was heated debate.

They discussed the value of revolution and brought up instances when revolutionaries were equally bad. The firmest despot arising from a Christian/Latino background could not, in good conscience, tolerate the rape of little girls and pregnant women.

Of course, this debate immediately brought on a defense of revolutions and as we anticipated. After this extended confrontation, the lead student offered to introduce our imbedded SEALS to their leader, who we believe is Carlos Minuro. Their argument? Our SEALS were far better versed in standard propaganda than the average university student. These guys did a masterful job.

A meeting is set for eight PM tonight.

Our other two SEALS went through a similar drill. One, I won't use his name, had to knock out an overly aggressive male student who's girlfriend had become enamored with him. They had mixed results and we'll have to wait and see if they end up in the introductions. Hector has friendly students standing by in case of mounting problems.

Bill, I have advised our SEALS to go as far as joining the rebels. We'll see.

Best to Kate,

The Encounter

There was nothing Bill and Kate Shepherd could do as they flew over the Atlantic. The training and experience of the Navy Seals and Agent Cory Danielson would have to prevail.

In the meantime, Drs. Maggie Brown and Raymond Morrissey had reached their stash of supplies. After last minute strategizing, they had advanced their planning to only a three-day layover to give them time to check and organize their gear for the trek into the Rainforest.

Maggie had been unusually quiet since they departed the Mayflower under a cloak of secrecy. Something had been on her mind and it wasn't until they were on Peruvian soil that she chose to share her disturbing thoughts with her traveling companion.

"You know Raymond, we are as qualified and capable as those other two, the Shepherds, and yet here we are working and they are off playing spy." Raymond hadn't observed Maggie so contrary since they had their misunderstanding on the South Island, once again, over money and power bartering. He didn't like what he was hearing but kept quite.

"Raymond, you know as well as me that we deserved some of that gold and I don't give a bloody damn about them. The Shepherds have stood in our way."

"You're obsessing. Look at it this way, Maggie, we already have the promised stipend deposited in our personal accounts." Pointing at the technologically superior scientific gear on the pallet, "And all of this fine equipment at our disposal. We're scientists first, Maggie and this could be a boon to our careers. We may very well make a major discovery." He was preaching to the goddess, like talking to a blank wall.

She mocked him. "Yes, Raymond, all this fine equipment. We could take it and go off on our own. We owe nothing more to the CIA and your friends." She hadn't heard a word he'd said.

"Are you quite serious? You want to go rogue?" Raymond stood facing her, wide eyed with disbelief. Had he read her that badly? "You must be delusional."

She didn't have the opportunity to respond because two well-dressed Peruvian men appeared from out of nowhere.

"Good morning Professors Brown and Morrissey. We welcome you to Peru and our lovely, gold laden rainforest!" The taller of the two gentlemen grinned unabashedly, "We hope, Professor Morrissey, that you will not take any antiquities from our country. Or worse still, try to sell them on the black market."

Raymond, caught completely off guard, couldn't mouth a retort. He could feel his skin go clammy as his throat went dry. "Who are you?"

"Oh, we apologize. Where are our manners? Let us first introduce ourselves. This is Juan Marta and I am Pedro Rodriguez. We are representative agents of the most recently formed Peruvian People's Government, presently also known as Sendero, formerly referred to as The Shining Path. We hope all these names and titles don't confuse you."

The imposing agents positioned themselves between the two scientists and their valuable equipment. "You are aware of us, are you not?"

Pedro Rodriguez did not wait for a response. "Senor, Senora, let me clarify. We are no longer a peasant uprising, but a well formed group of intellectuals who will teach our people how to live in a strong social compact. We pattern our thinking, not on Stalin but more on the doctrine of Mao, our great leader."

Raymond hadn't anticipated these men and their brazen posturing. He moved closer to Maggie and held his trepidation under control. "Gentlemen, a pleasure I'm sure."

"If you are unclear of our mission, we will presently change your mind." Juan Marta pulled out a small wad of tobacco and placed it under his lip. "A bad habit is difficult to break." His smile exposed yellow stained teeth.

"You are guests in our country but make no mistake, we know you are part of a US delegation sent here to foil the overthrow of our existing government." The men moved their right hands in unison, to the heavy weapons held securely in the leather harnesses belted beneath their military style jackets. With mounting alarm, Raymond's eyes followed their well-rehearsed movements.

The men pressed closer, invading the personal space of the two academics. "Now, Senor and Senora, you will please tell us all you know, we expect, in a most civil manner."

The quiet one fingered his weapon as Juan Marta measured his threats. "We do not wish to resort to violence unless we are provoked. Professor Morrissey, you may begin. So you are aware of our sincerity, please be aware that we were able to wire your rooms at the Mayflower Hotel and the domestic staff was more than willing to accept payment for information regarding your safe house, what you call the Hen House."

Pedro managed a smirk. . "What a strange name for the CIA."

Juan Marta, the assigned spokesperson, was enjoying the full disclosure and could see the effect on Morrissey's face. He ignored the woman. "Your representatives were eager to talk to us but at this moment we have more questions for you, Professors."

Raymond lost his composure and stammered. He knew nothing of value to these people. "I am sorry. We were only recruited to search for a lost burial site and the possibility of hidden Incan gold. I'm certainly not CIA. We're scientists. Archeologists, that's all."

The reaction of the Peruvian agents made it evident that they didn't buy his disclaimer. "You must believe me. Just take a look. Our scientific equipment has been delivered for that purpose, no other." Raymond was sweating profusely. He wasn't a good deceiver.

Throughout the confrontation, Maggie had remained in the background, planning her escape. Swiftly, she managed a bold step forward to confront the Peruvian People's Government agents. In a brazen tenor that caught the men by surprise, Maggie bellowed,

"Raymond, for God's sake, fuck those CIA bastards! Tell them about Hector and the spies they sent. Tell them how they cheated us. How we're not involved."

The men froze and Raymond was startled beyond words. Raymond could be a rogue but Dr. Brown's traitorous attack on his countryman was more than he could bear. "Maggie, are you crazy? What has happened to you?"

Maggie held her ground. She snarled. Her words disemboweled him. "Raymond, you're a damn fool. They have made a bloody puppet out of you. The Shepherds and the CIA have used you to meddle in this country's affairs. You stupid fool. You owe them nothing." Her eyes narrowed and her visage became the face of evil. "They can all go to bloody Hell. And you with them."

Raymond felt the world close in. He was suddenly a trapped animal, caught in the cruel snare of his former colleague and lover. "Maggie, you're mad. Don't listen to her. She's insane."

The unyielding men stood with their guns at the ready. Could there be a greater betrayal? To escape the horrors, Raymond did the only thing he could think to do. He ran. He broke loose from the small group and ran faster than he thought possible until a single report from Pedro Marta's powerful gun struck the back of his head and ended his escape.

Raymond Morrissey, the brilliant professor, archeologist, black marketer of rare artifacts, former lover of both Kate and Maggie was dead. His lifeless body was obscenely prone on the dirt road. A pool of dark crimson blood slowly soaked into the ancient Peruvian earth.

Maggie observed the slaying in slow motion. Raymond fell and his head exploded in a fine mist of blood and gray matter. "My lord, you killed him. How could you do this to him? I loved him." She dropped onto the pallet of scientific gear and sobbed. "I loved him. I loved him."

The agents laughed. "We will give you plenty of love Senorita. But first, tell us about the spies."

8 PM

Hector, Cory and the two Seals secreted themselves outside the university's administrative offices where the meeting would take place. Just out of sight, twenty of Hector's best-trained men waited for orders.

Precisely at eight PM, a black SUV stopped out front and unloaded its cargo of people, including the four-cloaked Seals. They jointly walked into the large assembly room where another twenty people were already seated around the large table. Against the unadorned walls stood four heavily armed men.

The four Seals scanned the room and each assessed the situation. They didn't want to appear apprehensive but it was more than heavy odds that they had walked into a trap.

As the meeting's leader, Carlos Minuro, prepared to speak, two field officers noisily entered the room accompanied by an acquiescent and disheveled Dr. Maggie Brown. The men, pushed her ahead of them and then halted in front of the group of incredulous faces.

Without further encouragement, Dr. Maggie Brown pointed and shouted, "There they are. The four spies, the Navy Seals. See, I told you the truth." The armed men lowered their AK 47's in the direction of the Seals.

Instinct took over and the four Seals split up and each took a hostage for cover. Maggie was pushed roughly to the side and made her way towards the door. A single shot rang out as she fought her way through the exit. She screamed then holding her wounded shoulder; she escaped before anyone could stop her. Her insane intervention was over. The leader of the Seals called out in Spanish, "Hold your fire or many will die." Everything happened in the measure of a second.

Their leader, Carlos, called out, "Let them go. Let them go. We must not descend to their level. Our revolution is intellectual, not militarist." As he spoke, the weapons fell to their sides and the

Seals released their human shields. Carlos Minuro's power through his words was broadcast loud and clear. His people listened and followed his command. Anyone who had doubted his leadership capabilities was convinced otherwise.

But the effect was short lived. The four-armed men, remembering their instructions, once again raised their weapons against Carlos and the American infiltrators and prepared to shoot.

Under their protective cover and through the Seal's listening devices, Cory and Hector had observed Dr. Maggie Brown enter the room under guard, then listened to her fiery accusations.

Carlos Minuro had temporarily defused the tense situation before they could rally and react. A single shot was fired with a different sounding report. It was not one of his men's weapons. No more than a minute had passed before Cory decided it was time to neutralize the armed men and take the rest into custody for interrogation.

Dr. Maggie Brown hysterically raced out the door into the waiting arms of Cory's comrades. She was bleeding profusely from a glancing gunshot wound yet she continued to struggle. They finally subdued her then hustled her out of the line of fire. The medic would stop the bleeding. They'd deal with her later.

Agent Danielson ordered his snipers to take out the armed men through the open windows as Hector's men surrounded the building and the exits. On cue, with weapons drawn, Cory and his remaining Seals rushed the main entrance.

The four armed men were taken down by the snipers and the room was left in turmoil. As Cory and his men entered to room, the two Sendero agents who had guarded Maggie, pulled their weapons and commenced firing at Carlos. Maggie Brown had escaped before Peruvian radicals were able to bring her down. They didn't want her loose tongue wagging about her colleague's murder.

Agent Danielson quickly cut them down with well-placed shots. He didn't want them dead. He wanted them talking and even under extreme circumstances he had the choice to shoot to immobilize or shoot to kill. His adrenaline pumping into his bloodstream produced clear and precise actions. They lay on the floor clutching their superficial wounds. Juan Marta and Pedro Rodriguez would live another day.

Before the students or faculty returned from their classes or from early meals, walked near the centrally located administration building, the unfortunate attendees of the clandestine meeting had been carefully searched, handcuffed, loaded into unmarked vans and spirited away. Three ambulances, their sirens on mute, removed the wounded and deceased and took them to an undisclosed destination.

Raymond Morrissey's body was discovered a mile from the campus, abandoned where he fell. He was placed in a black body bag and whisked away. There would be Hell to pay. The mission had taken a deadly turn.

For now, it was over. Cory and Hector sat in the vacated, blood-splattered room, assessing what had just transpired. There were tough questions to ask and tougher answers to extract. Thorough internal investigations would eventually tell the tale.

Kate and Bill Shepherd fastened their seat belts and prepared to land, oblivious to the disturbing events that transpired below.

Aftermath

As Kate and Bill descended the stairs from the Lear Jet, Peruvian Immigration and Customs met them. Standing to the side were Cory and Hector, neither with a smile on their faces. Hector made sure that the inspector correctly logged in the time of landing. After a cursory examination of their luggage, they saluted and left in their SUV.

When alone with the Shepherds, Cory quickly recited the events of two hours ago, the shoot out, the murder of Raymond Morrissey and the twenty or so Peruvian faculty they were keeping under guard in a nearby secure facility. They had recruited loyal Peruvian Federales to handle the interrogations, under Hector's guidance.

The loyalties of the various factions were clearly a dilemma, who supported whom? There was the constitutional government, the Sendero and interested faculty, lead by Carlos Monuro.

The agents wounded by Cory were of undetermined loyalty, but certainly not to the current governing power or Hector's men, who were nominally loyal to the government.

Lastly, there were the Federales who appeared to be loyal to both the sitting government and Hector's group. It would take serious discussion to sort out the players.

Maggie was hauled away for treatment and psychological evaluation. Raymond's assassins, who were wounded by Cory, were removed and treated in an unmarked ambulance while en route to a safe house obtained by Hector.

The meeting attendees, still to be sorted out by the Federales were bound, blindfolded and loaded into unmarked vans. When they reached their undisclosed destination, they were escorted to separate areas for interrogation.

Events moved so quickly, that Kate didn't have time to react to her professor's brutal death. She pushed her personal feelings of loss to the far reaches of her mind. She'd deal with those feelings later, once the crisis had passed.

Bill Shepherd, Cory, Kate Hector and the leader of the Federales met for an emergency conference to decide on a new plan of action. It was decided that the Federales would question the gunmen who killed Raymond Morrissey. They had witnesses to an actual crime within their jurisdiction.

Agent Shepherd reached into his pocket and withdrew a small, old fashioned tape cassette and handed it to the Federales Captain, Montez. "Captain, ever since the big water boarding flap at Guantanamo, we have eliminated overt torture. Unfortunately, it always worked."

"Agent Shepherd, the tape recorder?" Captain Montez turned it over in his hands.

"You see Captain, to get the same effect but without the actual torture, we have recorded thirty minutes of simulated torture, screams and all."

The Captain shook his head to cover a laugh. "The CIA is so clever."

"We think so. You can put the player in an adjacent room and activate the device by remote control. Just place one of your prisoners into the other room while you interrogate the other. We want him to think his buddy is being tortured." Bill Shepherd paused to let the ruse sink in. Let them believe their own propaganda."

"Agent Shepherd, I can supply some frightening tools, some instruments that can cause pain. That will help with our little, what you say, ruse." The Captain liked the ploy.

"Captain Montez, we deliver them to your competent hands. Of course, we want to know whom they work for and their mission. As you are well aware, critical to your government's requirements is timing. After we get the data, you can take them into custody for murder."

"Agents Shepherd, Danielson, you have my word. You will get your information very soon." He reached across the table and firmly shook hands. I like your methods. We will use them more often." The Captain was thinking into the future.

"Good, good, now that we've settled that, we have to get to the attendees and see how they're being processed. We don't want to be accused of kidnapping!" He faked a laugh but he knew that in a foreign country, charges could be thrown at them with little explanation and even less recourse.

When they left the meeting, Bill took Kate's hand and said, "Nothing is easy, is it? I hope we can get things under control and still be in the rainforest in a few days."

Kate's jaw dropped, "The trip to the Rainforest is still on? After everything that's happened? Raymond, Maggie, the shootings?" She was overwhelmed. "I don't understand."

"We're in Peru now and I think we keep going. Raymond can't complete the search but you can. "When things quiet down, we will check the equipment we gave Raymond and Maggie. After all, it belongs to Uncle Sam."

"I'm amazed, Darling. After all this, we still trek into the rainforest."

"No trekking. We fly. I still have the GPS coordinates stashed away. The gear will be airdropped." He put a comforting arm around Kate. "Trust me."

"I trust you. I guess I'm just overwhelmed. Poor Raymond. And Maggie Brown must be insane. She lost everything, even her mind."

Cory stood near enough to hear the pain in Kate's voice. "Morrissey ended tragically. I'm really sorry. He leaves quite a legacy behind. And Maggie Brown will be dealt with harshly." He felt his adrenaline level off but his heart still pounded.

Shepherd was thinking ahead. "Sweetheart, one more thing. I was wondering. I know it wouldn't be up to your standards but can we treat this exploration as a mining operation and use a bulldozer to dig up the first few feet of soil? I could get one down here real quick." He held his breath.

"You're kidding, aren't you? You are, right? You better be."

"Sorry I brought it up." He was serious but wouldn't dare let her know.

"You know, I'd be written out of the Archeologist's Union!

Cory didn't want to become immersed in their private affairs so he ran ahead to the building holding the detainees. The area appeared to be an abandoned industrial park, a series of single story structures covering two or three acres. The buildings were poorly maintained but sturdy enough to house and interrogate detainees without anyone being the wiser. The facility was securely fenced with a gate-guarded entry to the facility and a Federale agent had been assigned to check the credentials of anyone attempting to enter the grounds.

He was directed to the holding area and Hector's right hand man. Hector had just walked around the corner and they met at the closed door. "What have you found out?"

"Yes, while you were in your meeting we were able to obtain the names of all of these people but I'm afraid we must cross check to make sure of their true identities. Of the twenty being detained, only five appear to be students or teachers."

Bill quizzed him further. "Did they indicate what they were doing here?"

"Yes, Agent Shepherd, they seem to be from towns all through this part of Peru and were expecting a meeting of scholars."

"Did you believe them? Is that all they said?" Hector joined in the questioning.

"Well, one man who identified himself as an instructor finally admitted the subject of their meeting was peaceful revolution. We have collected all their papers and will do a thorough cross check."

Kate had been standing away from the conversation but spoke up, "Bill, gentlemen, do you think you can separate Carlos Monuro from the group and let me talk to him?"

Hector shook his head in the affirmative. "Of course, Senora Shepherd."

"I'd like to spend a few minutes with him. Maybe he'll open up regarding our mutual interests, namely the miner's letter and give me a hint at his true political intentions."

Cory spoke up. "This is a peculiar dilemma. Many of these people appear to be genuine intellectuals looking for a new order for their country. Were they guests or prisoners of the armed guards? Don't forget the guards shot at Maggie so they must have been involved with Morrissey's murder. They also shot at Carlos but gratefully, missed their target. I suspect now, that Hector and we were set up by the government to draw out their enemies. This meeting was more a trap for us than it was for Carlos. My recommendation is we take Carlos and our people and leave immediately."

Bill shook his head in agreement. "Hector, get your Captain and the pertinent interrogation papers and clear out with us. Kate, you can talk to Carlos at length when we relocate."

Within minutes, the US agents, Kate and Hector's men, lead Carlos through the rear door, entered the unmarked van and headed for the exit gate. Before they drove onto the main highway, they passed the Universite de Trujillo. The campus was teeming with military vehicles. Cory's suspicions were spot on.

Betrayal

"Get away from me." Maggie still fought through her pain. "They killed him. They killed Raymond. Shot him in the head." The anesthesia was beginning to take hold. "They killed my Raymond. The gold. Raymond, the gold."

She drifted into a drug-induced sleep as the doctors began treating the bullet wound. She was fortunate. The slug had entered the fleshy part of her shoulder, missing bone and exited through her bicep. She experienced blood loss but it was not life threatening. It was painful but then all gunshot wounds were painful except the ones that killed you. Besides leaving a nasty scar, once the wound was properly treated and patched, Maggie Brown would make a speedy recovery. Her psychological problems wouldn't be so quickly remedied.

Cory agreed to let Kate and Bill Shepherd visit the clinic to check on Maggie and make arrangements for the handling of Raymond Morrissey's remains. The van had traveled to a new location and the men, secreted away. Kate would speak to Carlos once the dust had settled. In the meantime, Kate and Bill Shepherd stood outside the emergency room.

It was unusual for the clinic to contain Raymond Morrissey's lifeless body. To keep his body out of the local morgue, a doable alternative was found. The small empty storage area behind the clinic became a temporary morgue until the CIA could make inquiries into the cause and those involved in his cold-blooded murder. Then his body would be placed on board a military plane and taken back to the States for burial.

"Dr. Brown's wound has been treated and we don't anticipate any complications. We've injected her with powerful antibiotics to avoid infection. Fortunately for her, it was a clean through and through. The Peruvian doctor, who had received his training at Johns Hopkins, spoke flawless English. "We will hold her overnight to make sure there are no other problems. She was hysterical when she arrived and I'm more concerned with her mental state. That may not be as easy to treat as the bullet wound. We're a small clinic but we can accommodate her overnight stay."

"Thank you, doctor, you've been very helpful under the circumstances. We appreciate that you turned your back room into a temporary morgue for our colleague." Bill Shepherd had been shaken by the news on what had taken place. "Our government will make the necessary arrangements and I hope that won't take long."

Agent Shepherd kept a strong arm around Kate's shoulder. Since they landed, events had come at them from all directions. The news of Raymond's murder had hit her very hard but she had to hold it together. They had history and Bill wasn't going to insist she remain callous. "You OK, honey? Hang in there."

Her cheeks were streaked with tears. "We shouldn't have included them in the plan. It was too dangerous."

"It sounds trite but hind sight is twenty-twenty. Sometimes things happen that are out of our control The doctor smiled meekly and returned to the ER letting the couple work through a vast range of emotion.

"But, we knew Maggie Brown was unstable. She should have been left behind. She killed Raymond." The tears began to flow. "I'll never forgive her for turning on him, on the whole mission. She put everyone's lives at risk."

"You're right. She has a lot of explaining to do but I think she's emotionally unstable and after what just came down, probably more so. What a mess." Bill Shepherd had trouble masking his feelings. Kate shared the depths of her soul and he couldn't pretend the events were of little consequence to him. "It will all come out. And we'll make sure Raymond Morrissey receives a respectful homecoming."

"He never told me much about his personal life with Helen. They had no children but he had a brother, who is ten years younger than Raymond. His name is Anthony and I remember Raymond telling me he lived on the west coast, I think Seattle. That was a long time ago so he may not live there anymore."

"I'll make a call and get them working on tracking him down. We just handed Raymond a million dollars. If there's a will or other personal effects, someone will have to take charge and sort it out." The legal details of dying unexpectedly crept into the tragedy.

Kate heard the sound of tires kicking up gravel. "Our driver is out front. We promised we'd meet Cory as soon as we handled things here. I'm ready." Kate was eager to leave the clinic. Raymond's cold, lifeless body made it all real. "I don't think we can do any more for poor Raymond or for Dr. Maggie Brown."

Dangerous Ground

Their unmarked van, with Cory at the wheel, merged into the heavy mid morning traffic and he skillfully maneuvered past the slow moving delivery trucks and vintage passenger cars. Hector sat behind him, feeding him directions to another building where they could gather their wits and decide on their next move. Cory kept one eye on the road ahead and the other, on the rear view mirror. "I think we've got company."

Bill Shepherd, sitting in the passenger seat, adjusted the other rear view mirror and immediately locked in on the dark SUV with tinted windows. "He's three vehicles back, Cory, can you lose him?"

"I can try but I doubt it. There's too much traffic to make a fast break or maneuver into the opposite lanes. This buggy is not going to outrun anyone." He put his foot to the pedal and the van slowly surged forward, a cloud of exhaust trailing behind them. "If I can make seventy, I'll be lucky."

Hector leaned further between the front seats, stared into the rear view mirror and caught sight of the chase vehicle. "Agent Danielson, that is an official government vehicle. They will call ahead for another vehicle to trap us. We have little chance to avoid them but if we exit up ahead, maybe we lose them among the narrow streets and old buildings outside the city."

Shepherd nodded and instinctively, Cory made a quick move into the far right lane and hit gravel. Cory fought to keep the van under him as his passengers shifted and hit the side panels. "Shit, sorry folks but we have a situation here." The tread caught solid concrete and managed a tight turn to the right. They bore further right and instantly found themselves on a quiet single lane road crammed with small, shabby private residences that surrounded a few tired factory buildings.

Kate, Manuel and Carlos remained silent yet the tension was malodorous. She tightened the seat strap and hoped for the best. Carlos stared ahead and measured his breathing. Manuel crossed himself and thought about Conchita and the twins. This could turn out badly.

"They're coming up behind us. I don't think we have a choice but to stop." Bill Shepherd realized their escape plan was futile. "Cory, let's see if we can talk our way out of this." Shepherd kept his voice steady and confident. Inside, his stomach was roiling. "Everyone, remain calm and maybe we'll get lucky."

Cory slowed the van and hit the hazard light indicator. He took a deep breath to calm himself and looked over his shoulder. "Please everyone, don't panic. We'll see if we can wriggle out of this."

The SUV pulled up and cut off their escape route. Four uniformed men hastily exited their vehicle and threw open the van's doors. "Out, everybody get out." The lead uniformed man held his AK47 at the ready. Please, line up beside your van, gentlemen and lady."

The troupe piled out of the van and followed the terse commands. Cory and Bill took the lead, "We don't want trouble. Look. We have our papers. The two agents handed over the official documents that had been issued to them previous to the university meeting. They both hoped the government issued paper would act as a *"Get out of jail free"* pass instead of an impulsive and messy mass execution.

The lead officer accepted the papers, briefly scoured them then handed the documents to his next in command who carefully studied them. When finally satisfied with their authenticity, the second in command handed them back to Cory and Bill. The man in charge observed the small party. As he inspected the lineup, he briefly paused in front of Kate; a roguish grin across his broad face then gave her a long, careful look.

The lead official nodded towards Carlos Minuro, as if he knew him intimately then passed him by. Manuel was greeted with a polite nod of the head. Then he paused in front of Hector Gonzalez. Hector was noticeably nervous. They exchanged a few words in Spanish then in broken English and he asked him for his papers.

The second in command suspiciously looked over the document and nodded his head towards the two armed men. With no obvious provocation, the uniformed men abandoned their mild demeanors, brazenly raised their weapons and pointed them specifically at Hector, skillfully extracting him from his comrades. Just as efficiently, the lead man shoved the gun between Hector's shoulder blades and hustled him in the direction of the SUV.

Both Cory and Bill held back. They were out manned and out gunned and for discretionary reasons, the determination was made to remain out of the line of fire.

"Gentlemen and gentle lady, you are free to proceed to your destination. We have no further interest in you." Hector was restrained by both arms and roughly pushed into the back seat of the SUV. It took only a few minutes.

The dark SUV with the tinted windows left a thick trail of dust and stinging gravel when it accelerated down the road. The remaining party, agents Bill Shepherd and Cory Danielson, Manuel, Kate and Carlos stood alongside the shabby back street. They systematically shook off the thick dust cloud and stared at the empty space where the SUV had vacated. Relief was written across the faces of both Carlos and Manuel. They were painfully aware of the harsh fate that awaited Hector, the same fate that could have been theirs.

"Someone higher up the ladder is threatened by Hector." Bill made a quick evaluation. "Your assessments were spot on, Cory. Somehow, his involvement is greater than we were led to believe. He's a marked man. Let's get out of here. We'll figure it out someplace else."

Carlos suggested a small residence, not far from where they were detained. Once under way, they traveled down a number of narrow, nondescript streets where they finally parked behind a battered storage shed. They followed Carlos into a small ground floor apartment. The back door led them through a dark, windowless kitchen and into a narrow living space. The one bedroom unit, a university student's off campus flat, was sparely furnished but tidy, a large professional photograph of Machu Picchu, the only wall décor situated over the green velvet covered davenport.

"Please, my friends, this modest apartment will keep us hidden for a while longer. It is the residence of one of my students." Carlos nervously cleared his throat, feeling the need to explain further. "She, Maria Anna Silva permits me to have her key." Obviously, the small apartment belonged to a student who was also Carlos' lover.

"It will do just fine, Carlos." Bill wasn't interested in whose apartment it was. It was time to lay out the facts and come up with a credible plan. "Carlos, do you know why Hector was taken?" There was no time to beat around the bush. "Who is he? And Carlos, who are you?"

Manuel had remained mute throughout the entire fiasco but now he felt the urge to make his voice heard. "Sir, if I may speak first." Manuel nodded towards Carlos to hold his response until he had finished. "Hector was a pawn, how you say? He was used to draw out and expose the revolutionaries, both those in the government and at the Universite de Trujillo." He paused to gather his thoughts. "And Carlos, I am sorry but you too were used to draw in other radical anti government intellectuals."

Carlos reacted by biting his upper lip and gripping the chair he was leaning against. "I only wanted my country to advance it's thinking and become a modern nation. I had no intent beyond that." His tenor was filled with regret.

"Manuel, please continue and tell us how or should I say, where you gained this intel." Bill Shepherd was surprised that Manuel, who had taken up residence in his Georgetown home over the past months, had gathered such detailed facts.

"It is the end of the Sendero revolt that I report to you, but in reality, it never occurred. It too was a ruse. There is so much deception in my country. Hector and his followers, will be executed to eliminate a piece of that deception."

"And the CIA and our Seals? What about their involvement?" Cory was certain he knew the answer.

"Agent Danielson, I think it is best to have your men prepare to leave the country to avoid any further fallout. The insurrection is over. You are best returning to your CIA headquarters to explain to these government officials that America's efforts were in support of their democratic government, not an effort to overthrow and replace it."

Carlos walked around the small room and stood next to Manuel. "My friend, you are correct in your estimation and I am sorry that so many had to suffer to return to the beginning of our struggle for a truly democratic country. I will return to my university responsibilities and only dream of the day." He spoke like a man defeated, a young man who thought change could come easily.

"Still, Manuel, you haven't told us where you received your intel." Bill pressed Manuel for more details.

"I'm afraid that I must keep that information to myself or else I would put you in more jeopardy. Let me say to satisfy the question, that my contacts are honorable people."

"I respect your concern for our safety and Manuel, I know you to be a man of honor." Bill Shepherd ended the inquest.

The small group took seats around the narrow space, first helping themselves to cold bottled water stored in the tiny icebox. Cory was on his satellite phone, contacting his key men, verifying their positions and instructing them to proceed according to their original exit strategy. He also made contact with CIA headquarters and listened intently to the commander on the other end of the phone. "Yes, sir. Yes, I understand. Yes. Very interesting." He hung up and compartmentalized the facts before he spoke.

"Hector has escaped. He was marked for execution and somehow, he was able to slip away. No one knows his position but our contacts believe he will find safe passage to a sympathetic border."

Manuel and Carlos shook hands and smiles of relief swept over their faces. Manuel spoke first. "Hector was betrayed and I am relieved that he will live to fight another day. He is a good man, a good soldier." There was more to their relationship but Shepherd had already closed his file.

Carlos had met Hector only one time and was unaware how vital a role he had played and now he sympathized with the risks he had taken on their behalf. "I hope I have a chance one time to speak with him."

"We have no control over Hector's future. He's on his own or more likely; he has friends who have helped him slip away. Most likely, some palms were greased." Cory knew the game. Money spoke loud and clear.

"To change tracks, the Peruvians want us out of the country. They'll forget we were here if we pack up and leave." Cory looked directly at Kate. That means you, too."

"But we can't." Kate felt her blood pressure rise. "There are too many loose ends. We have valuable research equipment waiting for us. With Raymond's murder and Dr. Brown still in the hospital, we have to take over the search."

"Kate, the situation has changed." Bill sounded reasonable.

"But the search hasn't. That had nothing to do with the coup or whatever you want to call it." Call them back, Cory, Bill. Call them. There's must be a compromising alternative."

Bill pulled out his sat phone and dialed up CIA headquarters. "Shepherd here. We have a concern."

Bill Shepherd walked to a secure corner of the small apartment and pleaded Kate's case. His voice was low and under control.

The group tried did not to eavesdrop. Kate exchanged ideas with Carlos and reassured Manuel regarding his family left behind in the states. "I'm sure everything will work out. Carlos, you have a brilliant future ahead of you and Manuel, if you decide to stay behind to help your country, Conchita will be pleased to finally join you in her birthplace."

"Bill Shepherd clicked his phone closed and approached the anxious gathering. They bought it. I arranged a conference call with our chief Embassy official, a government spokesman and my CIA representative. We knocked it around."

" Bottom line?" Kate was eager for an answer.

"Because of Raymond Morrissey's death and the wounding of his assistant, Dr. Maggie Brown, at the hands of rogue government representatives, they have rewritten the permits placing the expedition into the Peruvian rainforest into the hands of Dr. Kate Jenkins Shepherd, world renowned archeologist!" Bill beamed with relief. "You're going on a trek, my dear."

She hugged her man. "I am so relieved. After all the pain and sacrifice, maybe we can find something worthwhile. She looked around the group. "Cory, will you join us? We'll need security. And Carlos? She paused, thinking she might have spoken out of turn.

"Dr. Shepherd, I am honored that you ask but I must return to my students. But I will enthusiastically follow your adventure and hope you will be successful for many reasons." Carlos had played his hand well. "Would it be proper if I come speak with you privately before you leave for the rainforest? I have remembered something my father once shared with me when I was a young boy." A memory from long ago came to mind and he had nearly forgotten. So much had occupied his time and now that the crisis had diminished... "May I come to your hotel to meet for lunch tomorrow? Would your husband permit us to meet?

"Carlos, of course, please join me for lunch and we can have a good talk. I have questions. And yes, I will gladly keep you informed. Whatever we discover, you will be the first to hear. We are staying at the Intercontinental, located next to our Embassy. At noon?"

"Thank you, Dr. Shepherd. I will be there promptly."

Kate smiled warmly at the young scholar then turned her attention to Cory. "And Cory, what about you? Will you join us on our exploration back to the rainforest?"

Cory was overjoyed with the invitation. He fought the urge to grab her in his arms. His best friend's wife was off limits but there was nothing written that stated he couldn't enjoy her presence and fantasize.

"Yes, Kate, count me in. I will ask for volunteers from my Seal team before they leave the country. You will need a few strong backs plus added security just in case things get dicey."

"Wonderful. When can we leave?" Kate looked directly at her husband.

"Give us a day to regroup, to check the supplies and arrange for transport."

He turned his interest to Manuel. "One more very important development. Manuel, you have been granted amnesty, for you and your family." He paused to allow that revelation to sink in. "One stipulation, Manuel, that you stay out of the political arena. As you know, that can change and probably will. You're too valuable to put on the shelf."

Manuel listened intently and weighed his options before he spoke. "Dear friend, I stay and start a business. My country needs many things. I import from America many things and produce others. Conchita will be pleased to come home to raise our children in our true home." He firmly shook Bill's hand and proceeded to shake each hand and then he placed a light kiss on Kate's cheek. "I am home where I belong."

The Ancients

The bed in the hotel felt heavenly and unwinding in the loving arms of her husband helped the trials of the past several weeks fade away. Her body and mind were spent. The long flight to Peru ended in bedlam. The murder of Raymond, Maggie, psychotic and seriously wounded, Hector's capture and his unexplained escape from the government's death squad, all these overpowering events left her mentally exhausted. Making love to her husband helped restore a delicate portion of her being. She hoped another day or two of rest would prepare her to conquer the world.

Young Carlos Minuro would meet her downstairs at precisely high noon for lunch and that might prove interesting. Her curiosity was aroused. What did he suddenly remember? His father, the old Shaman, was a man of few words but his reflections were often revealing. What bead of wisdom did he pass on to his son? She'd wait to hear his story.

As promised, the young professor lingered in the lobby, anticipating his get-together with the beautiful, brilliant archeologist who he admired. Carlos felt his loins tighten as she stepped out of the elevator. He blanched and his limbs tingled at the sight of her. He indeed had a boyish crush on the lovely doctor. He knew he couldn't act on it. He was still a neophyte. She was both worldly and married. He absorbed her radiance and inhaled her lovely, feminine scent.

"You are beautiful." The words slipped out of his mouth before he could catch them. "If only..." he stopped mid sentence for fear she would turn and leave him standing alone.

Kate smiled at his youthful good looks and honesty. "I'm flattered, Carlos. Yes, if only I were a few years younger and you were available." She momentarily held his hand then carefully released her soft grip.

"Yes, a few years older!" His smile was alarmingly handsome, his teeth white and flawless. His skin smoldered with youthful anticipation. "I apologize for my infatuation."

"No apology needed but I admit, beyond your kind flattery, I am curious why you wanted to meet with me. Why don't we find a private table in the dining room and you can tell me what brings you here, besides to tell me how beautiful I am." A warm smile crossed her face as he guided her toward the café.

Ice teas and cool salads arrived promptly and Carlos initiated conversation regarding his father and his earliest memories that were beginning to surface. "When I was very young, my father told me stories about his father and his father's father but I paid little attention. They were gone and this was now. I was young and I admit, very foolish. I believed my father to be old fashioned and even odd. Like most youngsters, I thought he was somehow embarrassing."

"Carlos, you are no different than any of us. We all learned our lessons over time with life experience, the more we endure, the more we realize our own foolishness. I 'm sorry, please, go on with your recollections."

"Do not apologize, please. I value your thoughts. Yes, you are so right. When I sent you the miner's letter that belonged to my father, I thought it might endear you to me."

"That was your motivation?" Kate was surprised that youthful hormones had driven Carlos. Her husband was right.

"Silly, yes? Childish. But now I understand the implications of my generosity. You pursued the trail to New Zealand and discovered great wealth. That you have extended a sizeable reward to me is heartening. I am grateful beyond words. Because of you, I can instruct my students and still pursue my other curiosities."

Carlos spoke from his heart and she was moved. "I am gratified. You are worthy of the reward and then some."

"There is more." The young man leaned forward and lowered his voice. "I tell you something that no one knows, except my deceased father. He told me long ago and I pushed it to the back of my mind because it meant little to me, but now with you, I see great meaning."

Kate sensed the fine hairs on her neck prickle. "What is it? I'm curious to learn what could be so profound." She leaned closer to Carlos so he could experience her warm breath.

"Deep within the rainforest, there is a tribe, an unknown tribe who has never evolved beyond the Iron Age. Their name I do not remember but my father, long ago told me of their existence. They refused to venture out of the depths of the rainforest and to this very day, have managed to avoid contact with civilized Peruvians."

Kate heard her breath escape. "Carlos, are you sure? My goodness, a lost tribe?"

"There is more, Dr. Shepherd. The symbols you copied from the ancient gourd? My father told me about them and he drew copies from memory. Dr. Shepherd, there are similar symbols etched on the sacred gourds of the lost people. My father made contact many years before. He kept their identities secret but he remembered many small things."

"What else did he remember?"

"The young couple that buried the gourd? They were most surely members of the lost tribe. Chances are they were taken from the 'others' many years ago, more than two or three hundred years, and sold into slavery."

Kate's mouth went limp. She could barely form words to express her astonishment. "Carlos, how do you know all this?"

"I did my research at the university. My father told me many stories so after meeting you at the university, I began to write them down, to make sense out of them. He often spoke in riddles and I took my time to solve each one. The miner's letter and how you followed the clues inspired me to do the same. I hope you are pleased."

"Pleased? I'm elated! Carlos." Kate reached across the table and took the young man's hands. "Carlos, you have added joy to my life. I can't begin to tell you…"

" Dr. Shepherd, I have constructed a map for you." Carlos took out the folded piece of paper. "The journey from your research site is not so far but the terrain is difficult. It will take effort but the reward may be well worth your effort." Carlos held her hands and imagined her energy flowing through him. "I wish I could go with you but I will wait to hear from you."

"This is so amazing, A lost tribe. The source of the ancient gourd. What else could I ask for? Your research is invaluable." She was eager to share Carlos' revelation with her husband and Cory.

"There is one more ancient memory borne from my father. It may be nothing or it may be ..."

"Carlos, tell me, please. What is it?"

"The gold. At the time, I believed my father spoke of dreams and, mysteries, words that I could not grasp. But now I believe he knew for certain that great stores of gold were secreted away by the Ancients, as he called them, the lost tribe. Their spirit god demanded that gold accompany them to the other world. Like the Egyptians, they created golden symbols for their afterlife. Their Ka. This tribe does the same."

Kate envisioned a new kingdom waiting for discovery then she stopped in her tracks. "I can't, we can't plunder them. Imagine it. They have lived undisturbed all these many generations. They are entitled to keep the gold. All I desire is to make contact, long enough to return the gourd and possibly learn the gourds' history. I want to finally solve the puzzle."

"I too believe they deserve to be left to themselves." Carlos admired the beautiful archeologist more than ever before. She was not looking for wealth but rather, answers to great mysteries.

Kate imagined the information she could glean from an ancient Iron Age people. But she understood the physical risks exposed to them from contact with the outside world. "I have to sleep on this. It's all so unbelievable. Kate returned from her imaginings and saw Carlos focused on her. "How can I thank you?"

"You have already thanked me, Dr. Shepherd, just by meeting with me. I will wait anxiously for word of your encounter. Until then, I must get back to my students. Thank you for the satisfying lunch." He stood, bowed politely then exited the dining room, leaving Kate at the table, surrounded by a new wave of enthusiasm.

Rainforest Revisited

Bill Shepherd returned to the hotel suite after completing a short list in preparation of their rainforest departure. Cory and Bill supervised a thorough inventory of supplies and actual distribution of the scientific equipment aboard the four government issued Land Rovers.

Once that chore was completed, Shepherd and Danielson sat their men down for a last minute refresher. Four Navy Seals had volunteered to provide both security and muscle for the expedition and Peruvian officials insisted on two key officials to travel with the team, presumably to keep tabs on any discoveries made. The numbers swelled to twenty.

Cory recruited a Montaraz, a local jungle expert to help carve a path through the thick growth and also provide local knowledge. The reminder of their party consisted of porters and drivers to set up camp, prepare meals, and work the dig site under Kate's careful supervision.

It was nearly dark when he entered their suite. Kate was sitting over her laptop, immersed in her research so Bill slipped passed, headed into the bathroom, stripped down to his naked skin and stood under a cool shower. Five minutes later, Bill was startled to see Kate join him under the light spray.

"You were engaged. I didn't think you saw me come in." Bill couldn't help but reach out and hug her silky smooth body. "We'll be ready to pull out tomorrow morning, early."

"Honey, wash my back, will you? Kate seductively turned her back to him so her beautiful bottom was impossible to resist. "Gladly, if you'll wash my front."

Bill and Kate lay on the cool sheets, a light breeze blowing the sheer curtains back and forth. They had little time alone since they landed in Peru. The events were all consuming. Tomorrow, the trek would begin and privacy would be non-existent. They had satisfied each other and now she felt ready to talk. "Honey, I've got something to tell you."

"Carlos told me everything and created a map from his father's recollections. Once we've revisited our original dig site, I'd like to retrieve the ancient gourd and return it to the rightful owners. I've hardly thought of anything else. Can you imagine, a lost nation? Of course, our visit must be fleeting. If they, in fact, have never experienced contact with the outside world, the less interaction the better. Of course, I would love to research an Iron Age culture. Can you imagine?" She cuddled close to Bill.

"What about the original site? Do you believe it will pan out, like Raymond believed it would?" He stroked her arm sending little jolts of electricity down her body. "I hope there's something of value to make everyone happy. The government permits were issued because of our earlier deductions. I'd like to see them happy and less fractious."

"I'm hoping. As you know, there are no guarantees but I'll dream about it and maybe my dreams will come true." Kate rolled over, turned down the light and fell into a sound, satisfying sleep.

The caravan was on the road before the sun broke above the horizon line. It was a cool morning and spirits were running high. Bill, Cory and Kate drove the lead vehicle and before long, they turned off the maintained highway onto what looked like a drug cartel road, a roughly graded strip of washboard. When the road narrowed further and the foliage impeded their progress, a few men ran ahead with their machetes, hacking their way through the overgrowth.

The progress was slow but steady and the lead team had time to talk as they took turns behind the wheel. "This is pretty typical going. Before long, we'll be on foot." Cory skillfully maneuvered the Land Rover around various obstacles. "Kate, you've been here before but after the heavy rains, the terrain is choked with growth."

"Yes, it was a grueling hike in but we approached from a different direction. There were elevation changes that took some getting used to."

"Once we leave the vehicles, things will get interesting. Do you know how to survive in the rainforest?" Cory checked out Kate with his rear view mirror. He was smiling playfully. "Well, do you?"

"I suppose so, but Cory, why don't you give us both a lesson on survival. It will make the time fly." Kate leaned forward and rested her hands on the two headrests.

"OK! Who is that guy out there swinging his machete, the one with the colorful sash?"

"I don't know. I guess one of your hired hands. Who is he?" Bill joined in the exercise.

"Half right. He's a Montaraz, meaning a local jungle expert. When I say, *walk like a Montaraz,* what do I mean?"

"I have no idea."

"It means you incline your body forward and take long or short steps but never run. You always look down to avoid tripping or falling. A cut out here can lead to serious infection. And of course the Montaraz says, *never deviate your course more than 20 degrees.* So now you know about the Montaraces, plural." Cory smiled in the mirror? "More?"

"Yes, I'm enjoying this." Kate passed bottles of water to the men in the front seat. "Continue."

"Do you want to know about fording rivers or making camp?"

Bill piped in, "Cory, before we get involved in your "how to" survival manual, we better fill you in on something pretty remarkable. Kate, tell him."

Cory listened intently as Kate outlined her meeting with Carlos and the revelation regarding the lost tribe and the ancient gourd.

"Well, damn it all, that is incredible. I understand how isolated tribes can exist out of the public eye but to have never made human contact outside their little world is mind-boggling. I remember the Tasaday tribe in the Philippines, still living in the Stone Age. They fought wars and flew jets over the Philippines and still they remained untouched. Well, all the more reason for my tutorial on survival! Still ready to play?"

"Absolutely, yes!" He was right. Entering virgin forest would be challenging and survival knowledge was more than a parlor game.

"Good. OK! Let's talk fording rivers, which we will very likely have to do once we get into deep forest. Monunas is the local name for a strong whirlpool. Cocha means quiet waters. Both terms are important to remember. OK, your turn, what lives in calm waters? Bill, this is yours."

"A wild guess. Piranhas, a nasty, flesh eating fish."

"Spot on! Bravo! Do you know Carneros? Bill?"

"Refresh me."

"A Carneros is a small cylindrical shaped fish with two fins in the shape of the barbs of an arrow point. These little fish will bite if you cross the still water. They will twist and turn until they rip off a piece of your flesh. The blood you loose will agitate the Piranhas who will attack with a vengeance."

"Ouch!" Kate exaggerated a shuddered. I think I'll stay out of the water."

"OK, then how do we stay out of the water? Bill."

"We build a raft?" He knew the drill but was enjoying the informative banter.

"Spot on."

"And what do we build it out of, Kate?"

"I assume wood. Unless we can use palm fronds. No, I'll stick with wood."

"You're right choosing wood, but what kind?"

"I can guess but go and tell us. You're an excellent instructor." Kate shifted positions and sipped her water.

"Thank you for the complement. Balsa is the wood of choice. It's light and easy to work with. Most rainforest wood sinks because it is filled with water. So, to summarize, be careful crossing any waterway, river, stream or swamp. The fish will eat you and if they fail, the mosquitoes may succeed."

"Very informative. What about camping?"

"Glad you asked. The best place to build a shelter in the rainforest? Let me begin with the *don'ts* and *nevers.* Never camp on open banks or river beaches. They appear to be ideal sites but they also look ideal to caiman and big cats."

"What else?" Kate felt like taking notes.

"Stay away from humid earth or dry leaves. Why, you ask. A vast array of insects, love humid earth and snakes take refuge under the leaves. A side note. If you do have leaves to remove, always use a branch, not your hand or foot. The Peruvian rainforest has a number of venomous snakes. We'll cover that later."

"You told us where to not camp. Where's safe?"

"Well Kate, you're a great student, if you want to build a shelter in the rainforest, choose a high place away from swamps. Regardless of where we camp, there will be clouds of mosquitoes so we will use our netting and slather ourselves in Cutter's."

"How about setting fires?"

"Yes, Bill, fires are important. The smoke will keep insects at bay and discourage animals from entering the camp. Gather dried grasses and wood, not always easy to find in a rainforest. And never venture off alone. If you have to pee, take someone with you who has good hearing but bad eyesight. Seriously, the Rainforest is a very hostile place."

"Anything else?"

"Yes, a few more *nevers.* Never make camp under a tall tree. Old branches could fall and crush you. Never take off your clothing, even to sleep. Always tuck your pants into your rubber boots, even at night and if any bare skin is exposed, cover yourself with mud to avoid insect bites. Lastly, always dig a six or seven inch trench around the campsite for drainage. There's a valid reason why it's called a rainforest. "

"That was very informative, but what about contact with indigenous tribes?" Bill leveled the question at Cory but Kate answered.

"That's my territory, gentlemen. First, most native populations have had some contact with white men and women but where we are eventually heading, we may find ourselves to be the first contact made from the outside world."

If that's the case, we must walk with confidence and avoid aggressive motions. We should offer gifts, some object to attract their attention."

"Like colorful glass beads? I packed a container for that purpose." The beads were on the inventory requirements and he was pleased his supplier had filled the order.

"Perfect. Where was I? If we require it, ask for help using hand gestures to convey our needs. Always respect their laws and customs and never enter their huts unless invited."

"What else?" Cory caught her eye in the mirror.

"Let's see. No sudden or suspicious movements and never reprimand their potentially odd behaviors, like playing tricks on us or grabbing our belongings. But we should never pick up their belongings especially their weapons. By doing that, it could be interpreted as a threatening behavior on our part."

"What about food and eating and drinking?" Bill knew the answer but wanted to hear Kate outline it.

"Unfortunately, this is difficult for me. Never refuse food regardless of how much it disgusts you. The same with drink. If you are offered live bugs, eat them, drinks made from urine or animal blood, drink it and gag later. Refusing to share food and drink is considered a serious insult among nearly all indigenous tribes."

"We may have to put all of this information into practice before we're through. Seriously, the roads ahead will be filled with peril and our goal has to be vigilance. We need to come out the other end unscathed. Personally, my greatest concerns are simple cuts leading to infection or a snakebite that can be fatal. We've packed a pretty substantial first aid kit but out here, we're on our own." Bill felt protective of Kate and regardless of the nature of the adventure, he wanted it known that the untouched rainforest was a dangerous place.

Burial Site

The shelters were erected on a high place away from the swamp with everyone lending a hand. After two nights sleeping either in their vehicles or in a rough campsite that was too close to a wetland for anyone's comfort, the partially excavated site was paradise.

The three-team leaders leaned against the rocky promontory, the place where Bill originally discovered the ancient gourd. Kate had carefully extracted the small object and after wrapping it in a soft rabbit skin, she placed it in a waterproof satchel. "The dig is going smoothly."

The ground had been laid out in a traditional grid design and the workers were carefully removing layers of dirt and debris. When human bones were finally uncovered, a series of photographs were taken along with tiny bone samples that were tagged, wrapped in cotton and placed in small paper bags. Eventually, they would make their way back to the Smithsonian labs for DNA testing and carbon dating.

The bodies had been laid side by side in prone positions. They were not, like custom, buried in a sitting or fetal position dressed in traditional clothing and handmade footwear alongside their tools of the trade. The evidence suggested a massacre site, perhaps of indigenous people. The remains included small children and an elderly male.

Several pottery shards and beads were collected then the team rested and ate. It had been two days and still no signs of gold.

"Maybe Raymond's instincts were wrong. I was hoping we'd stumble upon something." Kate lay back on the rocks, "No guarantees. We'll give it another day then send the team back to the rendezvous site. The Land Rovers will livery them back to the city. Our little party will head in the opposite direction."

Cory had chosen his two best men and the skilled Montaraz, Yarro to join their mission into the deep rainforest in an effort to make contact with the lost tribe where Kate could return the gourd to its rightful owner.

Carlos' map had been computer generated and when Bill plotted a GPS course, they understood how difficult their trek would be. They'd have to ford rivers and streams, avoid the flesh eating fish and swat the Manta Blanca, the small mosquitoes that continuously plagued them.

"Did you notice that tree over there?" Bill was visually surveying the area and something caught his eye. "It's the only one like it in the area. Pretty unusual! Most trees sprout from acorns or some kind of seed pod. The young tree stands close to the parent."

"You know, that's pretty observant. An incongruity, but what are you thinking?"

"Kate, come with me. You too, Cory." Bill stretched his stiff back and walked along the perimeter of the dig. "I don't know but I have a funny feeling about this." He approached the tree and gave it a cursory inspection. "It's old and it's dying. Look at the insects burrowing into the bark and the moss around its base. The trunk is turning the bark to peat."

"I had no idea you were a horticulturist. How long have we been married?" Kate knelt down next to her husband, Cory over her shoulder.

"What's so special about this tree?" Cory hadn't grasped the significance of an anomaly, an unusual, old, dying tree within a stone's throw of a massacre site.

Bill pulled away the thick layer of moss and exposed bulging, rotting roots, the circumference of his forearm. "Please Kate, hand me your pocket knife." He took it from her and began to chip away at the root. "I see something shiny, maybe a stone or..." With his bare fingers, he pried out a shiny orb of gold. "Sweet Jesus."

Kate reached over and took the gold nugget between her fingers and held it to the light. "Well, I'll be..."

"Is that what I think it is?" Cory knelt down on the other side of Bill. "I can't believe you two!"

As discretely as possible, the trio chopped away at the thick root system extracting a dozen or more coin size globs of pure gold.

"Cory, call your best men!"

When the tree was finally felled, the golden nuggets increased a thousand times. Cory organized his men and carefully, as the gold was retrieved, each piece was inventoried and packed away for transport. Raymond had been correct even though the location of the find was a complete surprise.

"That's two for you!" Kate sat next to Bill observing the men hard at work.

"Oh, OK! First the gourd, and now the gold. Intuition is usually a woman's domain but somehow, probably luck." Bill was more surprised than anyone. He never considered himself particularly intuitive.

By morning, the gold site had been exhausted but the final count was astonishing. It would require strong backs to carry the bootie to the rendezvous point. The Peruvian government would be ecstatic. And so would young Carlos. A portion would go towards his personal educational fund. Bill, Kate and Cory, along with the members of their team would be rewarded for their efforts as well. And Raymond would receive credit, posthumously. It was a very good day.

The trail had disappeared a long way back and other than narrow animal trails, the machetes they carried cut a barely passable swath of earth. The hastily constructed balsa rafts carried them across the quiet waters and they avoided the flesh eating fish. The mosquitoes swarmed and Kate discovered mud did little to protect her exposed skin. Her pant legs were tucked into her rubber boots but still, she burned away half dozen leaches that found their way up her covered calf.

Their parlor game came in very handy. So far, the GPS and Carlos' map were on course. Another few miles of chopping and slicing through dense plant growth should bring them to the edge of the lost tribe's territory.

Yarro, the Montaraz, did a superb job guiding them along their route. Without him, the trek would have been more treacherous. His innate knowledge of the land was remarkable.

"Where's Yarro?" They had taken a short break so Kate could relieve herself within sight of the temporary camp. Yarro was asked to guard her while she was separated from the group. "Did you see him? I looked for him but he's not with me."

Bill and Cory undertook measured searches around the area but came back empty handed. "He's gone. He's vanished into the jungle. Just walked away. Damn. He's gone." Bill had put stock in the tracker. "Not much we can do. We sure as Hell can't go after him."

"Do you suppose we're getting too close to the lost tribe and Yarro ran off because, well, perhaps he's superstitious of the lost people or even fearful?" Her rational was plausible. "I imagine not all forest people are accepting of each other. Since he joined us, he's shared very little with us. There had to be a logical reason for him to high tail it out of here, don't you think?"

"Kate, you're probably right. Yarro's disappeared into the forest and I have to believe we've seen the last of him. But not to worry. We still have the GPS and the sat phones so we're OK. If we run into trouble, serious trouble, we can call in support." Bill gave Kate a reassuring hug. She was surrounded by a crack group of survivalists. Not to worry.

They picked up their machetes, repositioned their backpacks then proceeded further into the dense growth minus their native guide.

Contact

Kate and her crack team were not alone. Like ghost people, the small hunting party watched the white men and the woman with the golden hair. They stalked the white skinned strangers as they cut their way through the dense edges of the land. They silently watched as the intruders constructed sleeping platforms and raised strange cloth shelters.

The curls of smoke drifting from the campfires carried the scent of wild fowl. They continued to observe as the white men and the woman with the golden hair, picked at the delicate bones. The lost people strained to hear unintelligible chatter. Mostly, they concentrated on the odd, unusually tall female with the shiny gold hair and the pale skin.

The indigenous hunting party was one with their habitat, their deep burnished skin smeared with clay. Trial and error over eons guided them to natural protection from aggressive swarms of insects. Primitive scarifications displayed by individual members of the hunting party marked their status within the isolated society.

They debated what to do. Should they avoid the white intruders or boldly, with weapons raised, announce themselves? Would the encounter delay their hunting trip?

The lost people lived off the land and the land was generous. There was little need to venture far from the village. Trees were harvested and young seedlings sprouted and quickly grew in the rich, moist environment. The same was true of edible plants and tubers along with the small animals and edible insects collected from under the massive leaf carpet or deep within the recesses of tree bark. Of all the ecosystems on the planet, the rainforest is, by far, the most abundant producer of everything human beings require to survive and flourish.

The white men and woman, who cut a path closer to the settlements did not alarm the lost people, but rather, heightened their curiosity. This was a peculiar event. Deep forest was virgin and so were its people. Could it be the lost people displayed no fear? Could it be possible their unique, hidden society was so far removed from the other world, so isolated, they were able to feign death?

Still, the ancient stories recited over and over told different tales. Yes, their revered medicine man shared the ancient mythologies but to his audience, the stories were more dream than reality. Yet, a seed was planted. Beyond the depths of their rainforest world, danger lurked. The ancient memories held mysteries, frightening stories of lost people who vanished into the mist who forever walk the spirit world.

Within their secret society, stood six individual villages. Each chose a leader whose primary responsibility was to keep order and settle domestic disputes. The medicine man, a holy man, held court in the largest of the six villages. The mother of his mother had been medicine woman. Then she passed to the land of spirits. The old man of fifty had sat at her feet and now he told the stories, ground the herbs and roots and brewed the healing teas.

Pubescent males and females, brought together by their elders were ceremonially coupled for life but men could choose to take a second wife, most likely, an older, barren woman or young widow who would live under the same roof to help with the children and household chores. Both babies and women died often during childbirth or shortly thereafter. It was understood and sadly routine. The medicine man could only do so much. Isolation also had its benefits. There was no measles or other childhood illnesses that plagued the other world.

Children died of other things. Snakebites claimed young and old although some members of the lost tribe had been bitten so many times, they produced their own anti venom. Children and adults drowned, often victims of the deadly Piranha, yet still, the lost people bathed, washed their clothing and fished in the infested, quiet water.

Their shelters were large, round and communal, constructed from the materials of the rainforest. To ward off heavy downpours, they continually made repairs, piling giant leaves on the tilting overhangs.

The lives of the lost people were simple by comparison to the outside world. Ignorance was bliss. Primary was the search for food. They were hunters and gatherers. The rainforest provided for them but at a price. The price was effort. Harvesting the rainforest took exertion and their bodies suffered. The cuts and scratches earned while gathering a handful of edible tubers or mushrooms and the stings tolerated while smoking out a honey filled beehive took industry. Their small world was abundant and there was no reason to plant domestic crops. The concept was as foreign as the industrial revolution.

For eons, reverence for life and the power of the spirit world bound the indigenous peoples together. Departed tribal lives were celebrated with mystical and secret ritual. The bright gold stones, found in abundance within their hidden world, were collected, and polished then carefully placed on the bodies of their dead then they were laid to rest in an ancient burial ground.

The ancient myths promised the bright gold stones would guide the deceased from this world to the spirit world. Like stars in the sky, the brilliant stones offered a clear path to follow.

"Did you see that?" On alert, Hank, a member of the Seals, suddenly lifted his machete into a defensive position. Silently, like moths attracted to a flame, the small band emerged from the misty forest. Cory, Kate and Bill reacted to the slight rustle then in unison, they rose and turned to face the group of five who appeared curious and timid. The hunting party presented their spears in a non-threatening manner and the entire team took notice.

"Stand down, men." Cory followed Kate's tutorial. "Easy men, no sudden or suspicious movements." The lost people took a step forward, their apparent leader a full arm's length ahead. Kate stood and extended her hands, palms up. In turn the lost people raised their hands in similar fashion.

The military men were less comfortable laying down their arms but managed to set them down within arm's reach. "Hank, the glass beads." Cory hoped a gift would ease the strain. Hank slowly moved towards the waterproof pack and extracted a colorful handful of strung glass beads. He passed them to Kate who moved forward and extended her hand towards the leader of the slight group, a middle age male whose face and arms were ornamented with elaborate scarification.

He reached out and accepted the gift, ran his thick, fingers over the colorful, shiny surfaces, then smelled the unfamiliar stones. Finally, he raised the beads to his lips, sniffed the long strand then caressed the stones with his tongue. When satisfied, he handed the strings of glass- beads to the younger man standing behind him. The proud leader turned to face Kate, reached out and lightly touched her golden hair. A grin revealed a row of shiny gold teeth. Kate's team managed a collective gasp. They couldn't help but notice his gleaming dental work.

As quickly as they appeared, they melded into the rainforest. "Where did they go?" Kate's thoughts were flying everywhere. "Did you see the gold? His teeth were solid gold."

Bill moved alongside Kate. "Well, one thing's for sure. We've verified their existence! Carlos led us right to the door of their lost world."

Cory reached for the machete he had dropped at his feet. "And the gold. They must have a source close by." He dusted off his backpack and slung it over his shoulder. "What now?"

"Oh my God, I forgot. I had the gourd in my pack and I simply forgot about it. I was so taken aback by them walking out of the thick cover, I could barely keep it together. I was more fearful than they were."

"Kate, honey, you did great. I was worried when he touched your hair. It was the first time he ever saw blond hair."

"I'm certain we were all new to them. Dark eyes, dark hair and dark skin are the standard rather than the exception throughout this part of the world. I'm an oddity. It's reasonable that he wanted to touch my hair."

The two Seals had taken a short tour of the area and returned with news. Hank spoke up. "Agent Danielson, if I can interrupt, the small band of hunters rejoined our original trail and continued in that general direction. I could observe footprints but little else."

"Well, at least we know we were on the right track. Now the question begs an answer. Do we continue on?" Bill knew the answer in advance.

"Of course! We've come this far and the lost tribe is receptive, not hostile and I have something of theirs, the gourd. "

Cory watched Kate's face lit up at the sight of the lost tribe. "I'm willing, if anyone else is but I think once we get closer to their village, we remain along the perimeter and let Bill and Kate proceed to their chief or medicine man. They can make the presentation of the gourd without disturbing the order of things. That way, we make brief contact and leave quickly. We can move a respectable distance before we call for a chopper." They had spent hours debating the effects of outside forces on the untouched Iron Age culture and he knew both Kate and Bill, supported this minimal contact approach.

"If we take off now, we'll have a few hours to find a new campsite, get a night's rest then seek out the village. We can send our Seals out on a little search and discovery so we know what to expect. You saw how they were able to creep up on us. They'll probably see us before we see them again. They move through their forest like ghosts. Like Yarro." Bill Shepherd was eager to press on. The insects were beginning to swarm

Bill led the way, still glancing around for Yarro, in case he was still lurking nearby. They covered another grueling mile, checking the GPS and Carlos' map to make sure they were deadheading. The foreign landscape became claustrophobic as the swampland pressed closer to the makeshift trail and the air reaked from rotting foliage. They marched on even though their bellies growled with hunger.

Bill Shepherd, tired to the bone, rounded a thick overgrowth of trees supporting a tangle of vines that wound through and over the saddled branches and canopy. Out of this mass of moisture-laden leaves, a luminescent object suddenly dropped towards the ground but instead, landed on Bill's broad shoulder. Instinctively, he turned his head to the left, in time to catch a glimpse of a small, green snake. Before he could react defensively, the snake latched into the soft tissue below his ear.

Bill's hand punched the snake to the ground where it slithered into the thick groundcover. "It bit me, the snake, the Green Tree Viper caught me on the neck."

Cory grabbed Bill's shoulder and forced him around. His eyes were already loosing focus. "Are you sure it was a Green Viper?" He was immediately searching his pack for the anti venom syringe filled with polyvalence. The properties worked on most venomous snakebites.

Kate froze in her tracks. She heard "snake". The rainforest was home to many poisonous varieties. The Green Tree Viper had a reputation for being one of the most deadly. The reaction to its bite ran the gamut from a painful, deep edema at the source of the bite to unbearable pain followed by loss of consciousness, loss of kidney function, very high fever and eventually death. "What kind of snake?"

The Seals cleared a small area and had Bill on the ground. Cory uncapped the syringe then administered the clear anti venom in his thigh. "Green Tree Viper." He pulled away Bill's shirt and studied the position of the fangs.

""What can I do? Kate felt helpless but she didn't want to panic. Everything happened so quickly. The accompanying Navy Seals sprung forward and swiped at the branches to make sure the snake didn't have a friend. "Cory, let me help." She dropped to the ground and rested Bill's head in her lap. He was lapsing into a coma. "Bill, honey, don't sleep, please. The anti venom will work soon." She wasn't sure about that.

Cory barked orders to his men to lift and carry his best friend and fellow agent. They had to find a high, level area to treat him further. The point of penetration was problematic. The toxic venom was likely pumped directly into the jugular and even with the anti venom being quickly administered it might not neutralize the effects of the deadly Green Tree Viper.

"Please don't leave me. Don't die." She stayed at his side as they moved his slack body.

The Seals discovered, level, dry ground a hundred yards west of where they were heading. They quickly formed a MASH unit, fashioned a makeshift bed, draped it with mosquito netting then combined a plastic water bottle with a length of PVC tubing to Jeri rig a useable IV drip. Bill Shepherd lay fitfully, one moment grimacing in pain, the next, drifting into a restless sleep. Kate gently wiped his hot brow with a dampened cloth. His fever was dangerously high enough to be concerned about seizure.

"The sat phone won't pull up a signal." The battery was charged but for whatever reason, the *no signal* flashed. "Keep trying." Cory did all he could do. They had to summon a chopper into the area for an emergency extraction. "Damn, keep trying."

"He's burning up. The anti venom isn't working." Kate held her husband's limp hand. "Is there anything else we can do?"

"Kate, we have him on saline fluid drip so he won't dehydrate and he got the full dose of anti venom. Now it's up to Bill." He wanted to sound more optimistic but the location of the bite was the worst possible. He wasn't a praying man but he figured this was a good time to start.

"There should be a satellite overhead. Why the hell can't we get a signal?" It was getting dark, the mosquitoes were coming in waves and Bill was failing. "We have to do something before it gets dark." Cory and his men were growing more frustrated as the sun lowered in the sky. Bill could hang on for a few days but if his kidneys failed, it was all over for him. One dose of anti venom was powerful. A second dose could be dangerous.

Bill was his best friend. They had always been there for each other. Cory could count on two hands how many times Bill had pulled his ass out of the fire. It was Cory's turn to come through but he was in deep water. A skilled crew surrounded him but, like he told Kate, fighting off the effects of the snakebite was now up to Bill.

"No signal." The state of the art gear was failing at a critical time. "Try again."

The lost people came out of nowhere. They had been watching, saw the snake fall out of the tree and leave its deadly mark on the white man's neck. The dreaded Green Tree Viper was killed and the leader threw the snake on the ground at Bill's feet.

As if in a trance, the tribal leader with the unusual scarifications, moved forward and dropped to his knees directly alongside the stricken man. He stuck his right thumb in the soft loam then pressed his toughened thumb against Shepherd's feverish forehead. He rubbed the remaining earth over each of his closed eyes. All the while, he was mouthing peculiar words. Then he grasped the small, limp snake and placed it against his lips then against Bill Shepherd's ugly wound. He was willing the poison back into the snake.

Kate, Cory and the two Seals, stood silently, enthralled as the tribal leader worked his magic over Bill's stricken body. The tribe of lost people stood opposite their leader, solemnly observing his sacred ritual that to this point had only been performed on members of their ancient tribe.

On cue, one tribal member gather dried grass, and with a flint, ignited a small fire that grew as more fuel was added. Once the fire blazed, he stepped forward, took the dead Green Tree Viper from his leader and lowered it to the flames. The sound of skin-popping as the snake was consumed made Kate's skin bristle. Within minutes, the small snake was reduced to a blackened, twisted mass.

The lost people surrounded the makeshift gurney then lifted it and without a sound, followed the old path. They caught Kate and her team by surprise but without question, they retrieved their backpacks and filed after the tribal men who were transporting Bill Shepherd's stricken body.

Kate felt herself drift back in time, drifting far away from the familiar world she occupied. The ancient world she entered bore remarkable similarities to the books she read as a graduate student, those with exploratory articles and elaborate artist renderings of what ancient tribal life was perceived to be.

The faces of the children were bright and curious. They exhibited the same curiosity as the sunny faces playing in Central Park. As the interlopers followed Bill Shepherd's prone body, villagers surrounded them and touched their strange clothing. The leader raised his hand and the curious onlookers stepped back to let the strangers pass.

The tribal leader motioned to lower the gurney outside the draped entry to the largest and most central lodge. The roughly constructed lodge was built with hand formed mud brick, animal dung, dry grass and massive leaves that covered the slanted roof and overhang that protected the entry and sheltered a stone fire pit from frequent, soaking rains.

Kate was numb. She held Bill's hand as they approached the village and could feel his weak pulse tracing through her body. Cory stood by her side with the two Seals. Nothing had gone according to plan but well trained military were skilled chameleons. The situation changed, they adapted. Right now, the primary concern was Bill's condition and his chances for recovery. The administered anti venom should be taking effect, if it was going to work. Cory would inject a second dose in another hour. The primitive IV drip had been refilled once along the way and was nearly empty. Kidney failure was a concern and it was important to continue to flush his system and keep him hydrated.

The leader of the lost people had contributed the best spiritual medicine could offer. If nothing else, the character of the lost people was elevated to a higher plateau. They were gentle and caring people.

The leader disappeared inside the main lodge, presumably to confer with others regarding their encounter with the white strangers. Moments later, the leader appeared, draped in a ceremonial cloak, his face dyed brilliant shades of blue and deep sienna. The leader assumed the imposing role of medicine man. It made sense, considering the snake ceremony and the firm control he had over the hunting party.

The Holy Man knelt down and placed his palm on Bill's feverish brow then mouthed the same words spoken during the snake ritual hours ago. Kate could not decipher the language but the nuances were revealing. A prayer is a prayer in any language. She smiled at the impressively cloaked Holy Man and in turn, he leaned forward and touched her golden hair.

Kate felt a pang of regret, not only for Bill's plight but also for their intrusion. These people had been able to avoid the mean spirited 'other' world and observing their concern over a strange white man was heartening. She reached for her backpack and extracted the fur wrapped bundle and carefully placed it in the Holy Man's hands.

He stared at the gift, stroked the soft rabbit fur then rubbed the pelt to his cheek. He grinned with delight, showing once more, the even row of gold teeth. Kate motioned that he should unwrap the bundle and as he began, Kate held her breath. Would the gourd bring back ancient memories or would he regard the carved, burned gourd as an odd, foreign object?

The Holy Man let the fur fall away as he took the smooth object in his hands, turning it round and round. He rose to his feet and disappeared behind the draped entry of the lodge. Kate sat on the ground, perplexed. The Holy Man reappeared with an elder who was carrying a strange bundle of dried moss.

They squatted on either side of Kate and the old man pulled away the moss covering, revealing a nearly identical gourd. Kate found it difficult to control her joy. She held both gourds in her hands and examined their likeness. The symbols were nearly identical, the deep stained surface a perfect match. The Holy Man pointed at his face and Kate realized the symbols were replicated in his scarification.

She had spent months speculating the meaning of the symbols and why the gourd existed. Now it was clear. The sacred gourd had been hidden away before a massacre took members of their lost tribe to their spirit world. The perpetrators were presumably from the outside world.

Kate scanned the boundaries of the village and admired a grove of beautiful, tall trees that cast deep shadows over the settlement. The trees were the same variety that stood alongside the burial site and marked the location of the gold. They had estimated the lone tree to be approximately two hundred years old, the same time as the massacre.

Cory caught sight of the two identical gourds and signaled an affirmative thumbs up. He knew how important this moment was to Kate. She had placed her professional reputation on the line along with her trust in Carlos and his father's revelations. Now, if Bill would recover.

He was resting peacefully and the fever was lessening. While he slept, Kate spent time with the Holy Man and the elders. She didn't try to understand their language. It was as unique as the people. With hand signals and facial expressions, they described their life in the rainforest.

After so many villagers had tried to touch her hair, she produced a small knife and cut a lock of her hair. She handed it to the Holy Man and his spirit turned solemn. Reverently carrying the lock of hair, he walked with Kate to the main lodge, where he carefully placed her hair in the newly returned gourd. Reciting a short prayer, he took her hand and led her to a smaller lodge that sat on the edge of the village.

He paused at the draped entry. There were sounds emanating from within the shadowed lodge. The nameless Holy Man pulled the drape aside and they entered. Kate withheld a gasp. A male child lay on a bed of green leaves. His body was cold and ash gray in death. Two females, one the child's mother, the other perhaps a grandmother, carefully prepared his body for the spirit world. The Holy Man motioned Kate to a corner of the lodge where she sat and observed the solemn ritual.

Trouble

The small caravan arrived at the rendezvous site and unloaded the gold they had carefully guarded. The driver's were trusted government agents, ordered to cart the find back to Lima, to a secure vault for final tabulation. The find had been well documented by Kate and Bill Shepherd and their accounts would assure the gold would end up in the proper hands. But corruption was still an issue.

The planners of the expedition were still embedded in the deep rainforest for reasons, not fully understood. But their participation in the original find plus their thorough reports would determine who would be eligible to the lions' share of the find. If they were *permanently* lost in the treacherous rainforest, the distribution of wealth would be much simpler.

The remaining two Navy Seals' responsibilities ceased when they delivered the gold and their party to the Land Rovers and the waiting Peruvian government representatives. They were dismissed with little ceremony and being well-trained agents of the USA, red flags went up immediately.

As the trucks were being loaded the two men worked their way out of sight and pulled out the secure sat phone. The screen flashed *no signal*. Impossible. The equipment had been checked out from top to bottom. They were professionals and no detail got past them. They sensed a serious situation developing. As they observed the greedy faces of the government agents, they knew their instincts were correct.

It had been two days since they abandoned the burial site and parted company with the other two Seals, Dr. Jenkins Shepherd, Agents Danielson and Shepherd and the field guide, Yarro. The small search part had another day or so to go before they would reach their destination. According to Agent Danielson's vague description of their destination, they understood it to be an undercover op. The Seals punched in GPS coordinates and noted a looping river that would connect to the established position of that destination. They had time if they moved out now.

The thrill of a gold treasure had the party engaged. The Seals repacked their gear and secured the cache of weapons and grenades. Without raising suspicion, they disappeared into the rainforest.

Recovery

Twelve hours after arrival in the ancient village, Bill opened his eyes. Kate wrapped her arms around him and kissed him. "I was so worried. I thought I lost you." He reached up and wiped a tear away.

"Where am I?" Bill tried to sit up but found his head loose on his shoulders.

Kate sat next to him and described the events of the last two days. He remembered the Viper, but from that point forward, his memory was foggy. He listened as she described the gentle ancient tribe, the snake rite and how they made their way into the village. She emotionally described the presentation of the gourd. She spoke about the identical gourd, cutting her hair, the beautiful grove of trees and lastly, the heart wrenching funeral preparation. She described in detail the constellation -like golden pattern that covered the young body.

Cory and his men joined the couple. Bill got to his feet and with some assistance, took a walk around the small village. Young and old alike approached and touched their clothing, then giggled in delight. They welcomed an assortment of foods, primarily vegetarian and exotic. They shared the remainder of the colorful glass beads to the delight of the women who put them around their necks. Black hair, straight and shiny as onyx capped the heads of every member of both sexes and all ages. Clothing was simple and layered when the temperature dropped. A few lost people wore leather sandals that were cut from the rugged skins of the caiman, attached with strips of cord that wrapped around their sturdy ankles. Everything they needed was gathered in the surrounding area.

The Last Battle

"Bill, we have a problem." Now that he was up and recovering, Cory and his Seals had to let him know about the problem with the sat phones. "We tried when you went down and nothing. Our only conclusion is sabotage. Yarro deserted camp around the same time and I've got that itch, the one that tells me trouble's brewing.

Cory and his men had come to the same conclusion as their counterparts overseeing the gold shipment. "By now, they've loaded the trucks and my men have tried to make contact with us. When the sat phone failed, I am certain they drew on their experience and came up with "Plan C". According to my GPS, there is a river that skirts the area. It winds in and out but eventually it takes us back to the cartel road. My men by now are making their way to us."

"What are you thinking?" Bill was still putting the scenario together.

""We don't believe in coincidence. Yarro, abandoning camp gave it away. He disables the phones, marks our position, and takes off to meet his small war party that is eager to take us out. It makes sense. And by our calculations, we are cutting it close. If we leave first thing in the morning, we should meet up with my men in time to take on the insurgents. But there's a chance we'll have to hold them at bay while we wait for reinforcements."

"So you think we've been marked." It wasn't a question. "Does Kate know?"

"I had a talk with her and laid it out. She wants to get as far away from this village as we can. She's bent on keeping it a lost society. She's grown fond of the people and she wants them unaffected." Cory shifted his weight as they walked along the perimeter. She felt guilty leaving the beads. She likened it to the movie, "The Gods Must Be Crazy", the indigenous tribe with the Coke bottle falling from the sky."

"I remember it. I can see her point but I'm not going to be an Indian giver. The tribe will covet those beads for centuries."

"Regardless, I suggest we pack up, say our fond farewells then make our way to the river. Maybe they will provide a guide to point the way. Kate can handle a machete and we may need it. We'll have to construct a substantial raft and plan on poles to get up stream. It won't be easy but it's doable." Hiking exposed them to a variety of creatures that could kill them. They found that out earlier. At least, in the river, they knew the enemy, sharp-toothed caiman and two very aggressive fish, who traveled in schools, and who could devour a human in minutes.

The departure was poignant. The nameless Holy Man, surrounded by the elders and children, walked the small group of strangers to the edge of their kingdom, where the calm river twisted through the rich foreboding forest. The lost people abruptly stopped and their leader reached into a small pouch he wore around his neck. He extracted an orb of gold the size of a robin's egg. He placed it in Kate's hand then turned on his heels. They were gone.

Kate stared down at the smooth object; it's coolness warming her heart. The lost people would remain lost. She would never divulge their location or the ancient customs that made them unique. She hoped the beads would remain their only gift from the outside world.

The Holy Man left three strapping young men to help construct a raft and it took a couple of intense hours to build a useable, sturdy raft that could handle both the river's unpredictable current and also provide a viable fighting platform. The lost people gathered balsa and the Seals cut it into manageable lengths. They lashed them together with vines as tough and strong as cable.

The river would run against them so they cut and stripped green saplings to make long, supple poles to propel the raft forward. To steer the craft, they fashioned a rudder and firmly strapped it to the aft section of the raft. It was a substantial accomplishment.

Kate allowed the able-bodied men to construct the raft. They were powerfully built and worked well as a unit. She sat in a small clearing by the water and fingered her two keepsakes, the carved bone she discovered in Arrowtown and the beautiful, solid gold egg given to her with such reverence by the Holy Man of the lost tribe.

She chose not to learn his name or the names of his people. That would make them real and she wanted them to remain invisible. The funerary stones. If rumored to exist, the so-called civilized world that ardently sought the precious metal would destroy their ancient world.

The three youthful tribesmen sensed the completion of the large, sturdy raft. Before the team could express thanks, they became ghosts and vanished into the verdant forest.

They took inventory of the small cache of weapons stowed in their backpacks. The numbers were adequate to confront a well-armed raiding party. Besides two short barreled Glocks, with four boxes of hollow tipped ammunition, Cory carried six grenades, an eight inch finely honed knife and his machete. Bill Shepherd carried the exact weapons minus the long bladed knife. He preferred a six-inch blade that tucked neatly into his pant leg.

Kate carried extra ammunition for the hefty handguns and her field-tested machete. Each Navy Seal was equipped with a short-barreled AK47, extra munitions, a knife, grenades, flares and their machetes. Their best weapon was the superior training and discipline of the men manning the hand built raft. The small company counted on support from the outside, trusting the Seals were on their way, but when they would connect was anybody's guess.

They set sail on their maiden voyage and the raft handled better than expected. It was light and maneuverable and traversed the shallows well. The only problem was their exposure. They were sitting ducks and after negotiating a mile upstream, they decided to pull alongside a sheltered bank and make a few alterations.

The men spotted a stand of bamboo and proceeded to collect a substantial quantity. They lashed the bamboo together into a bullet resistant super structure that attached to the raft like a manageable sail. They allowed for openings, large enough to sight their weapons and hoped it would give them a level of protection.

The tributary of the Amazon took them further from the ancient settlement and Kate was relieved. They were sailing into a dangerous encounter yet the lost people of the rainforest would be assured a peaceful, undisturbed existence.

The group discussed Yarro's suspected betrayal and who exactly, secured his allegiance. Most likely, Yarro was a pawn, promised whatever his heart desired to switch loyalties to a corrupt government faction. They would never deliver. By consensus, they planned for a combined government/insurgent attack, presumably by water, the most efficient traveling route. Yarro's men would be superior mounting a land attack, with a force of at least twenty soldiers but a water attack would benefit the smaller American force.

As they guided the vessel further upstream, they noted locations for resting and also obvious sites for ambush. They kept watch for both hostile forces and their comrades in arms. Each person was assigned a position and a weapon and remained alert. The twenty-mile journey upstream was plodding. The enemy and their allies would most likely travel with the current and make greater headway. No one could venture a guess regarding who got out of the starting gates first. They hoped the advancing Seals would not engage the enemy until they had joined forces.

The scenario rapidly altered. The enemy had traveled a second tributary and joined the river three hundred yards downstream, behind them. The GPS suggested a merging rivulet but they hadn't thought it large enough to be instrumental in their planning. The inflatable craft was large, motor powered and heavily manned. In its wake was a second craft of similar dimensions and equally armed. The operation was more sophisticated that they anticipated.

No sooner had they spotted the two inflatable crafts that they heard a loud report. Instinctively they ducked and took cover behind their rigged bamboo shield. The well-trained soldiers were battle prepared and kept calm, as the gunfire grew closer. The balsa structure took fire but held. Kate stayed low so the men could sight their weapons through the shield. The moment of truth was approaching and Kate longed for the peace.

Cory and Bill took two grenades each and checked their weapons. The bamboo structure continued to absorb enemy rounds but in time, it would begin to fail. At a hundred yards, Bill and Cory launched their grenades, followed by two more launched by the Seals. The first two came up short.

The concussion grenades blew up under the first inflatable as it raced forward. The six insurgents were unable to react quickly, were thrown off balance and tossed into the water. Within seconds, the water churned with Piranha. The screams were unnerving. Everyone on the handmade raft had combat experience except Kate but no one had experienced such screams.

The second craft cut its engines and tried to aid their compatriots to no avail. They headed for the bank to regroup. The initial surprise attack hadn't gone as planned. They hadn't expected the small force to be as well armed or battle ready.

A third similar craft followed the wakes of the first two. They spotted blood and bodies in the water and headed for the opposite bank. The small group judged their intent and maneuvered closer to the opposite bank but they were slow to maneuver and took fire from both banks.

A trap had been inadvertently set. Yarro was a clever strategist and made a decision to overpower the raft with sustained firepower but he didn't take into consideration, the Navy Seals' superior aim and ordinance. The battle strategy altered, Cory commanded his men to take aim and make it count. At the same time, Kate looked up river and spotted reinforcements. "We've got company, the cavalry has arrived!"

The two approaching Seals, manning a hand constructed raft, assessed the situation and moved into an offensive position, protecting the first raft's flank. They carefully took aim and decimated the second inflatable. The third inflatable, carrying Yarro, launched and moved closer to the Americans. His soldiers lay dead or dying along the banks and he realized that his head would be delivered on a plate if he failed this mission.

Bill's attention was focused on the last men reaching for their weapons on the shore. One insurgent raised his gun and sighted Cory but before he could release his payload, Bill placed a bullet between his eyes.

Yarro, with his remaining insurgents fired wildly into the air then he circled the rafts, shooting through the disintegrating bamboo shield. Suddenly, the combat was too close and the maneuvering, too risky to use firearms. The weapons of choice were knives and the long bladed machetes. The Seals used their rifle butts to ward off the wild attackers. Kate leveled her machete at the advancing force and sliced off an ear. The rebel bellowed as he fell backward into the water. The water roiled as the evil flesh eating fish devoured him.

Cory was pinned down by one of the raiders but Bill was able to reach him and drive a knife into his chest. The snakebite had taken its toll and he could feel his body tire. But he fought the urge to lay off. Directly to his left, another rebel lunged towards Kate, and tried to grab her machete. She struck back but he knocked her to the ground. Bill Shepherd's adrenaline reserves surged, he screamed his rage and deftly threw his knife, embedding the blade in the attacker's Adam's apple. The warrior silently fell backwards into the water and disappeared beneath the froth.

As Bill regained his footing, the last man standing, Yarro fired point blank into Agent Bill Shepherd's back. The image of Bill's body thrust forward was surreal. Kate screamed louder than she had ever screamed. Cory lifted his handgun and took aim. He cut down Yarro but it was too late.

Bill Shepherd was seriously wounded. Reacting to the crisis, Cory applied all his training to stop the bleeding. The battle with the rebels was over but the race to save Bill was just beginning. Kate stripped the clothes off Bill to determine the extent of his wounds. Two rounds entered his body. To the best of their combined knowledge, no vital organs appeared damaged. All they could do was stop the bleeding and rush him to the nearest hospital. The chopper was on its way and would land in less than five minutes.

Going Home

It was a quiet and painful journey back to Lima. The chopper arrived shortly after the functioning sat radio ordered it to extract the remaining party. The insurgents were left on the banks, their bodies, if still in one piece would be removed by embarrassed government officials.

Kate stared out of the chopper's window as it flew low over the deep green wilderness. It was so beautiful from high up. So pristine, but its depths held so many secrets. She held the golden egg and the small-carved bone in her hands, praying they would give her the courage to go on. Her greatest love, William Shepherd, so much a part of her life was lying on a cot with IV tubes and blood dripping into his veins She ached for him, holding his hand as if she could somehow force her energy into his wounded body.

They would arrange to stay at Walter Reade Medical Center and Cory would be at her side to help her make it through. It would be a difficult recovery but she owed it to the most courageous man she ever loved.

Cory was already on the phone rounding up the best medical teams in Peru and securing the CIA jet that would get Shepherd back home as soon as he was stabilized.

Cory stared out the opposite window. He was a seasoned military man and had seen death but the possible demise of his friend impacted him deeply. A leave of absence would help him sort things out.

There were loose ends but this was not the time. Dr. Raymond Morrissey's body had been flown home and Dr. Maggie Brown was recovering back in Auckland. The gold had been found but Kate seemed not to care about it anymore.

Kate did care about young Carlos and hoped he could rebuild his life. She thought about the resilient people of Christchurch and wondered how the rebuilding of their lives was going. Manuel and Conchita would be shocked by news of Bill's nearly fatal wounds.

And she thought about the lost people and prayed for their longevity. They had been kind, gentle and unaffected by greed and she prayed they would remain that way forever.

The End

Coming Soon!

Port Royal
An Unexpected
Tale of Discovery, Intrigue & Passion

There is no peace for the wicked or for that matter, a young archeologist and her CIA Operative husband when their pleasurable escape to an exotic island turns into a mystery so deep and disturbing that Kate and Bill Shepherd are forced to abandon their holiday to chart another perilous course.

The *She Quester*, a beautiful schooner, along with her crew, has vanished. The affable captain, Sam O'Doole, is left to ponder the fate of his prized ship and its valuable cargo, his two sons. The Shepherds, absorbed in his plight, develop a daring plan to locate the schooner and unearth the shocking intelligence behind its capture.

Join the Shepherds as they brave the high seas and the tyrants who threaten to drown their hopes and dreams.

CPSIA information can be obtained at www.ICGtesting.com
Printed in the USA
BVOW082150181012

303413BV00001B/99/P